ACTS OF ACCEPTANCE

S.W. Leicher

Twisted Road Publications LLC

Copyright © 2025 by S. W. Leicher
All rights reserved

ISBN: 978-1-940189-37-6

Author Photo by Joyce Ravid
Cover Photo by iStock Photo
Cover Design by Babski Creative Studios

www.twistedroadpublications.net

Praise for *ACTS OF ASSUMPTION*

"The grace and delicacy of Leicher's prose, the honesty
and humor of her characters' voices, and the abundance of
carefully observed detail make this book a joy. The people
and worlds in *Acts Of Assumption* are singular and universal
at once, and vividly drawn. Leicher is a novelist to watch." ~
SJ Rozan, award-winning author of *Ghost Hero*

"Serach's and Paloma's voices are so eminently engaging and
alive that ...despite the toll of living against expectation...the
novel assumes their right to a happy ending—together." ~
Letitia Montgomery-Rodgers, *Foreward Review*

Praise for *ACTS OF ATONEMENT*

"*Acts of Atonement* ... proves just how vibrant and connected
the lives of New Yorkers are." ~ Sonia Manzano, "Maria" on
Sesame Street, and author of *Becoming Maria: Love and
Chaos in the South Bronx*

"In the novel's clever, satisfying conclusion, Paloma takes
control at last, having learned to use strict cultural traditions
to her advantage to bring everyone closer together—a
perfect ending to a complex, touching story about the
difficulties of navigating one's identity. *Acts of Atonement* is
a novel about accepting yourself and others for who they are,
not who you want or expect them to be. "~ Eileen Gonzales
for *Foreword Review*

"The core beauty of Ms. Leicher's brilliantly written *Acts
of Atonement* lies in how deftly it draws us into the pain,
irrationality, and joy of family, captures the nuances of love
between two women, and tests our personal capacity for
tolerance, acceptance, and empathy. " ~ Michael J. Coffino,
author of the award-winning novel *Truth Is in the House*

ACTS OF ACCEPTANCE
a novel

S.W. Leicher

For Chris, who saw it coming.

And for New York City, the heartbeat of the tale.

CONTENTS

Definition of Acceptance

1.   *Facing and dealing with situations and emotions that may be uncomfortable or painful.*
2.   *Including someone in a group or something in a belief system.*
3.   *Welcoming, receiving, favoring, and approving.*

Based on Merriam Webster Dictionary

CAST OF CHARACTERS

GOTTESMAN FAMILY, in order of appearance

Rav Shmuel Gottesman, AKA Shmuely—youngest sibling in the original Gottesman family. After a childhood in Boro Park, Brooklyn, he moves to Jerusalem to study and teach Talmud.

Reuven Gottesman—Shmuely's first cousin.

Ruchel Seligson Gottesman—Shmuely's wife.

Asher Gottesman—Shmuely's son.

Shoshana Gottesman, AKA Shoshi—Shmuely's daughter.

Yehuda Seligson—Shmuely's father-in-law. He lives in Jerusalem and runs a jewelry empire.

Gittel Gottesman—Shmuely and Serach's mother, now deceased.

Shlomo Gottesman—Shmuely and Serach's uncle, now deceased.

Hulda Seligson—Yehuda's mother, now deceased.

Serach Gottesman—the eldest daughter in the original Boro Park Gottesman family. She lives with her partner Paloma in Prospect Park South, Brooklyn, and is an accountant.

Beile Pinsky, Mierle Rapoport, Chava Krauss, Shayna Posner—Shmuely's and Serach's sisters.

Bluma Pinsky—Beile's oldest daughter.

RODRIGUEZ FAMILY, in order of appearance

Paloma Rodriguez—South-Bronx-born daughter of a Colombian immigrant mother. She lives with her partner Serach in Prospect Park South, Brooklyn, and is an oncological nurse at Manhattan East Cancer Research and Treatment Center.

Manny Rodriguez—Paloma's older brother. He lives in the Fordham area of the Bronx with his wife and sons and is the co-owner and manager of the Los Milagros Auto Repair Shop.

Ramon Rodriguez, AKA Anteojitos (Little Eyeglasses)— Manny's youngest son. He is a young man with special needs, placed at a residential treatment center in Rockland County following his arrest for mistakenly firing a gun at Manny's childhood friend, Fernando.

Oscar Rodriguez, AKA Negrito (Little Blackie)—Manny's adopted eldest son. He lives with his girlfriend, Gloria, in Ridgewood Queens and is the founder and owner of a start-up software development business.

Roberto Rodriguez, AKA Gordito (Little Fatty)—Manny's adopted second son. He lives with his parents in the Bronx and works at his father's auto repair shop.

Gloria Isabel Mendez—Negrito's girlfriend. She lives with Negrito in Ridgewood, Queens and is the founder and director of a fashion design collective run by women of color.

Beatriz Gallego Saenz—Manny's wife, and the mother of Anteojitos, Negrito and Gordito. She works as a cleaner for individuals and institutions.

Dolores Rodriguez Gonzales—Paloma's and Manny's mother. She lives in a trailer park in Upstate New York and does occasional bartending.

José (Joe) Cuesta—Dolores's first boyfriend in the Bronx. Current whereabouts unknown.

Jeff Adam—Dolores's current boyfriend in Upstate New York.

OTHER FIGURES OF NOTE, in order of appearance

Annie Heymann—Runs the Canine Rescue Team of Hackensack and sells Serach her car.

André Johnston—House Parent at the cottage in which Anteojitos lives at The Excelsior School.

Frayda Goldblatt—Serach's friend from the old Boro Park neighborhood.

Etha Burnett—Paloma's friend and former colleague at Maimonides Hospital.

Frank Davis—Paloma and Serach's friend and erstwhile housemate. He is a concert pianist.

Malka Siegelstein—Frayda's friend.

Shprintza Bernshteyn—Daughter of Malka and Human Resources Director at B'Sevah Tovah, an assisted living residence for Orthodox men in Boro Park, Brooklyn.

Dov Bernshteyn—Shprintza's husband and owner and director of B'Sevah Tovah.

Dr. Marcus Pessin—dentist at B'Sevah Tovah.

Reb Avram Bernshteyn—resident of B'Sevah Tovah, Dov's father and Shprintza's father-in-law.

Father Kevin Byrnes—chaplain at the Brindisi Funeral Home.

Bobby Santiago, Father Byrnes's assistant.

Luis Montero and Levar Wilson—gravediggers at Woodlawn Cemetery.

Eugenio Puente and Tobias Martinez—car mechanics from the Los Milagros Auto Shop.

Fernando Eduardo Reyes—son of the co-owner of the Los Milagros Auto Shop. Permanently disabled by a gunshot fired by Anteojitos, he lives in the Bronx with his father.

Fernando's father—founder and co-owner of the Los Milagros Auto Shop. Permanently disabled by a series of strokes, he lives in the Bronx with Fernando.

Carlota Quiñones Regalado de Bianchi—major donor to Manhattan East.

Kae-Dang Jeung—Frank's clarinetist boyfriend.

Judith Skollar—Renowned opera star and Paloma's former employer and benefactor. Upon her death, she bequeathed Paloma her Prospect Park South house and all that it contained.

Van Binh—sexton at the Church of St. Nicholas of Tolentine.

Alyosha Sokholov—Frank's cellist friend.

Yan-Xiu Chen—Frank's piano student.

Penina Pearlman—Kitchen supervisor at B'Sevah Tovah

Giulio Lazzaro—head waiter at the Stelle di Mare Ristorante in Sheepshead Bay, Brooklyn.

Reb Lazer Buchbaum, Reb Chaim Lillien, Reb Heschel Cohen, Reb Yitzhak Tannebaum, and Reb Issur Belinsky—past and present residents of *B'Sevah Tovah*.

Dalisay Hipolito—Ruchel and Shmuely's Filipina housekeeper.

Dr. Lewis Botwinick—Ruchel's obstetrician.

Ahmed al-Khatib—driver for hire in Jerusalem.

Gary Mitchell—receptionist at Manhattan East

Amalia Bonilla—Nurse Manager in the Pediatric Department at Manhattan East.

Dr. Sherman Silverstein—Admitting Physician in the Pediatric Department at Manhattan East.

Emma Corbin—pediatric patient at Manhattan East.

Jane Corbin—Emma's mother.

Reb Ephraim Fishman—member of the synagogue at which Shmuely *davens* when he is in Brooklyn.

PROLOGUE: AN UNUSUAL NAMING

*"May He who blessed our forefathers ... bless the woman
who has given birth to a daughter who has been born at
an auspicious time ... May she and her husband raise the
daughter to a life of Torah, marriage, and good deeds. And
let us respond: Amen."*

Mi Shebeirach prayer recited at a daughter's naming

March 2020: Jerusalem

"I have been reviewing all the arguments," declared Rav Gottesman (Shmuely, to his familiars) as he paced from the doorway of his study to the windows at the back, cellphone plastered tightly against his ear. "There are those who say that a father should ask to announce his daughter's name at the first *Torah* service following her birth, regardless of when it occurs. Weekday *Torah* service, *Shabbos Torah* service—it doesn't matter which one it is. What matters is simply doing it as soon as possible."

He stood still for a moment before turning to pace in the opposite direction.

"But ..." he continued in the sing-song voice that befits such a discussion, "there are those who say the father should specifically ask for that first *Shabbos* service—even if it means delaying the naming for a few days. For it is only on a *Shabbos* that he can sponsor a full festive meal."

Shmuely fell silent and Reuven, on the other end of the call, knew to hold his tongue. He was well acquainted with his cousin's rhetorical style.

"And then," Shmuely eventually resumed, "there is Rav Shlomo ben Joseph Ganzfried of Ungvár, who agrees that the father should request to do it at a *Shabbos* service but notes that it should be the first *Shabbos* service that the girl's mother can attend—not the first one following the girl's birth. He notes that since the mother is explicitly cited in the blessing made at a naming, a request that supports that mother's presence will carry the greatest weight."

Shmuely moved the phone aside briefly to scratch beneath his beard.

"It is a compelling argument," he sighed, "but things being what they are with Ruchel, who knows when she will be up to returning to synagogue?"

This time, Reuven knew to take the cue.

"Shmuely," he said. "You are a pillar of our congregation. You will be granted the honor of announcing your daughter's name whenever you ask for it. Ruchel's presence is irrelevant."

Shmuely gave a rare, mischievous smile that his cousin could not see.

"That was my thinking as well. So being that I don't want my daughter to remain nameless for any longer than is necessary, I will announce it at this Thursday morning's service."

"How is Ruchel, by the way?" Reuven ventured, after a moment.

"Coming along, *Baruch Ha-Shem*. And meanwhile," he added wearily, "whatever she cannot manage, her mother manages. She has moved back into our house, my mother-in-law. Any excuse and there she is again."

Reuven almost responded, but Shmuely broke in before he could.

"Anyway, Reuven," he concluded, briskly, "the reason I'm calling is to let you know that you also will be receiving an honor that morning. Along with my father-in-law. So be prepared."

Reuven didn't waste any time wondering why he was being recognized. He was, after all, Shmuely's sole blood relative in Jerusalem—and almost as much of a *macher* in their synagogue as his cousin. It only made sense.

Still, he felt both startled and humbled when he heard the daughter's name revealed for the first time. For Shmuely had not opted to call her "Gittel" in memory of his own late mother, as had been universally expected. He had decided to name her "Shoshanna," after Reuven's father Shlomo, who was long deceased and who already had a bevy of grandchildren named for him.

The pleasure that Reuven received from that decision, however, was not universally felt. When Shmuely first informed his wife Ruchel of his intention, for example—as she struggled to find a more comfortable position for herself and the squalling infant on her narrow hospital bed—she had colored fiercely.

"For your Uncle Shlomo?" she had exclaimed, irritably shifting the child yet again. "If you didn't want to name her for your mother, couldn't you have chosen to do it for my grandmother Hulda? You know how much I suffered when she passed away last October. You know how much such a gesture would have meant to my father."

Shmuely had taken a deep breath so as not to respond with equal sharpness. He then let it out again, very slowly, and said that—in the absence of his own father—his Uncle Shlomo had been like a father to him. End of discussion.

Which was the same explanation that he offered to anyone else who ever asked about it. He had learned that brevity is the best approach in matters of a personal nature. That it minimizes the possibility for either pain or gossip.

Besides, how else could he frame it?

How could he possibly admit that giving his daughter the name of the mother who had declared his beloved sister Serach forever dead to him would dredge bile into his throat every time he spoke it? Or that naming her for the uncle who had privately asserted that Serach was neither dead nor worthy of condemnation would help keep Serach alive for him, if only within the depths of his own heart.

No, of course he could not have confessed to any of that. Any more than he could have put words to the blast of shock and longing that he had felt when he picked up his little girl for the first time and found Serach's lovely gray eyes staring straight back at him.

PART ONE: IN PERSON

"Mary is our mother, the cause of our joy. Being a mother myself, I have never had difficulty in talking with Mary and feeling close to her."

Mother Teresa, Saint of Calcutta,
speaking of the Virgin Mary

July 2020: Brooklyn

-1-

Every day for the past four months, Paloma's evening routine had been the same.

She would charge off the subway at Church Avenue, run down the platform, climb the stairs to the street, and rush the three blocks to Marlborough Road—holding her breath within her mask whenever she passed through a crowd or when any solo walker veered too closely in her direction.

She would bolt down the short stretch of tree-lined sidewalk to reach her house, skid around to the back, leave her nurse's crocs just outside the door and stand in the middle of the kitchen, peeling off her pearl-gray scrubs, her underwear, and her socks.

She would throw her balled-up clothing into the washer-dryer in the small closet just outside the kitchen, toss in a detergent pellet and turn it on.

Once the washer started churning, she would dash up the stairs to the second floor, lock herself in the bathroom, soap down every inch of her body till it practically blistered, and shampoo her mass of glossy black hair twice before wrapping herself up in big white Egyptian cotton towels and making her way into the bedroom to throw on a clean set of underwear, some sweat clothes, and a pair of sneakers that had not ventured more than a few steps beyond the house for several months.

Then and only then would she call up to Serach—holed up in her third-floor study and seemingly oblivious to everything except what was on her computer screen—to announce that she was home and would be downstairs fixing supper.

The fanatic sanitizing routine was carried out partially for therapeutic reasons: an attempt to wash away some of the chaos, the misery—the fear—with which she'd grappled all day. She wasn't a nurse in the newly established COVID ward, thank God. Those nurses faced the worst of it. But too many of the cancer patients for whom she cared so tenderly had been disappearing into that ward and only a handful were re-emerging.

The routine also served, however, to reassure her that she would not risk infecting Serach with even a single one of the trillions of germs with which she had inevitably come into contact during her eight-hour shift at the Manhattan East Cancer Care and Research Center and her back-and-forth subway commute between Prospect Park South and the Upper East Side.

It may have been fifteen years since Serach had battled her own case of cancer, but pre-conditions are pre-conditions and extended bouts of chemotherapy can have unexpectedly long-term debilitating effects.

Serach generally gave Paloma a good half hour of solo fussing before slipping downstairs to ask how she could help. She had quickly realized that her partner required a solid dose of decompression time each workday and was determined to do whatever it took to support that need.

On that Thursday in late July, however—practically jumping out of her skin with excitement—she flew down the stairs from her study as soon as she heard Paloma's voice and planted herself in the arched doorway of the kitchen in such a way that Paloma would have no choice but to notice her.

"I have a surprise for you!"

Paloma glanced up. Serach was looking absolutely electric. As electric as she herself felt drained. She forcibly cleared her mind of some of the more frightening images of the day.

"What kind of a surprise?"

"A lovely surprise. One that will open up whole new vistas to us."

Paloma smiled.

"And what could that possibly be?"

"I got my drivers' license today!"

It wasn't like Serach to brag. But in this instance, how could she help it?

"I filled out all the paperwork, I took the lessons, I took the drivers' test and passed it on the first try—which almost never happens—and the license arrived in this morning's mail!"

She waved the little card around like the prize that it was.

Paloma put down the spoon, switched off the flame, and turned fully around to face her partner.

"You what?"

"Oh, Paloma! It's been so incredibly hard not to say anything! But I didn't want to breathe a word about it till I'd succeeded."

Paloma's look of stupefied disgust intensified.

"You're telling me that you've been spending the past I-don't-know-how-many weeks in closed cars with driving teachers who have been God-knows where before they got into the car with you? That you've been absorbing liters of those teachers' potentially contaminating breath for hours on end?"

"It was always the same teacher, Paloma," Serach responded softly, after a pause. "It was only once a week for five weeks. We kept the car windows wide open. Both of us wore masks the whole time. K95s."

"Not to mention that you've been traipsing off to the Department of Motor Vehicles to stand in line with hundreds of strangers blowing viral strains at you for hours on end?"

Serach shook her head.

"Almost everything was done remotely, Paloma. I had to go to the DMV only once and that was by appointment. They keep the numbers in the room strictly limited and everyone has to wear a mask."

"What's more, you were doing all that while I thought you were safely holed up in your study, far from any source of danger?"

"Oh, Paloma! I may be an introvert—I may like to work at home—but I've never been a hermit. I haven't told you what I've been doing because you tend to get so crazy about so many things these days. But if I hadn't begun going out, I would have gone crazy myself. I walk around the block at least once a day, every day—rain or shine—and sometimes I even stop to talk to people. I've also... been doing our shopping in person for weeks."

She glanced at Paloma and then (quickly) away again. Paloma looked so horribly angry. Still, once she had embarked on this confession, she couldn't take it back. She forged on.

"Paloma, I just couldn't bear getting deliveries anymore. All those environmentally-damaging plastic bags!"

She took a breath and looked straight at her partner.

"Paloma! I know what I am doing! I always keep my mask on. I keep a distance between myself and anyone with whom I interact. I'm a very cautious person. I—"

"You have no idea what it's like out there!" Paloma finally responded, in a tone that Serach had never heard before.

"Paloma!"

Serach walked forward to plant her hands firmly on her partner's shoulders. Unwillingly—and then willingly—Paloma allowed herself to be soothed by their familiar warmth.

"Paloma, of course I haven't experienced the worst of the pandemic in the way that you have," Serach continued. "Nor have I gained much insight from you, since you refuse to share what you've been seeing with me, no matter how often I ask."

Paloma tightened her lips.

"I'm not complaining," Serach quickly added. "I know you need to just get away from it all when you come home. But I do read the papers. I listen to the news. I... hear the sirens."

She let go of Paloma's shoulders.

"Paloma, I'm careful. When—in all the time we've been together—have you known me not to be careful?"

She didn't wait for an answer. Their entire partnership was the result of the monumentally risky initial decision that she had made to break with her community and flee into Paloma's waiting arms. She kept going before Paloma could point that out.

"You need to think of what it will mean for us. We'll be able to drive into the countryside and find some secluded spot all to ourselves and... rip off our masks!"

Paloma couldn't help but smile. She looked down for a moment and then picked up the stirring spoon and switched the burner back on.

"Well," she murmured, as she began stirring again. "I don't see what good it does for you to learn how to drive, since we don't have a car. Plus, since—from everything I hear—buying a car these days is next to impossible."

"I'll tell you what good it will do, if you'll only calm down for a moment."

Serach paused.

"And if you'll stop bristling long enough to congratulate me for what I've achieved. It's not so easy passing a drivers' test the first time you take it, you know. Especially if you've been conditioned since earliest girlhood to think that it is unseemly—if not downright wrong—for a woman to occupy the driver's seat."

She paused again.

"My mother never learned to drive. Nor did any of my sisters. According to Frayda, even the two sisters who moved to Long Island—where not knowing how to drive is like not knowing how to use a fork. Many observant women now do it, out there. But not Chava and Shayna. They'd rather depend on their husbands and Lyft and home deliveries than meddle with the traditions that their grandmothers followed."

Paloma would have bitten off her own tongue sooner than confess that somewhere deep in her own mind she also still thought of driving as something strictly reserved for men. For her brother Manny. Or for her nephews Negrito and Gordito. Not something for her or Serach.

She hung her head.

"Jesus, Serach. You're right. I'm impressed as all hell."

She swallowed.

"And of course I trust that you've been careful about the whole thing. It's just that...."

"It's okay. I understand."

"But you still haven't answered my question. The car? The impossible-to-buy car?"

"The car is arriving here on Saturday."

"Serach—what are you talking about now?"

"There are websites on which you can buy all sorts of things if you just persist. I began the search at about the same time that I began taking my lessons. It took a while, but I finally located just the right car at just the right price. I've been budgeting for it for months and now I'm going to pay for it."

"Good heavens, Serach! You shouldn't have to do that all alone. How much will it be?"

"Paloma, this is my *meshugas*. Leave it to me. And no worries: it's quite affordable. The seller is itching to sell it. We reached a fair price with no problem."

Paloma looked away. They would work out the payment arrangements later. She'd make sure of it.

"So... what kind of car is it?"

"A little silver 2018-model Subaru."

"How the hell—how the hell did you even know what to get?"

"Subaru has been carrying out a campaign for years to get you and me to buy their cars. Don't you know that? It's on all the lesbian websites. There's this whole network of fellow lesbians who swear by them. They call them 'Lesbarus.'"

Jesus—what else has Serach been looking up on lesbian websites while I've been sealed up in my own little whirling, painful cocoon?

"The seller lives in Hackensack, New Jersey. She runs a nonprofit that matches rescue dogs with foster parents. Evidently, rescue dogs are also a major part of the Subaru image. Anyway, Annie—that's her name—and I saw eye-to-eye right away. She's driving into Brooklyn on Saturday to deliver one of the dogs to a foster family in Fort Greene before arriving here to settle up with me—and leaving our new car parked right in our driveway!"

Paloma shook her head and smiled the smallest of smiles.

"Serach, you still take my breath away."

Serach smiled to herself as well for a moment, and then—emboldened by what she had just accomplished—continued.

"That's good," she said, "because there's something else that you need to do for me."

"Sure, Baby. Whatever you want."

"It's five minutes to seven, and I want you to stop cooking for a moment again and come stand with me outside."

"You know I don't do that."

"I know that you've avoided it. But I want you to do it this evening. I really do believe that things will improve, Paloma. I know you can't feel it from where you stand and given what you see every day. I understand that you've had to shut down entire parts of yourself, just to keep going. But you deserve this. Our neighbors have been asking me why you stay inside every evening. They know that you're a nurse, you know."

She paused.

"I never know what to answer them. How to explain what holds you back. I don't understand it myself. But tonight— please do it! Please!"

Paloma turned off the flame and put the spoon down once again. She masked up and followed Serach around the side of the house to the pavement out front. She stood by Serach's side as their neighbors came out of their own houses, one by one, and couple by couple, and whole families, and—along with everyone else in the city—began to applaud for those who were on the front lines of the epidemic.

At first, she kept her head down. But eventually she looked up again and smiled and nodded in brief acknowledgement.

Then she and Serach walked back into the house, hand in hand.

August 2020: Piermont

- 2 -

Paloma adjusted to Serach's new role as family chauffeur with surprising ease, happily accepting her partner's every invitation to go for a spin. Hopping into her seat, she would roll down the window ("it still stinks of dog in here," she invariably claimed), turn on her favorite playlist (Celia Cruz, Tito Puente, a few Bad Bunny hits) and begin to sing along.

"I guess it's only fair," Serach had sighed. "I chose the car. You choose the music."

Nonetheless, on that watershed summer Sunday morning, Paloma was having none of that. She slid silently into place, buckled up, and stayed perfectly mum for the whole first leg of the journey.

"Paloma, must you sulk so?" Serach eventually muttered, as she merged assertively onto the Brooklyn-Queens Expressway.

"I'm not sulking," said Paloma. "I'm mad. What was André thinking, ordering us up to Anteojitos' school like that, right in the middle of this pandemic?"

"It wasn't an order, Paloma," Serach replied, gently. "It was a suggestion. He said it would be a 'good idea' for us to come. We haven't been there in ages, you know. I'm sure our nephew really misses us."

Paloma said nothing.

"Everything will be outdoors. Everyone will be masked. There's really nothing to worry about."

She gave her partner a quick glance.

"You were okay with everything by the time we went to bed last night. What's changed?"

Paloma tossed Serach a swift look back, and—despite all her best intentions—was momentarily unable to retort. Her partner had been looking so damned attractive since she'd started this whole driving thing. It made it hard to think straight.

Part of the appeal came from the vintage wraparound Ray-Bans that Serach had taken to wearing ("the sun's glare can be so disruptive," she explained)—a move that lent an enticing edge to her normally sweetly-boyish face. Part was the way she had begun gelling her short-cropped curls into a near-perfect version of a 1950's ducktail. Part was the way that her dancer-graceful posture seemed to morph into Marine-Corps-steely the moment she wrapped her slim fingers around the steering wheel. Thoroughly disarming.

"What's changed," Paloma eventually resumed, "is that I've had a few more hours to think about it, and where I keep landing is that this was no nice little suggestion that we should go visit Anteojitos. This was André himself wanting to see us. Face-to-face. Because he has something to say that's too terrible to say on the phone. Or by Zoom."

"Terrible like what?"

'I don't know," Paloma said, suddenly rushing through her words. "Like that Anteojitos is talking about guns again? Or has a case of COVID so bad they don't think he'll pull through?"

Serach shook her head. It was so like Paloma to get angry when she was scared.

"Paloma!" she said softly. "Our nephew will never touch another gun. You know that. And if he were really sick—God forbid—André would have said so right away."

Paloma shook her head.

"My love—there was nothing in any of his texts that was the least bit worrisome. It was all perfectly calm."

"Everything about André is always perfectly calm. He's the original Mr. Cool. It's how he manages to stay sane while house-parenting all those idiot kids."

Serach, with some effort, made no comment about Paloma's choice of words.

"I'm also ticked," Paloma added, after a beat, "that he texted you instead of me. And that you didn't grill him about what he's after, so we could be better prepared."

"It's always been me that he texts," Serach replied, keeping her eyes on the road. "Probably because he knows I don't do things like grilling him."

The area around the cottage where Anteojitos had been housed for the past two years was showing clear signs of neglect. There were patches of bare earth where there once had been a lawn. There was a blanket of cigarette butts surrounding the picnic table at which they would be sitting. Large swaths of weathered wood showed through the dark green paint of the table itself.

André, however, appeared as well-put-together as ever, sitting with his back pressed up against that table and his long legs stretched out in front of him. His elaborate dreadlocks were held cleanly away from his face by a cheery red bandanna. The sleeves of his white tee-shirt were rolled up to showcase his darkly-gleaming, formidably-muscled arms. His mask—rather than obscuring his good looks—drew direct attention to his outrageously long-lashed black eyes.

He stood up as the two women approached and extended a hand to each. Paloma was tempted to grasp the one he was offering her—André's big warm hands were so marvelous. Nonetheless, she held back. Skin-to-skin germs. God forbid.

She gave him a brilliant (if masked) smile, instead. It would have to do.

"How good it is to see you," André said in the voice that had never lost the cadences of Trinidad.

"It certainly is," said Serach. "It's been far too long."

She regarded him for a long minute.

"You're looking well, André. Have you managed to stay healthy through all of this?"

"Oh, I had a major bout of the thing earlier this summer. But I seem to have survived."

The two women nodded sympathetically.

"And how is Ramon?" asked Serach—using the given name that everyone outside of Anteojitos' immediate family used for him. "Why isn't he down here waiting for us? Is he okay?"

"Ramon is up in his room, glued to his computer screen. I haven't told him that you were coming. I'll clarify everything in a moment. But first let's sit down, shall we?"

He motioned to the picnic table, and they all clambered over the attached benches to take their seats—Serach and Paloma on one side and André on the other.

"I will get right to the point," André began. "I have some tough news to share with you."

Serach dodged Paloma's knife-sharp look.

"The Excelsior School has suffered some blows during these past months," he continued. "Eleven staff members quit. One died."

"Oh, no!" said Serach, and André nodded back at her sadly.

"We've been advertising everywhere to find replacements, with little success. Safety concerns, I suspect. We've been left without the personnel to cover all our needs."

He spread his hands and looked at them for a long moment.

"There is also the matter of space," he eventually added.

"We have traditionally accommodated our students two or three to a room. That isn't possible anymore. We need to room them individually now, so they can be isolated whenever anyone falls ill."

Paloma stopped glaring at Serach and threw a glance at André. She saw what was coming.

"Long story short: we have been forced to pare down the size of the school." He sighed. "We've begun by lowering the age at which students age out. It is now eighteen—not twenty-one, as it had always been."

"Ramon turns eighteen at the end of this month!" said Serach, very softly.

"Yes. We're planning a little outdoor party for him. Perhaps you'd like to—"

"André, please don't sugar-coat this mess," said Paloma, standing up and freeing her legs from the bench. André replied nothing but just looked up at her from under his eyelashes.

"Sorry," she eventually added—but without changing her tone. "I know it's not your fault."

"No offense taken,"

"Have you told Ramon?" asked Serach.

"Yes, we have," André answered quietly. "He didn't react very well. He doesn't like change, as you know." He paused. "It is why I didn't ask him to join us. We would not have been able to discuss things freely."

"How about my brother?" interrupted Paloma, still standing. "Have you told him?"

"Yes, of course. We told him before we told Ramon."

"He hasn't mentioned it to me."

"He's been very pre-occupied," André said gently, "from everything he tells me."

"But this is a catastrophe! Why didn't he tell me about it?"

"Does he tell you everything that is going on in his life?"

Paloma grimaced.

"Also, from what I know, he doesn't think it's a catastrophe," André continued. "He seems very glad that his son is finally returning to him. He has missed him."

"Okay, André," said Paloma, after a small pause. "I think we've got the whole picture, now. Anteojitos is headed back home—where he'll get into God knows what new messes and where no one has a clue as to how to help him. No more learning. No more support from you. But we should all be happy because Manny is happy. So, are we done? Can Serach and I take off?"

"Paloma." André murmured. "Please bear with me."

Paloma, unwillingly mollified by the richness of that voice, sat back down.

"Things are not as grim as you paint," he began. "To your point about Ramon's academics: truth to tell, for most of his time here, Excelsior has not been able to truly support him in that area. Some of our lessons would go too fast for him. Some would go too slow. His classmates would distract him. Or would intimidate him. He would fall behind. He would lose interest. Short of providing him with a private tutor—which was never possible—there was little we could do."

He sighed.

"But then," he continued, his tone brightening, "almost miraculously, everything turned around once COVID forced us out of classroom teaching and into on-line instruction. It turns out that studying within the privacy of his room—and working strictly at his own pace—is just what Ramon needed all along. The computer became his private tutor. He was able to concentrate. To repeat as necessary. To absorb the material."

He grinned.

"And best of all—going home will not mean interrupting all that wonderful progress. We can send him off with a whole range of tools and resources."

"You're absolutely right!" Serach crowed. "He's been making such terrific strides, recently! Not just keeping up—forging ahead in some areas. Math-related, mostly. Right now, he's deep into studying the Fibonacci series."

Paloma whirled around. How did Serach know those things?

"And of course he'll be able to continue all that once he's home," Serach continued, ignoring her partner's expression. "We'll get him a laptop."

André beamed at her words.

"That is exactly how I hoped you would react," he said. "Now to your point about Ramon losing my support," he added, pivoting back to Paloma. "How can you possibly think that I would abandon him? I will stay in touch and offer him help and encouragement in any way that I can, for as long as he allows."

Paloma looked away.

"Finally, regarding your brother's being happy to have his son back again—for heaven's sake, Paloma, that's a good thing."

Paloma reluctantly nodded.

"That still leaves one major issue," said Serach, after a moment's silence. "What about Ramon's job? Losing that will be a huge blow for him."

"As usual, we are on the same wavelength, Serach," said André. "That has been my main concern as well."

"What are you two talking about now?" Paloma asked, more annoyed than ever. "What job?"

"When the pandemic first hit," said André, taking in Paloma's displeasure and speaking carefully, "and communal eating became dangerous, we had to begin delivering meals to students in their rooms. We lacked the staff to manage it with any kind of efficiency, so we asked the students themselves to help out. Ramon was the first to volunteer—and the only one who managed to stick with it. He's proven remarkably steadfast. Also, remarkably adaptable. He finessed the move to bringing the trays outdoors, once it became warm enough to do so—while being willing to go back to the room-to-room routine during periods of bad weather, or when somebody falls ill. For a boy who hates change, he has managed very well."

"Not just managed!" interrupted Serach. "Flourished! He says that when the students see him now, they start chanting: 'Here comes Ramon! He brings us all our trays! Hooray, hooray, hooray! Let's give him our hoorays!' He says that sometimes he chants right along with them."

"Jesus, Serach!" Paloma finally couldn't hold back. "How do you know all that? And why haven't you said anything to me about it?"

"I know it because I call Ramon every Thursday," Serach replied, softly. "And I haven't told you anything about it because you've been too caught up in what you've been going through to pay attention to much of anything else."

She paused for a beat.

"Not that you've ever shown much interest in Ramon, once he was safely ensconced here."

André knew to keep silent. He hadn't gone through years of conflict resolution training for nothing.

"Ramon also loves the fact that we pay him for his efforts," he ventured once he deemed that the moment was right. "He keeps what he earns in a special box in the main office. He never spends any of it in the canteen, like the other students with campus jobs. He does, however, come in regularly to count it. It makes him feel very proud."

Paloma shook her head. Had her blockhead brother ever thought to pay his son when he "employed" him to sweep out the auto shop? No, he had not. Well, too late for that. Too late for a lot of things, evidently. She brought her hands down on the table and leaned toward André.

"All right," she said. "Now that we know the true, full extent of the catastrophe, can Serach and I finally leave?"

"No," André said, shaking his head and giving her a smile broad enough to be clearly discernible beneath his K95. "Not quite. For we have finally come to the heart of the issue. To the reason I asked you to come all the way up here today."

He looked straight at Paloma, smiling pleasantly.

"I need to ask you ladies to do something. Something that will take some doing. And I've always found that it is best to make tough 'asks' in person."

Paloma regarded him back, steadily and suspiciously.

"The school is drafting a discharge plan for Ramon," he continued. "It is my hope that you will be the two central players on the implementation team. Perhaps the only real players, since—as Paloma so astutely points out—everyone else in his family is totally clueless."

Paloma looked down and grinned, despite herself. André was almost never catty.

"I think you'll agree that the most important thing is to keep Ramon working," he added, pivoting toward Serach.

Serach nodded vigorously.

"It can't be just any work, of course. It has to be something that offers clear expectations, careful supervision—fair compensation. Supportive work, basically."

He paused for a moment, keeping his eyes fixed on Serach.

"There used to be a number of programs like that in New York but I don't know which ones have survived the current crisis," he sighed. "Your task is to find one that has. Then, to convince Manny to enroll Ramon. Then, to make sure everyone sticks to the arrangement."

He waited for a moment while he looked back and forth between the two women.

"Do you think you can do all of that?"

"Of course we can!" Serach exclaimed, deeply relieved to have a plan of action. "We managed to get him into Excelsior, despite all Manny's initial reservations, didn't we? We've made sure that he's stayed here, despite Manny's ongoing desire to bring him back home again."

She placed two light fingers on Paloma's wrist.

"That is, Paloma has managed to do all that. She can be very persuasive, you know."

"Oh, yes," said André. "That I do."

"Jesus, you guys," said Paloma, brushing Serach's fingers away. "You don't have to butter me up. You're clearly right about this. I'm on board."

She stood up and once again disentangled herself from the bench.

"But now we absolutely must get ourselves out of here before Anteojitos gets the sudden urge to stroll downstairs, sees us, and throws a fit."

Serach and André nodded and stood up as well, and then they all hovered in place for a long awkward moment. Finally, André cleared his throat.

"I will miss seeing you two almost as much as I will miss Ramon," he said.

"We can't thank you enough," said Serach. "For everything."

Paloma pulled off her mask, looked straight at André and gave him a smile he wasn't likely to forget. She then placed a hand on Serach's shoulder, turned her gently around, and led them down to their car without either one of them allowing herself to look back.

March 2021: Brooklyn and The Bronx

- 3 -

*P*ing!

When the chime of the phone and the sight of Gordito's chubby-cheeked icon jolted Paloma out of what she'd hoped would be a Sunday sleep-in, her reaction was immediate, strong, and strange.

Was it the unnaturally hot weather of that early spring that prompted such an off-kilter response? The second large glass of wine that (atypically) she had permitted herself to drink at dinner the previous night? The tail end of some swiftly-dispersing dream featuring sultry singers and sun-scorched sand?

Whatever the source, all Paloma could think in that first wave of muddled semi-consciousness was that her middle nephew was waking her up to say that he and Manny were on their way to whisk her off to City Island—the Bronx's very own version of a New England fishing village—to resume one of their summertime lunches at Chulo's Seafood and Salsa Shack.

Suddenly, she was once again awash in the scent of deep-fried lobster tails and *tostones*. In the sound of trumpet riffs by whatever fabulous *conjunto* was playing the house on that day. In the taste of the mojitos that had earned Chulo's the title of "best cocktails in the Bronx."

She was basking in the awareness that every man in the place had swiveled around in his seat to catch a better glimpse of her as she sashayed in between her brother and his son—one hand resting lightly on each of their hefty forearms, high heels flashing, skimpy red sundress flicking around her knees. That every one was scratching his head ("how the hell did that kid get so lucky?") at the sight of the portly, teen-aged Gordito—fueled by stolen sips of his father's mojitos—pulling her out of her seat to *merengue* her across the dance floor with unexpected macho grace.

She was, in short, back in that once-upon-a-time when the Bronx was still pulsing with life. When no one had heard of the word: "COVID." When spending time with Manny and his sons was part of her normal routine.

Then she looked down at her screen for a second time to read what it actually said.

They broke into Papito's shop again.

Paloma punched her finger at the phone icon as hard as she could and waited for that familiar, snuffling voice to answer.

"Gordito! What happened? Did they trash the place again?"

"No. Yeah. I guess. But that's not...um...that's not the problem. It's um..."

Paloma knew that yelling at her nephew's incoherence would only make things worse. She clamped her lips together and eventually he found his way back.

"So, you know how Papito—how he gets when the alarm company calls?" he began again. "How he—like—drops everything and runs right down to the shop?"

Paloma nodded into the phone.

"And how when the cops bring him home again, he's always—like—still all jumpy, and how he always yells a lot?"

"Yes, I know all that! For Christ's sake, get to the point!"

"Well," said Gordito, suddenly articulate. "This time, it wasn't like that. When the cops brought him back, he didn't start yelling or anything. He just sat down and started making all these funny noises. Wheezing, I guess you'd say."

He swallowed hard and Paloma held her breath.

"He can still walk," Gordito eventually continued. "He was just able to walk to the bathroom. But not very well.

"Jesus!" Paloma closed her eyes. "So who's there now besides you and him? Who's helping you look after him? Anteojitos? Negrito? Your mother?"

"Anteojitos is here but he's still asleep. Negrito is at Gloria's place. You know—his girlfriend? And Mama—didn't Papito tell you? She got this cleaning job at Montefiore Hospital on Sunday mornings. She leaves the house real early. Like, just after three o'clock. She was already gone when the call came in."

"Well, damn! I'll be right there."

"You don't have to come, Tía..."

"So why did you bother texting me? Of course I need to come."

"Well, yeah. I guess. Look, gotta go. He's coming back into the living room."

"Oh, for God's sake," said Paloma to the suddenly dead screen.

She sat very quietly on the bed for a moment, pondering her next move.

Should she run right up to Serach's study where her partner was undoubtedly already hard at work on some tax return and risk the barrage of concern that would shatter the steel-rod self-control required for this crisis? Or should she just text Serach something non-committal from the train and tell her more about it when she arrived back home?

No contest. She couldn't afford to let anything deter her. She threw on some clothes, bolted downstairs, and set off.

She then stood shivering uncontrollably on the platform for the full eighteen minutes that it took for the Q train to arrive. It made no difference that the mid-March temperature was already registering a freaky seventy degrees. The trembling wouldn't stop.

Once on board, she found herself one of only three passengers in the car—the other two being a pair of small, dark Latino men in Yankee caps, half-dozing in their seats after their late-night shifts. She was, similarly, the sole person out on the sidewalk when she arrived at Bedford Park Boulevard. The only movement as far as could be seen came from the crumpled pages of a dismantled Daily News gusting down the pavement.

Normally, she took great pleasure in the sensation of early morning urban solitude—of owning the cityscape in every direction that she looked. On this morning, however, it all just felt ominous. She clutched herself tightly as she walked the five blocks to her brother's building, wondering what she would find when she arrived.

Years before, when she had camped out with her brother and his family following a two-year stint with her grandmother in Colombia, he had given her the key to the lobby door and the two keys—top and bottom lock—to his apartment. She had never offered to return them and he had never asked to reclaim them. They still hung on their own little hoop on the key ring that she now fished out of her shoulder bag and jangled nervously in the palm of her hand.

Better to use these, she thought, than to press the lobby buzzer and alert Manny that I am on my way up. Better to glide into his apartment unannounced and get that initial diagnostic view before he put on an expression of total unreadability.

It nonetheless proved harder than she thought to just barrel in. It had been so long since she'd been in that apartment—

longer still since she'd been part of that apartment's daily life. She took a deep breath before unlocking the door and crossing the foyer into the living room that she once had known so well. She looked warily around, afraid of what she might see.

At first glance, nothing seemed drastically different from what she remembered. Her sister-in-law Beatriz was a splendidly obsessive housekeeper despite all her other failings and the place was as neat and clean as it had always been—even in the days when three messy little boys had dominated the premises.

On closer inspection, however, there were definite signs of change. Manny had somehow managed to keep his business afloat over the past few years, but he had clearly been unable to maintain his home in style. Not with two sons to put through college. Not with inflation up and gasoline prices skyrocketing and the city's economy practically grinding to a halt.

Not with all those break-ins.

The carpet was stained in ways that even diligent Beatriz had not been able to address. The armchair onto which Paloma had routinely draped herself as a teenager had threads poking out from its upholstery. The couch on which she had slept during the five months that she had lived there had faded from dark red to a shade of dull near-pink and was sagging deeply.

Not as deeply, however, as the figure now seated on it.

Manny was wearing a set of gray sweat-clothes not all that different from what Paloma herself was wearing. In a past epoch, such a coincidence would have been grounds for a great deal of pleasant bantering about their parallel outfits and their parallel good looks. Not now.

It was clear that her brother had put on a good forty pounds that he could ill-afford to add to his already ample form—forcing the fabric of those sweat-clothes to gap and stretch in ways that broke Paloma's heart. His face and neck were almost the same dismal color as that stretched-out, fraying fabric.

Paloma—for the first time since she was a parochial school student routinely making such gestures—was suddenly seized by the desire to cross herself. She shook it off, ran to the couch, sat down beside her brother, and threw her arms around him. How could she help herself? She drew as close as was humanly possible to his bloated, warm shape. She pulled down her mask to kiss him on the cheek and took a full half-moment before pulling it back into place.

"Manny! Hermano! How are you?"

Manny looked at her with shock tempered by exhaustion.

"What the hell are you doing here, Hermana?" he muttered. "How did you...? Gordito asked you to come, didn't he? Damnit! Gordito!"

"He didn't ask me to come, Manny. He just told me you'd been broken into. I—"

"GORDITO!"

Paloma was relieved that her brother could still release such a fierce shout—he had been looking as if he didn't have enough air in him for any such thing. But she was not pleased at the fit of unhinged coughing that immediately followed.

Gordito appeared in the archway of the living room. The two men looked at each other for a long time, both panting a little.

They were not blood relations. Gordito—like his older brother, Negrito—was Beatriz's son by one of Manny's predecessors. But the effects of having lived almost all his life with Manny as his adoptive father were unmistakable in Gordito's overall appearance and mannerisms. He was as stout as Manny—though there was a visible layer of muscle under all that bulk now. He was taking the same stance that

Manny always took—rocking back and forth on his feet as if he couldn't decide whether to propel his large frame forward or stay put.

"Gordito—why the hell—?"

"Manny, stop! He didn't ask me to come. He didn't even want me to come. It was I who insisted on it, despite all his protestations. I am *pura Rodriguez* just like you. Nobody tells me what to do. Or what not to do."

Manny brought his lips together hard. Had she angered him further, or was he trying to suppress a smile?

"Okay, Hermana. Okay."

Gordito twisted his hands briefly and continued to rock.

"It's okay, Gordito," Paloma repeated back to Gordito—since Manny was clearly not going to do so. "We're all fine, now. You can go back inside. I bet your father could use a glass of water. Could you get him one?"

Manny put up his hand.

"No water, Paloma."

Paloma paled. Was Manny having trouble swallowing? Was he having chest pain?

"All right, never mind, Gordito. Why don't you just go into your room or something?"

Gordito nodded and slipped away.

"Manny, you don't look so well."

"Shit, Hermana, they just broke into my—" he dissolved into more coughing and put one hand on his chest. "Into my shop. Third time since last summer. The fuckers."

She tried to place her hand on his and he shook it off. She drew a deep breath.

"Look," she finally resumed. "Are you sure you don't want something to drink?"

He tightened his lips, nodded, and looked down. But this time when she reached over, he let her take his hand.

"Manny, this really isn't good. What you actually look is ... terrible. And you sound even worse. We need to take you to an emergency room to get you checked out. You look like a man who has just had..."

He raised his head.

"I would rather die right here and now," he took a breath, "than go into a goddamn hospital where—" he coughed again, "where that goddamn China virus is killing all the patients."

There were so many things in his statement that needed correcting, but what good would it do? They sat in silence for a long moment.

"So they got the guys who broke in?"

"Yeah. The cops arrived right away and dragged them off. Showed them what was what."

Paloma closed her eyes, envisioning Anteojitos' long-ago arrest in that very same shop.

"Yeah," she said, and this time she couldn't stop herself. "I'll bet they did."

Manny's face almost reclaimed its full vivacity.

"Don't you dare..." he said. "Don't you dare badmouth the cops."

"Manny, you weren't there when those officers tackled Anteojitos and twisted his arms behind his back and yanked him back up again by the handcuffs. You didn't watch as they jerked him around—right and left—parading him in front of me so I could see him writhe and hear him howl."

"And you weren't there, Hermana," said Manny in a tone that chilled her to her core, "when I arrived in my shop this morning and those thugs had broken in—again—and were standing in my space with their guns drawn, looking at me like I was—"

He began to cough. She reached for his hand again and he shook her off.

"If it wasn't for the cops... "

Paloma held her breath. Her brother was going to cry and she couldn't bear it. But he pulled himself together before that could happen and looked at her directly for the first time.

"When the cops grabbed those shits and took their guns away and kicked them down, I felt…"

"What?" whispered Paloma.

"Safe," he said, almost as softly.

It was a long time before either of them could speak again.

"Manny, is there anything at all that I can do for you?"

Manny sighed and it didn't turn into a cough. Paloma took his hand again and, once again, he let her.

"Yes, Hermana," he said. "There is. If I die from whatever the hell this is, I need you to tell Mama about it."

Paloma gasped. This was definitely not what she expected. He couldn't have asked for anything more terrible.

"And," he added, paying no attention to her reaction, "you need to tell it to her in person. I'll get you her address and instructions for how to get there."

Paloma squeezed her eyes together.

"It won't be necessary, Manny," she finally said. "You aren't going to die."

But she said it in a voice far flatter than she intended. She had seen his aura. She knew.

"Do you promise to do it?"

She nodded.

"¡*Hablame duro,* Hermana! Say it out loud! Do you promise?"

"Yes, Manny. Of course I do."

She lifted his hand to her mouth and kissed it through her mask. He turned their hands around and kissed hers, skin to skin.

"Okay, then—get going. I don't want you here when Beatriz comes back. I got enough trouble on my hands without that."

"Jesus!"

Manny flashed his sister a dimple.

"Yeah, Hermana, just the sight of you back in her living room—even without your Jewish girlfriend—and she'll become a ballistic missile. First, she'll wipe you out. Then, she'll wipe Gordito out for calling you. Then, she'll explode into a million pieces, herself, and I'll be stuck paying for a triple funeral."

His half-smile slid into a full-fledged grin, and—for one brief moment—he looked like his old self. Paloma tucked the image into her mind in case she needed it later and then leaned toward him.

"God bless you, Manny," she said, pulling her mask down again for a quick second and kissing his forehead. She ran her hand back and forth over his irresistibly bristly crew cut and began murmuring a prayer to the Virgin. He ducked his head away before she could finish.

"No, Hermana," he said. "Leave it be."

He raised his head and looked briefly straight at her. His eyes were clear, but they were tired and sad beyond measure.

Then he looked away and Paloma stood up slowly and walked out of the room.

April 2021: Brooklyn

- 4 -

The arrangements that Serach had made with her old Boro Park friend, Frayda, had been working out very well despite all Serach's initial doubts.

"Paloma and I are forming a pod," she had ventured on one of their weekly phone calls, a few weeks after the crisis first materialized. "We would like you to join it."

She drew a breath before continuing.

"But only if you promise to wear a mask whenever you are anywhere outside your apartment, and to avoid large indoor gatherings—even with a mask. Also, to get yourself vaccinated as soon as you can."

Serach was well aware of Boro Park's strong early reputation for rebelliousness in all matters related to the pandemic. The members of her old community had been openly and collectively flaunting the City's mandates on mask-wearing. They were loudly contesting the State's efforts to ban large indoor gatherings (including, particularly, religious services). They ranked among the most vociferous and consistent of all New Yorkers in voicing skepticism about the value and safety of any developing vaccine.

She had no idea how Frayda felt about any of those sticky issues and no desire to pick a fight with her friend. She nonetheless needed to be clear about the conditions for joining their pod. Paloma had been unyielding on that front.

"I'm asking you to agree to those measures so that we can all feel safe with one another," she added, after a pause—

fervently hoping that those words would soften any potential resistance.

Frayda, however, had been seemingly unfazed by what Serach was requesting of her.

"What does 'being part of a pod' mean?" was all that she'd asked.

"It means you are part of a small group of people who stay very careful and therefore feel comfortable socializing with one another," Serach had replied. "Indoors. Without masks."

Frayda had remained silent.

"I'm not ready to go into a restaurant yet," Serach continued, "but if you join our pod, you and I can go back to seeing one another. You can come to our house and we can eat together in our kitchen. Please say you'll do it! I miss you so much!"

Frayda had mulled it over.

"Who else will be in this 'pod'?"

"Only Paloma's friend Etha. She's a nurse, just like Paloma. She lives alone and is even more careful about contagion than Paloma is."

Frayda grunted.

"Not Paloma's dear friend, Frank?"

"No," said Serach. "As far as I can tell, no pod would be safe enough for him. He hasn't as much as poked a toe out of his apartment since this whole pandemic began—or so Paloma says. I suspect he will stay inside till he's sure that the whole city has been vaccinated."

She waited a beat as Frayda considered that piece of information.

"So Frayda!" she finally exclaimed. "Do you say yes? Please do! I've been missing our get-togethers so much!"

"Let me think about it."

It hadn't taken long for Frayda to decide, however—nor to promise to abide by all of Paloma's rules. She had been missing Serach as much as Serach had been missing her. More, perhaps. By June, they were lunching together again once a month, same as they always had—except that they were now doing it in Paloma's kitchen.

Frayda would happily dispense whatever gossip she was able to garner from the neighborhood. Which merchants had set up new shops along 13th Avenue and which ones had failed. Which rabbis were ascendant and which ones were no longer in favor. Which community leaders were suffering from which ailments—and who had died of what.

She would also report back on what she managed to cull from local sources regarding Serach's sisters. ("Mierle is now a grandmother. Shayna and Chava are doing fine in Cedarhurst, Long Island. They've each had two more sons and Chava has launched her own catering business. She's some businesswoman, that one. Definitely your mother's daughter.")

She would even provide regular news bulletins about Serach's brother Shmuely.

She would fill Serach in on the progress of Shmuely's expanding family—on the exploits of little Asher and of his new baby sister, Shoshana. The Israeli branch of the Gottesman family had remained a topic of major interest in the neighborhood, after all—its apparent growth a source of relief after that long, long worrisome period when it seemed that Ruchel would never conceive.

She would also offer glowing accounts of Shmuely's ever sky-rocketing reputation as a Talmudic scholar—for the neighborhood also never tired of *kvelling* over the ongoing success of their talented favorite son.

And she would offer regular updates about the performance of Ruchel's father's jewelry empire. Shayna and Chava evidently both regularly shopped at the store that he had established on the street that Cedarhurst locals proudly called: "the Rodeo Drive of the Five Towns."

They were duly impressed.

The one question that she never touched upon, however—and that Serach assiduously avoided raising herself—was the one that plagued Serach the most. The question of whether Frayda thought Shmuely would ever get in touch with her again, following their brief reunion at his son's *bris* in the unimaginably long-ago spring of 2019.

The risks of broaching that particular question were far too great—the most likely answer far too upsetting. Neither woman wanted to talk about something that could cast such a huge pall upon the pleasure of once again sharing a meal.

The only issue that caused any friction or discomfort between them, therefore, was that of who should provide the food—and who should pay for it.

Serach initially volunteered to take responsibility for all the relevant preparations. She was essentially the host, after all. Frayda, however, wouldn't hear of it.

"What you serve us might be properly labeled as Kosher," she had retorted. "You might buy it at the right store—in a place where everything is Kosher, where there is no room for doubt. But then what? You bring it home and it ends up right there in your refrigerator or microwave? Or gets touched by one of your spoons? *Toi, toi, toi!* No. You need to leave the food to me."

To drive the point home, she promptly purchased a big plaid insulated picnic basket at the Target Store in Midwood. In preparation for every visit, she would fill it with a pint of chopped liver—or of tuna fish or egg salad—plus one pint apiece of cole slaw and of potato salad. She would add in two challah rolls, several new pickles tightly wrapped in cellophane, a ginger ale for Serach and a Cel-Ray tonic for herself, and a half-pound box of *parve* vanilla cookies with dabs of bright red jelly at their centers that they always managed to polish off between them.

She would also stick in all the materials and utensils required for the initial sanitization of surfaces, the serving of the food, the making of the appropriate blessings, and the eating itself.

She would think of everything, in short, and there was nothing Serach could do.

Serach nonetheless persisted in asking to at least help pay for what Frayda was bringing. She had no idea of the source of Frayda's income, and she imagined that no matter what it was, it couldn't possibly be very substantial. Plus, it was only fair that she should chip in.

Those requests, however, were consistently rebuked as well.

"If I can't treat my friend to a proper Kosher lunch once a month..." Frayda would begin—and the pride with which she said both "friend" and "proper Kosher lunch" would force Serach to swallow hard and say: "Okay, okay," before Frayda could even finish her sentence.

The matter was not irrevocably settled, however, until that rainy Tuesday in mid-April—slightly over a year into the pandemic—when Frayda arrived at the Rodriguez-Gottesman front door with an announcement that allowed for no opposition.

"You must never again offer to pay me for the food that I bring, Serach," she proclaimed, as she pulled off her shoes in the mud room, handed Serach her coat and umbrella, accepted the slippers that Serach handed to her, and strode into the kitchen. "I absolutely will not hear of it."

Serach said nothing as Frayda began to unpack her basket—vigorously spritzing and wiping down the two placemats with the disinfectant and sponge that she fished out from the basket's side zipper compartment.

She continued watching in silence as Frayda deftly pulled out the paper plates, assembled the chopped liver sandwiches, opened the salad containers, arranged the pickles, put out the silverware and glasses, and poured them each some soda.

She sat quietly as Frayda brought out the two-handled cup with which to do the pre-meal hand washing and the prayer books for *bentching* once the meal was over.

The moment that Frayda finally sat back to contentedly survey the oasis of *kashrut* that she had created, however, Serach posed the question that Frayda's words demanded.

"So, Frayda," she began. "Why is it that I must never again offer to pay for our lunch?"

"You must never again offer," Frayda answered, "because I am now employed and bringing in a solid income. Just like you. Better than you, probably, since you work for yourself—which means who knows what."

"Frayda!" Serach said, ignoring her friend's last comment and beaming warmly back at her. "How wonderful for you! Where is your employment—and what kind of work are you doing?"

Frayda picked up the two soda cans once again and determinedly shook the very last drops into their glasses.

"Wait," she said. "First the blessings, then the explanations."

She walked over to the sink with the two-handled cup, filled it carefully from the faucet without allowing any part of it to touch any part of the sink, poured the water over her hands three times—first over the right hand, then over the left—mumbled the blessing for ritual handwashing, returned to the table and handed the cup to Serach.

Serach took the cup and followed suit.

Frayda then made the appropriate blessing over her sandwich and took a careful bite.

"Okay, Frayda!" said Serach—as soon as Frayda swallowed. "Enough with the suspense! Talk!"

"So," said Frayda, leaning back in her chair, "one month ago this Sunday, I run into Malka Siegelstein in Edelman's Fresh Food Station on 12th Avenue—do you remember that store?"

"No, I don't remember that store, Frayda. It must have opened after my time."

Frayda shrugged.

"You may be right. Definitely right—now that I think of it. Well, in the meantime, it has made quite the name for itself. Only the best, it carries. I don't shop anywhere else anymore."

Was Frayda having fun with her by dragging her story out this way? Or was she just savoring it so much that she wanted it to last and last? You could never tell, with Frayda. But then Serach caught the little smirk of satisfaction on her friend's face and gave her a stern look.

"Frayda! Stop stalling! Tell me about the job!"

"Everything that I have told you is relevant."

Frayda waited for another narrowly-calculated couple of beats and then continued.

"So I run into Malka," she said, "whom I know from shul—her, you must remember. She's *davened* there for years."

Serach sighed and nodded.

"Yes, Frayda. I do remember Malka."

"We're not really close, she and I—never were—but she's a very friendly type, as you may also remember. Always smiling, always with the 'hello.' You can't as much as look at her before she begins a whole long conversation with you."

Frayda took another bite of her sandwich.

"However," she resumed, after carefully chewing and swallowing the bite, "on the Sunday that I see her at Edelman's, she is definitely not smiling. Or conversing. She's got this big frown plastered all over her face, up and down the aisles as I follow her. I wonder should I say something, and then I think: 'You don't ask, you don't find out.' So I say: 'Malka, you're looking so *farmisht*. What's wrong?' And Malka answers: 'It's Shprintza.'"

Frayda squinted at Serach.

"I don't know whether I ever shared this with you, but eight years ago Malka's youngest girl, Shprintza, married one of those big social service executive types. Dov Bernshteyn? The widower who lives in that big house on 53rd Street off 14th Avenue? Malka was really upset at first, even though she had been so completely *bazorgt* that here was her Shprintza already twenty-one years old and still unmarried. 'Why should my daughter settle for used goods?' she kept saying about the widower."

Frayda drew a breath.

"But Shprintza insists on it, says she really likes him—he's a good prospect, he's got this wonderful house—and it turns out she was right. Not only is she happy with the widower and the accommodations—she also lands herself a very good position working in one of Dov Bernshteyn's organizations. *B'Sevah Tovah*. Do you remember *B'Sevah Tovah*—that assisted living residence for men, up on 12h Avenue? Very solid—very good reputation?"

Serach nodded.

"Yes. I remember it."

"So Shprintza becomes head of the Human Resources Department at *B'Sevah Tovah* and is doing an excellent job. I can't tell you how many times Malka has shared that particular fact with me, even though we only talk in *shul* and not as much as she'd like because some *yenta* always shushes us."

Frayda took a much larger bite of her sandwich, ate a good half of the potato salad and most of the cole slaw, finished it all off with a pickle and then reached for her soda to take a big swig.

"But as it turns out," she finished and continued, "at this particular point in time, having that particular position in that particular place has not been such a great thing."

She paused and shook her head.

"Because of what is happening with the COVID," she resumed, sotto voce—as if she were saying something dirty. "All the patients are getting sick and half the staff are packing up and leaving. Like rats from a ship"

"That seems to be the story all over the place."

Frayda grunted.

"So you say. Well, in Shprintza's case, the situation is causing her all kinds of *tsoris* as you can well imagine, because she's the person responsible for making sure they can still do all the things they need to do to stay in business. Even without enough staff. And, of course," she added, "if it's causing Shprintza *tsoris*, it's causing Malka *tsoris*."

Frayda paused and began wiping the remains of the potato salad up with the remains of the challah from her sandwich.

"So, I ask Malka—just to make conversation, you understand, I wasn't angling for anything—I ask: 'so, what kinds of positions are empty?' And Malka answers: 'All sorts of positions. It is a total catastrophe.'"

Frayda polished off the challah and took another long sip of her soda.

"'But where we need help the most right now,' Malka goes on, 'is in the dental department. Because' as she explains, 'not only has the receptionist quit, but so has the dental assistant who has been there for years and who has always known how to handle everything.'"

Frayda paused, wiped her mouth, and took another sip.

"It seems that Dr. Pessin—that's the dentist who's in charge—is threatening to quit, himself, he's so upset by it all.

Can you imagine what would happen if that were to happen? If there were no dentist, either? Dental issues wait for no one, as you know. Especially when you're dealing with old people. It's a constant stream of crises."

She nodded to herself several times in quick succession.

"But what can Shprintza do? How can she find the staff she needs? Who wants to work in a dental department these days, with patients sitting there with their mouths wide open and all those germs flying all over the place, you can't possibly control the contamination?"

"Okay, Frayda," said Serach, suddenly intuiting what was coming, since she knew Frayda's family history. "I'm getting the idea. So what did you respond to all that?"

"I responded: 'As it turns out, Malka, I have some experience in that particular field. I was the dental receptionist and the dental assistant for my father—the best dentist in Washington Heights—for two decades before marrying my husband and moving to Boro Park...'"

Frayda finished off her soda.

"And the next thing you know," she added, popping a couple of cookies in her mouth, "I am interviewing for a position and they are asking me about my experience and my qualifications and my availability and...."

"And they hire you!"

"And they hire me. On the spot. Dr. Pessin (he's such a nice man besides being such a good dentist) has been training me to use all the fancy-shmancy equipment they now use—you wouldn't believe all the advances they've made in thirty years. He's shown me how to put on my special protective equipment, so I stay safe—you shouldn't worry. He's taught me how to answer the phone just the way he likes it, and how to make the appointments and how to handle the cancellations. He's also teaching me how to deal with the billing, which has also changed a great deal over the years—you should know, you're an accountant."

Serach nodded and Frayda gave her a smile wider than any that Serach had ever seen on her face, and then leaned back in her chair.

"So once again, I am working within my profession," she resumed, after a brief satisfied moment. "As the dental receptionist and the dental assistant and the dental file keeper and the head of dental billing for the *B'Sevah Tovah* Assisted Living Facility. The *ganze megillah.*"

"I'm so proud of you, Frayda."

"Friday, of course, we end the day early for Shabbos," Frayda continued. "And Sunday is just a half-day. And I get every other Tuesday off—which is why I moved our monthly lunch date to Tuesdays instead of Mondays. But, other than that, I am there full-time, doing everything that Dr. Pessin needs. And then some."

"I think it is all terrific, Frayda."

"Yes, it is. Out of this whole COVID *balagan*, something good emerges."

Frayda licked her fingers, wiped them with her napkin, and then folded the napkin and stuffed it back in the picnic basket along with her glass, silverware, and placemat.

"So now you need to finish up your lunch as well and we need to *bentch* so I can pack up your things, too, and go home. I can't spend the whole afternoon schmoozing with you anymore. Not since I became responsible for all the dental issues of sixty *alte kakers* who never learned to floss properly."

"No, Frayda," said Serach, putting down her fork and reaching for the prayer book that Frayda was handing her. "I don't suppose you can."

September 2021: Brooklyn and the Bronx

- 5 -

"I won't be going to the wake," Paloma announced when Gordito called her with the news.

God forbid that I should have to see my brother's body lying on gold satin in a fancy casket in some stuffy funeral chapel—his face all pumped up with embalming fluid, his body crammed into a stiff black suit, those wonderful, square workman's hands folded reverently over the heart that betrayed him.

"I won't be at the funeral Mass, either."

God forbid that I should have to sit in mock devotion in the Church of St. Nicholas of Tolentine—scene of so many of my parochial school traumas—as an off-key choir burbles through a pop-enhanced hymn and a fat, white-faced priest drones on about the piety of a man who hated religion. What the hell was Beatriz thinking, anyway, commissioning a full-blown Catholic Mass in that place? She never goes to Mass, herself. It's all for show.

"I will, however, come to the burial."

That, at least, will be held in Woodlawn Cemetery, the secret turf that Manny and I shared on so many sweet, hot summer evenings. How bold we were—slipping between the gates just before the skies darkened, daring one another to get right up close to those terrifying mausoleums with their perpetually dank interiors! How deliciously I would shiver as I peered into those dark depths! How comforting Manny's arms would feel when he finally stopped laughing, caught me up in a monster hug, and whisked me out again, just before the gates closed for the night.

"That's okay, Tía," mumbled Gordito. "You don't have to come to all the different parts. But I did have to tell you about them. I mean…"

"Of course you did, Gordito," said Paloma, suddenly contrite.

For Gordito was, of course, going to be a loyal soldier for his beloved father, every step of the way. As he had been during all those unspeakably difficult past months in which Manny had been so ruthlessly—so heartbreakingly—stubborn in refusing her visits and advice. ("I'm fine, Hermana! I don't need you here, being the bigshot nurse and telling me what to do!")

He would be sitting by his father's open coffin for as long as it remained stashed in that incense-reeking chapel—late into the night and all the way into the morning—if they let him.

He would be sitting at the Mass in his own too-tight black suit, responding to the service in all the right places—God alone knows where he got his faith, given the parents he's had.

He would be manfully helping to bear the coffin from hearse to gravesite.

"Of course you did," she repeated.

"Uh, well then I guess I'll see you on Wednesday morning," muttered Gordito.

Paloma nodded at her phone.

"Yes, Gordito—you will."

She took a breath.

"And may God bless you for all that you are doing for your father and for everyone else," she finally added. "May God bless us all."

Wednesday dawned hot and humid, a covering of gun-metal-gray clouds foreshadowing the heavy rains that would inevitably follow. By the time Paloma reached the cemetery, scrutinized the map, and found her way to the gravesite, it had begun to sprinkle.

Standing on one side of the gash in the earth was a slender woman in a daffodil-yellow slicker and long black hair whom Paloma had never seen before, a priest as fat and white-faced as Paloma had imagined, and a small dark man in a small dark suit standing with a boom box in one hand and a canvas bag full of black umbrellas in the other.

Across from them was a female figure in a too-short black dress and high black heels, and a tall skinny creature in a black hoodie. Both were looking at the ground so intently that their chins appeared to be wedged into their chests.

Oh my God—that must be Beatriz! How squashed she looks! And—oh sweet Jesus—that's poor Anteojitos!

A moment later, several things happened—seemingly all at once. The heavens opened to let down a torrent of water. The priest's assistant flew around the group distributing umbrellas. Six black-clad men appeared ten yards back on the walkway and began trudging slowly toward them, casket on their shoulders, at the full mercy of the rain.

Paloma recognized Negrito, Gordito, and the two mechanics from Manny's shop—God bless them for paying this last tribute to their late boss. The other two pallbearers were strangers to her—anonymous cemetery workers brought on for the job, no doubt, since there were no other males among Manny's small circle of family and friends to assume those two last somber positions beneath his casket.

The downpour cascaded onto the pallbearers' heads and shoulders, running down their backs and their legs. It flooded over the casket—a dismal affair of dull gold and ostentatious brass trim—to land on the rapidly-drenching ground with enough force to be heard.

A few feet before the pallbearers reached their destination, however, the drumming of the rainstorm was overpowered by an explosion of music from the boom box in the priest's assistant's hand. Trumpets, guitars, maracas, an accordion—and a full-voiced contralto pleading in Spanish to be remembered—accompanied their last steps forward to lay the casket down on the complicated mechanical device that would eventually lower Paloma's brother into the ground.

As soon as the coffin was in place, the pallbearers dispersed. The two graveyard workers grabbed umbrellas from the priest's assistant's black canvas bag, unfurled them, and moved a discreet distance away from the core group of mourners. The two mechanics did the same with the umbrellas and assumed spots near Beatriz. Gordito ran to Paloma's side and attempted to squeeze his rain-soaked bulk under the umbrella that she had shown the foresight to bring. Negrito—sleek as an otter in tight black pants and a drenched long-sleeved black shirt—bolted toward the still-blasting boom box and switched it off in a gesture dramatic enough for all to see.

"What the hell are you doing playing that Mexican shit at my father's burial?"

He swept the hank of his dripping hair away from his forehead and stood face-to-face with the priest for a long tense moment. The priest reached out from under his own umbrella to touch his confronter's shoulder.

"My son," he said, softly. "We were told that this was an Hispanic service. We always..."

"This is not a goddamned Hispanic service! We are all Americans here. Or don't you think so?"

"No, of course not, my son. Of course you are all Americans."

Negrito strode over to the girl in yellow, shaking himself out as he walked. She put a hand on his arm and attempted to accommodate the umbrella's span over his head. He pushed it aside and then stood very straight as the rain continued pouring down his face.

"I'm okay without it, Gloria."

Ah, thought Paloma. Gloria. The girlfriend.

The priest returned to carrying out the service, seemingly unperturbed. He said some prayers, recited some psalms, muttered some platitudes about the dearly departed, then returned to saying some prayers.

The mechanics joined Gordito, Anteojitos, and the priest's assistant in bowing their heads where appropriate. Beatriz, Negrito, and the girlfriend remained stanchly upright throughout. As did Paloma. Instead of praying, she used the opportunity presented by the gathering to carry out a good long evaluation of the girl she had never met and the woman she had pointedly avoided since Beatriz had made clear her scorn for Paloma's life—and life partner.

Jesus, she's gorgeous, she thought as she eyed Gloria up and down—feeling suddenly old in her own little tan trench coat and in the presence of such youthful panache. Negrito has done very well for himself. And Jesus, Beatriz looks tired and spent.

Eventually, the priest—having offered a few final platitudes about Manny and reciting a couple of final psalms—seemed to be wrapping up.

"Let us conclude with the words with which our Savior taught us all to pray some two millennia ago," he was proclaiming. He then launched into a heavily-American-accented Spanish version of the "Our Father."

At which point, Negrito shook off Gloria's hand and once more bolted forward.

"Maybe you haven't caught on yet," he growled—clenching and unclenching his fists. "But we all speak English here. In fact, some of our families," and here he gestured toward Gloria, "have been living on what is now U.S. soil a hell of a lot longer than yours. So kindly cut out all that fake Spanish shit. My father would have hated it and it's getting on my nerves."

The priest looked back at him mildly, nodded briefly, and—impressively—resumed the "Our Father" in English, at exactly the spot at which he had left off. When he had finished, he tilted his head toward the two cemetery workers and they stepped forward to lean over the casket, loosen certain straps, and turn certain cranks on the metal structure on which it rested.

Slowly—ever so slowly—the coffin began its descent into the earth to land without a sound. When it had reached its final resting place, however—and when the two workers had stepped back again—the soundlessness was broken by an otherworldly wail.

The wail hovered directly over the mourners for a brief moment before sweeping across the full three hundred acres of the cemetery, tilting precipitously upward, and soaring through the wall of plummeting rain to reach the heavens themselves. It then kept going—crescendo-ing ever more wildly—until Negrito bounded forward to reach Anteojitos, smacked him forcefully on the side of his head, and pulled him into a rocking, shaking embrace that finally returned the world to silence.

At which point, the rain began to let up.

"I think it's all over, Tía," came Gordito's muffled voice. "I think the gravediggers will do the rest."

"Not yet," said Paloma. "There's something I have to do before they start in."

She folded up her umbrella and stuffed it into her raincoat pocket. She then bent down to pick up a fistful of the well-soaked earth that had been excavated from the gravesite and threw it into the abyss over the coffin.

"Catholics sometimes do this and sometimes they don't," she murmured as she came back to Gordito's side. "But Jews always do. Serach says it helps. Try it."

Gordito nodded and followed suit—and then Negrito, Gloria, and the two mechanics did so as well. Beatriz and Anteojitos stayed rigidly in their places, however, and when it was clear that they weren't going to move, the two cemetery workers—now armed with shovels—stepped forward to start heaving the rest of the pile of soil back into place.

"Okay," Paloma sighed to Gordito after watching them for a moment. "Now it really is all over. Let me just touch base with your mother and brothers and I'll get myself out of here."

She briskly walked over to Beatriz. It took an effort to take those few steps—and to extend her hand—but she heard Serach's voice in her head telling her to be the adult in that space and she acquiesced.

"I'm very sorry, Beatriz," she said. "I know this must be very hard for you."

Beatriz shrugged and looked away, and Paloma swiftly turned on her own heel and reached for Anteojitos. She had almost as little success with him as she'd had with his mother.

"You need to remember something, Anteojitos," she said, as he squirmed uncomfortably out of her arms. "Serach and I will always be there for you. You can count on us. I mean it."

"Tía Serach," he said, after she had let go, "didn't come today."

Paloma's lips tightened briefly.

"Serach wanted to—she really did," she said. "She loves you. She loved your father. But no way was I going to expose her to the kind of abuse your mother is capable of dishing. With me, as you saw, she was simply rude. Thankfully for her. With Serach, God knows what she might have said or done—or what might have happened next. Graveside or no graveside."

Anteojitos glanced sideways at his aunt for a half-second—the fog and raindrops on his glasses obscuring the expression in his eyes. He then dropped his head and the wet black hood of his sweatshirt fell forward to shield his whole face. Paloma reached out to squeeze one of his bony shoulders and—receiving no response—sighed and walked briskly to the other side of the grave to reach Negrito and his girlfriend.

"You've certainly become The Man around here, haven't you?" she grinned, before catching her oldest nephew up in a fierce embrace that he didn't resist. "Good for you. Your father would have been proud."

She paused to gaze at his serious, handsome countenance. Then she turned to Gloria.

"Thank you for being here for my nephew, my dear," she said. "He may never admit it, but he's always needed someone like you in his life."

Gloria smiled briefly but warmly back, and Paloma whirled around to face Negrito again.

"Call me when you next find yourself in trouble," she said. "And call me even when you don't. Don't you dare forget about your old aunt."

He nodded.

"And behave yourself, *Pendejo!* Stop being such a goddamned bully with Anteojitos! He deserves your support—not your bullshit. Especially now that your father is gone."

Negrito bent down to give her a kiss on the cheek. He then straightened himself up again and attempted a cocky smile. It looked incongruous with his sad, sad eyes.

"I'll be good. I promise," he said. "Fabulous, even. You just wait. You'll be hearing nothing but good things about me. All the time."

"I'll give you a ride home, Tía," said Gordito, suddenly re-plastered at her side.

"No need," she said. "Though it's very sweet of you to offer. I can easily manage the hike back to the subway now that it's stopped raining. The exercise will help me shed the weight of this abysmally sad day. Besides—don't you need to bring your mother and Anteojitos home?"

"Um, Negrito will take care of Mama and Anteojitos," Gordito replied, looking back in their direction. "And see, there's something in my truck that you need to—that I have to talk to you about."

She raised an eyebrow.

"And that would be?"

"See, Papito left a will and I'm the executor, and you need to see it because—see—there's something in there that's about you that you should know about."

Paloma suddenly stumbled, forcing Gordito to catch her.

Oh, shit, she thought. Manny's left instructions about my telling Mama that he's dead. It's all in writing. It's all in his will. Shit.

"Okay, Gordito," she finally managed to mutter. "Let's go."

They began heading toward the main Webster Avenue gate—Paloma (generally as sure-footed as a cat) stumbling so many times that Gordito eventually placed one thick arm around her shoulders to help steer her forward. All across the slippery wet cemetery paths they moved forward within that clumsy embrace. At the entrance, Gordito made a move to lift his arm away, but Paloma leaned up against him so insistently that he refastened his grip, and—firmly glued together—they continued navigating the ten blocks of Webster Avenue till they reached the narrow street on which he had parked the dark green Los Milagros Auto Shop pick-up truck.

Gordito steered his aunt to the passenger door, unlocked it, and stood by while she pulled herself in. He then lumbered around the front, climbed into the driver's seat, and reached across her lap to open the glove compartment.

"It's, um—the will is in that tan envelope."

Paloma retrieved the envelope, unfolded its flap, and pulled out a piece of paper that had clearly been creased and re-creased many times.

"I'm the one who's holding the will because Papito made me the executor," Gordito repeated, and the pride in his voice was palpable.

"So you say," said Paloma, distractedly, before remembering herself and adding—with the proper degree of admiration, this time: "That's a really important job he gave you."

"Well, he trusts me," Gordito said, fumbling over his tenses—as he would for many months to come. "He knows that I'll do whatever he needs me to do."

He paused.

"See, when he got so sick, I was the one who... I mean, I've basically been running the shop for him ever since."

Paloma reached over to hug her nephew's heaving shoulders for a long moment before turning her attention to the document that was burning a hole in her hand.

It was a single handwritten page. Not much of an official will. It was, however, properly signed, witnessed, and notarized. She recognized the signatures of the two mechanics and the seal of the notary from the bank on Jerome Avenue that her brother had always used.

It was also, unmistakably, Manny. Abrupt. Illiterate. Straight to the point.

June 28, 2021

I leave all my shares of the Los Milagros Auto Shop Business to my son, Roberto Victor Rodriguez who is the Executor of this Will on Condition that he keep Suporting His Mother and His Brother Ramon Ernesto Rodriguez as long as They need it and that He Sends half the proffits to Fernando Eduardo Reyes and his Father my business partner like I do every Quater.

I leave Everything in my Savings Account and IRA to my oldest son, Oscar Gregorio Rodriguez, to Invest in his new Computer StartUp Business.

To my sister Paloma Belén Rodriguez who Doesn't Need anything I leave Joe's Phonograph which is in the Storage Room in the Basment of my Apartment House. Everything else I leave to my wife Beatriz Gallego Saenz.

Signed: Emmanuel Alberto Rodriguez

Paloma stared at the page for far longer than should have been necessary. Had she missed something? No. She had not. There was absolutely nothing in it about their mother, Dolores. No address given for her house. No directions on how to get there. Not a single traceable, guilt-inducing word about Paloma's promise to tell Dolores that her only son was dead.

With no one any the wiser about that foolish, involuntary promise, Paloma was free to do as she wished. Which was to leave her mother in the full selfish ignorance that she had seemingly always craved where her two children were concerned.

"Are you done, Tía? Have you read it?"

"Yes," Paloma said, suddenly yanked back from her reverie. "Yes, I have."

She carefully re-folded the paper, re-inserted it in the envelope and put the envelope back in the glove compartment.

Gordito nodded and reached for the gear shift.

"So who is Joe?" he asked after they had pulled out of the parking spot to hit the road. "And what is a phonograph? What was Papito talking about?"

Paloma was so relieved at his question that she burst into giggles.

"A phonograph is—God, it's so before your time that I can't even begin to explain it. A phonograph is like a turntable for records that...."

"Oh, yeah, sure. I know what a turntable is. The D.J. at the Club Los Piquantes up on Westchester Avenue uses one."

He took one hand off the driving wheel to briefly scratch the back of his head.

"But I never knew that Papito had one of them. I guess he just kept it in the storage bin and didn't talk about it. What are you going to do with it?"

"God only knows!" Paloma snorted. "Probably throw it out. I have no idea why he hung onto it or why he would care what happened to it after he was gone. He wasn't particularly sentimental, your father. Plus, he and Joe didn't exactly get along."

"And who is Joe?" Gordito repeated, as he began heading out toward the Major Deegan Expressway.

"Oh yeah. You wouldn't know about him either, would you? Joe is—well, he was a long time ago—your grandmother's boyfriend."

She paused.

"Not your grandmother from your mother's side. Your father Manny's mother."

"Abuela never mentioned anyone named Joe to me."

It took Paloma a moment to fully absorb what her nephew had just said. But when it finally hit her, she whipped around to face him.

"And when would your Abuela have mentioned Joe to you?"

"Uh, I don't know. On one of my visits."

Paloma's left fist flexed, her arm drew back, and then she caught herself. She had actually wanted to punch him! *Jesus, Paloma—get a hold of yourself!*

But then again, how dare he? How dare he have had a history of cozy little visits with Dolores? Of sitting and chatting with that monster of a woman?

She caught her breath.

"And when exactly do you pay those visits to your Abuela?" she finally managed.

Gordito shrugged.

"I go up to see her at the beginning of November to make sure her thermostat is set right and the vents are okay because if you don't, well, the propane costs—you can blow through hundreds of dollars in those mobile homes if you aren't careful. Then in May, I go back up again to check on her A/C and make sure the vents are okay again, because—"

Despite her mounting rage, Paloma couldn't help but note (not for the first time) that when Gordito talked about something about which he felt confident, his speech became perfectly coherent. She quickly brushed those musings away, however, to return to the matter at hand.

"And did your father go with you on all those lovely little visits?" she said, before he could drag out his explanation of vents and costs any further. "And do your brothers accompany you?"

Every kind thought that she had ever had about Manny suddenly evaporated at the idea that he and his sons had continued to visit Dolores over the years, despite all his claims to the contrary. At the thought that he had continued to cater to the woman who had rejected her only daughter—Manny's only sister—with such devastating thoroughness.

"No, Tía. It's been just me for, like, ages. I mean—since I learned to drive. And to fix things. Papito and Abuela don't—I mean they didn't—get along so well. They...."

"Yes?"

"Fight a lot. Fought a lot. Once he got really nasty with her."

Paloma's heart swelled. *Okay. Less of a betrayal than I feared.*

"And—I mean—he couldn't do much of anything after..."

"After he got sick," Paloma finished his sentence.

Gordito nodded.

"Yeah. After that. And then Negrito..." he began again.

"Is Negrito." Paloma cut him off, even more abruptly. She had suddenly lost all patience with this conversation. Just wanted it to be over.

"Yeah, well," Gordito forged ahead, anyway, "Negrito never really cared about Abuela. So I don't ask him to come with me."

He drew a long and labored breath and ploughed on.

"And Anteojitos..." he began

He stopped and this time Paloma waited for him to finish.

"With Anteojitos," he concluded, suddenly super-lucid, "everything is always harder. So I don't try to bring him, either."

He stopped again.

"Anyway, so it's best if it's just me," he concluded. "Abuela and me, we've always been okay."

He finally fell into silence and Paloma felt grateful. Before she could fully relax, however, her equilibrium was once again assaulted by a long, piercing wail. It had nowhere near the dimensions of what Anteojitos had produced earlier in the day—Gordito had always been the quietest among Manny's three sons. But it definitely had some substance.

"Oh, noooooooooooo!"

"Jesus, Gordito! What's wrong!"

It took some seconds before he could stop. Paloma handed him a tissue and he blew his nose hard before taking another gigantic breath.

"Abuela doesn't know what's happened to Papito!" he finally sputtered. "When I saw her last May, he was—well, he was weak, but he was still...so I didn't say anything. I didn't want to worry her. But when I go up to see her this November, I'm going to have to tell her that he's...."

Manny—damn you! You knew that you didn't have to put anything about my promise into your will because you knew that all of this would eventually come out and that I wouldn't let Gordito face that terrible task alone.

¡Pendejo!

"No you won't have to tell her, Gordito," she finally breathed. "I'm the one who needs to do it. I'll go up with you when you drive up in November. All you need to do is get me there. Since you're the one who knows the way."

October 2021: Brooklyn and Manhattan

- 6 -

"What do you mean, you can't go?"

"I mean that I can't go! That particular Thursday is the day of my re-certification exam. I'm all signed up for it. I've been studying for weeks. I'm sure that I told you about it."

"You told me about the exam. Not about the date."

"Well, perhaps not. But then how was I to know it was the same day as your luncheon? You didn't tell me anything about the luncheon till just now, either."

Serach caught sight of her partner's downcast face and paused.

"Paloma, I'm really sorry," she said. "You know how much I support Manhattan East and how proud I am that you work there. Haven't I been making sizable donations to them for the past few years now?"

Paloma shrugged.

"But going on that particular date is totally out of the question. It's the only time that this exam will be given this fall. Taking it—and doing well on it—are critical to my practice. I can't afford to miss it!"

"So what am I supposed to do with your ticket? We were going to be sitting together at a nice little two-person table with clear sightlines to both the lake and the podium. I paid a lot for those tickets. They weren't the most expensive in the house, but they also weren't the discounted employee tickets that would have landed us at a table way at the back, jammed right up against three other couples. You've always wanted to dine at the Central Park Boathouse and we've somehow never gotten around to it. This was going to be your big chance."

"Paloma, it is not my fault that you didn't consult me before buying my ticket. Why did you just presume that I would be free to go with you?"

"You work for yourself. You're always free."

Serach tightened her lips. Why did everyone always think that?

"Well, on that particular day I'm occupied," she said. "You're going to have to invite someone else."

"Who am I supposed to invite?"

"How about Etha?"

"Etha is in Jamaica visiting her cousins that week."

"Well, then—how about Frank?"

"Frank is so uptight about the dangers of social gatherings that he makes me look reckless by comparison. We haven't as much as met in person since this all started."

"Well, this function might just do the trick. It'll be fancy— just as he likes. It'll be held outdoors, with just you and him at a table—safe as can be. Give it a try. Tell him he needs airing out."

Serach spoke deadpan, but Paloma grinned.

"Okay, okay. You're right. It might be just the thing to finally spring him out of his cave."

As it turned out, it was. Frank agreed to it. Quietly, but definitely.

Which is why Paloma felt so anxious as she sat there at her pricey two-person table for a good twenty minutes without any sign of his arrival. It wasn't like him to be late. She checked her phone for the eighth time and sent him a second text. He hadn't answered the first.

`Where R U?`

On my way.

Well, thanks for finally deciding to respond. Hurry up! Almost everyone else is seated—they'll be starting any minute.

She closed her eyes, opened them up again, nibbled at her roll, sipped at her ice water, and waited some more. Finally, she spotted her former housemate ambling down the path toward the restaurant as if the word 'hurry' was unknown to him. He sidled into the restaurant's front entrance where he took his good time signing in and then made his way out the back door and onto the terrace.

"I was ready to give up hope," she said, rising to hug him.

Frank ducked away from her arms and sat down.

"Please," he said, shaking his head. "These things never start on time."

He looked around him with the practiced eye of a performer counting the house.

"Well, darling, this certainly beats the last fundraising luncheon that you described to me. That one at which you spoke? That one that was held—where again? In the cafeteria of the hospital laboratory—a place in which no one in his right mind would want to eat a single olive?"

He delicately peeled off his mask, reached for a roll, buttered it, took a miniscule bite, and looked around him again.

"So tell me. What did it take to make the powers-that-be change their fundraising approach? Why are we here and not slumming it in some empty operating room?"

"Shush, Frank. Not so loud!"

"Oh, please," he continued in the same unregulated register. "We are the only ones at this table and no one is paying us any mind. You can answer with a clean conscience. Why the change of heart?"

Paloma sighed. He wasn't going to stop till she answered him.

"The luncheon that I described to you, once upon a time," she said, keeping her own voice pitched well below his, "the luncheon that you are remembering in such detail—was basically an information-sharing session for Manhattan East's most elite donors and board members. People who are congenitally incapable of being impressed by anything. People who are dedicated to keeping a tight rein on every penny that we spend. Why would we have bothered springing for a deluxe venue for that particular crowd, at that particular time?"

She paused and ate another piece of her own roll.

"This event is different. It's designed to thank and impress our 'minor' donors (the ones who probably had to think twice before shelling out $700 or more for lunch) while reassuring the elite group of truly mega-donors (the ones who have been fueling our recent capital campaign) that we are still alive, kicking, and capable of pulling off something like this. Plus, it's a way to cheer everyone up—the rich and the less-rich—after our long collective hibernation. We're all a bit desperate for some celebration, aren't we?"

Frank made a face. "Well, I guess I must rank among the riffraff, because I'm seriously impressed," he said. "The Central Park Lake lapping gently away not a stone's throw from our seats. Those quaint little rowboats bobbing up and down. The towering buildings of Billionaires Row peeping out over the trees to our south. Very impressive—the whole thing."

He adjusted his tortoise-shell glasses and peered at the program.

"Then, of course, there's the menu! Why do you suppose they've opted to top the salmon with both a lemon-butter glaze and a sprig of candied violets? Is it the color scheme that they're after? Or the taste? I adore candied violets. But I would never have thought to put them on top of salmon. More appropriate for a wedding cake, wouldn't you say?"

His voice remained several degrees louder than it should have been. He sounded almost drunk—and Frank was a teetotaler.

"Frank, will you please keep it down? And will you please stop making fun of everything?"

"I'm being perfectly serious, Paloma. I love a good presentation."

He glanced down at the program again.

"I also can't wait to hear about all the breakthroughs that you're making in that laboratory of yours—dismal as its cafeteria may have been as a party venue."

"Frank—what is the matter with you? Why did you even accept my invitation if you're going to behave in this way?"

Frank had the good grace to look chastened. But then he leaned over and spoke once again in a stage whisper.

"My only regret is that you haven't made a move to introduce me to that donor who nearly seduced you back in that long-ago epoch before everything fell apart. What was her name? Carla? Charlotte?"

"Frank, stop it! Please! Pipe down!"

"Or is she not in attendance this afternoon?"

"Oh, she's here all right, Frank," Paloma finally sighed. What was she going to do with him? "I saw her name card at the reception desk. I also caught sight of her back as she glided onto the terrace. She must have been shriveling away for the past two years with no live events to go to. She's a real party girl."

She paused.

"But I'm not going to introduce you to her, Frank, so you can totally remove that hope from your naughty little mind. She and I parted on very bad terms. As you must recall."

Frank raised an eyebrow.

"So what table is she at, dear?"

Paloma couldn't help herself. She had, of course, made note of Carlota's place card.

"Table 5. Down at the front with the other super-big shots, of course."

"Well," said Frank, and he stood up. "Then I guess I have no choice but to take a little stroll down to Table 5 to catch a glimpse on my own. The speeches haven't started. The main course hasn't arrived. People are still picking at their fruit salad and dinner rolls. I'm sure I'll be able to spot her. She's a blonde, right? Rail-thin like one of the Social X-Rays in Tom Wolfe's *Bonfire of the Vanities*?"

Paloma had no idea what book he was alluding to but she caught his meaning and nodded, despite herself.

"And what color will Carlota be wearing?" he continued.

"Frank—don't! Please don't!"

"What color, Paloma?"

His sternness caught her off guard.

"White," she sighed. "Head to toe. She only wears white. But Frank—"

"Don't worry, dear. I'll be subtle as a minnow, swimming hither and yon. One glance in her direction and I'll speed immediately back to your side. She won't suspect a thing."

Then he slipped away.

What was up with him? His behavior was far beyond odd. It was bordering on downright crass—a startling departure from his normal bone-deep sense of Southern decorum.

Even his appearance was off in some way.

Yes, his navy-blue suit was as exquisitely tasteful as always—its cut neatly poised between Italian movie director and British banker. The tie that he'd chosen was both subtle and eye-catching. His tobacco-brown cap-toe oxfords were buffed to the appropriately muted shine.

But something—something subtle and unplaceable—was wrong.

As Paloma watched him wend his way forward toward Table 5, it finally came to her. That tasteful suit—that suit that must have put him back a small fortune—was sagging ever so slightly around his shoulders and his hips. Not so much that a casual viewer might catch it. But enough to alarm someone who knew Frank's commitment to maintaining the impeccable figure required to showcase an impeccably tailored jacket. In the past year and a half during which Frank had basically kept himself out of Paloma's sight, he had apparently lost most of his muscle tone.

In a disturbing flash of insight— and for the first time since she had known him—Paloma could picture her best friend as an old man.

He slipped back into his seat before she had the chance to digest what all that might mean.

"Well, Paloma, you clearly escaped with your life," he said in the outrageously boisterous tone that was beginning to scare her deeply. "How could you even contemplate having an affair with such a creature? She has 'harpy' written all over her. Not to mention 'Botox.'"

Paloma responded before she could help herself.

"I didn't 'almost do it' because I in any way desired her, Frank," she said. "As you may remember. I 'almost did it' because I thought her assistance might be useful in keeping my nephew out of prison. It would have been a seduction of convenience—nothing more."

Frank arched an eyebrow.

"Well thank God you didn't start anything major with her. She would be a terrible companion for you. You are so much better off alone."

"Frank," said Paloma, feeling her cheeks flame. "Let's get out of here."

"Good heavens, Paloma! Why would we leave right now? Don't you want to hear about all those medical advances they're going to describe? Don't you want to sample that enticing salmon with violets? Aren't there scads of people with whom you need to network?"

"I already know about all those advances," Paloma replied, enunciating deliberately. "I don't want to eat—I seem to have lost my appetite. There is no one here that I want to chat up. The only person I need to talk with is you. Let's go!"

Frank picked up his fork and then put it down again. By the time it reached the napkin, Paloma had stood up, pushed back her chair, and begun walking toward the exit. Frank rose reluctantly as well and trailed her out of the restaurant and into the park.

When they had reached a spot suitably far from the event, Paloma whirled around to face him. The setting was hardly conducive to serious conversation. Crowds of New Yorkers and tourists were whizzing by on the road in front of them on scooters, in pedicabs, in horse-drawn carriages, on bikes, and on foot. Someone nearby was crooning "New York, New York" along with a boom box playing at full volume and one of the cyclists was circling around and back with Edith Piaf songs blaring out at them at an equally penetrating pitch.

Paloma tuned them all out to lock eyes inescapably with her friend.

"Okay, Frank. Here goes. Let me begin by saying that I was absolutely thrilled when you agreed to come with me today. For many reasons."

She monitored his face. It registered nothing. But he was clearly listening.

"I thought it would be good for you to finally get out of the house. I thought it would be blissful to finally see you in person. Damnit, I've missed you! More than I can say."

She paused and caught her breath.

"But now that I am seeing you, I'm worried sick. What has gotten into you? Why are you behaving so badly? It's always been fun to trade wicked remarks with you, but today it's like your inner monologue has totally evacuated."

Still no reaction.

"And for goodness' sake, what did you possibly mean by saying that I'm 'better off alone'? I'm not alone! Serach and I are closer than ever. Frank, what's up with you?"

Frank remained standing, eyes closed—tilting back and forth slightly and giving the impression that he was about to keel over entirely.

"Frank?"

Frank opened his eyes and looked out over her head to the landscape around him.

"There is truly nothing more beautiful than Central Park in the fall, is there?" he said in his most melodious drawl. "The trees. The fall flowers. The dark greens and the dandelion yellows and the red-oranges of all hues."

He sighed.

"Not to mention that from this particular vantage point, we also have the chance to enjoy New York's stunning new Midtown skyline. Trees and skyscrapers all packaged together in one vast seamless vista. Sunlight glinting through delicate yellow leaves and sunlight glinting on massive glass facades. Absolutely stunning, wouldn't you say?"

"Frank! Talk to me! What is going on with you? What is wrong?"

She waited while he licked his lips, straightened his tie, and finally closed his eyes.

"Kae-Dang and I have parted ways," he finally breathed. "He no longer wants to continue our relationship."

"Good Lord, Frank. When? When did that happen?"

"Three months ago."

"Three months ago? And where have you been living ever since?"

Frank's voice went up a good five notes.

"I've been... I'm still.... living in his apartment. Well, he needs my share of the maintenance costs, and..."

Paloma barely controlled her face.

"Frank—for God's sake, why haven't you just packed up your things and moved out? You don't owe him a thing! Why should you care about his maintenance costs!"

Frank went back to licking his lips.

"Where would I go?" he eventually whispered.

"Frank! Back to us, of course. You have a forever home in our house—don't you know that? The Bösendorfer Grand has been crying out for your touch for ages! I've been dying to watch you savoring my meals. How could you possibly doubt that Serach and I would want to have you living with us again? How could you stand to keep living in Kae-Dang's tiny apartment for three months, while—"

"While I was forced to move from our conjugal bed to the living room couch? While Kae-Dang was dating other men? While I was continually being exposed to... to..."

Paloma was left wondering whether he was going to say "all that humiliation" or "all those germs" because he snapped his mouth shut and turned his face determinedly away from her.

"Yes," she pushed forward when it was clear that he wasn't going to finish the sentence. "How could you possibly have stayed while all of that was going on?"

"Because I loved him, Paloma," Frank replied in a voice so soft she barely heard it. "Because I kept hoping that he would change his mind. Because I love him still."

My poor Frank! Paloma shook her head. How could he possibly have made himself so vulnerable? How could he possibly still love that schmuck? Well, this damned pandemic has skewed so many of our perspectives, ripped away so many of our choices—diminished us all.

"Okay, Frank, okay," she finally said, out loud. "It's okay. I understand."

He reached into his pocket, pulled out his spotless folded handkerchief, and wiped his face.

"Besides," he said, his face returning to something approximating its usual color. "How was I supposed to get all my things safely out of there and into any other dwelling in the midst of this world crisis? How was I going to transport my clothes, my books—my music! My Modigliani! Was I supposed to take all of that with me on the subway? Was I supposed to hail a taxi and spend an hour in traffic with some horrible unwashed driver breathing all his germs at me in that small, enclosed, inescapable space!"

"Well, no more fears on that front, Frank," Paloma said, watching his face closely for reactions. "Serach and I have a car now, and we will whisk you and the 'Modi' and all your clothes and all your other possessions back home with us— safe, sound, and germ-free."

His face had returned to blankness and she glared at him.

"Frank, I'm talking to you. I've just proposed a total solution to all your problems. A form of transportation, a warm welcome—a home tailored to your needs. What do you say?"

He gave a slight, almost sleepy, nod. Clearly, he was out of practice at a great many things—showing gratitude being near the top of the list. Paloma's annoyance emboldened her to ask the next few tough questions.

"Frank, tell me something. Over the past three months when we've been on the phone together at least once a week— sometimes twice—why didn't you as much as whisper to me that all this was going on?"

"I didn't tell you," he murmured after a very long pause, "because I was ashamed."

Paloma breathed in, breathed out, stepped back and looked a tiny bit less fierce.

"Well, you've told me now," she said. "So the only remaining question is: 'Does what I am proposing make sense to you?"

No answer.

"Are you going to do what I am suggesting?"

No answer.

"Frank! You have been totally, royally dumped by that man. You need to take your life back. Are you or are you not going to do that?"

"I..."

"Frank—pull up your big boy pants! Are you contemplating staying with him? For real?"

Frank looked down and shook his head.

"No. You are right. I need to get out. It's time."

He paused.

"But I want to do it at a moment when he is nowhere in the vicinity. I don't want a scene."

"So, we'll make sure that he's away when we do it. When's the next time he'll be out of the house for a solid chunk of time?"

"He's supposed to go out to the Hamptons for the day on Sunday to play in some chamber group for some private function. He'll be gone by ten thirty in the morning and he won't be back till late. Or perhaps he'll even stay over that night. I suspect he has a thing for the viola player. Who lives in Montauk."

"Jesus, Frank! Why do you even care anymore?"

Paloma glared at him and he dropped his gaze.

"Serach and I will be on your doorstep at ten forty-two. Start packing tonight."

"I don't even want to do that while he's around," he sniffed. "I want there to be absolutely no warning at all. I want him to come home all excited from his rendezvous and have it hit him like an arctic blast that he's lost me for good."

"Okay, then just hold tight and we'll do the packing when we arrive. We're very efficient at organizing things, you know. Well, Serach is. You'll be packed, transported, and re-installed with us by dinnertime."

Frank said nothing. She took it as assent.

"Rouse yourself early that day and prepare for our arrival."

Frank took a deep breath.

"Bring bubble wrap," he said. "For the 'Modi.'"

Manhattan and Brooklyn

-7-

Serach and Paloma piled into their Lesbaru on that Sunday morning well before ten o'clock, filling the back seat with all the boxes that Paloma had managed to cadge from their local wine store. They drove across the Brooklyn Bridge, headed uptown, miraculously found a parking spot just across the street from Kae-Dang's apartment house, and waited.

Right on cue, Kae-Dang strode out the front door, Satchel-and-Page green canvas briefcase slung across his shoulder and clarinet case in hand. His cognac-colored bomber jacket was the perfect length to emphasize the tight contours of his hips and the long litheness of his legs. His patent-leather-black hair rose slightly in a sudden gust of October wind and then settled down again, exactly in place.

"Well, he certainly doesn't look any the worse for wear," said Paloma, watching him glide down West End Avenue, swing left at the corner, and head toward the 79th Street subway station.

Serach shook her head sadly.

"No. He doesn't."

She turned toward Paloma and pulled off her sunglasses.

"I know you said that Frank was frustratingly vague, but did you get any sense at all about what happened between them?"

"Not from him, but I have my theories. I would guess that it was a case of Kae-Dang chomping at the bit against all of Frank's neuroses. As far as I know, Frank didn't move an inch outside the apartment till he'd been properly vaccinated and—even then—continued to behave like a nun in a cloister, most of the time. While Kae-Dang is this dashing young thing who would want to resume his old social habits as soon as he could. Or sooner. It must have been hell for Frank to witness Kae-Dang gallivanting about. And it must have been hell for Kae-Dang to be subjected to Frank's reprimands every time he returned home again. His dramatic sighs. His accusatory looks."

Serach held herself back from making any comment regarding the still-fraught topic of partners acting tyrannically about COVID prevention practices. She slid her shades back on and stared straight ahead through the windshield.

"I've often wondered about the age difference," Paloma continued, oblivious to Serach's train of thought. "Frank always contended that it wasn't a problem, and it probably wasn't while they were traipsing around Europe like kids or taking nice long breaks from one another on their separate concert tours. But once they were stuck together 24/7, month after month...."

She paused.

"It's not just that Frank is considerably older than Kae-Dang. It's that he's of a totally different vintage. The only thing he's ever been even slightly modern about is being gay."

She undid her seat belt and rolled up her window.

"But enough of all the—what is it that you guys call gossip? *Lashon Hara?* Let's get everything out of the back and get ourselves upstairs. Frank must be hysterically pacing the floors by now, wondering why we aren't ringing the bell."

"I've been preparing an amazing dinner while you two spent the afternoon putting everything where it belongs," announced Paloma, once they were back in Prospect Park South and Frank and Serach had collapsed into the living room's pair of Louis Quinze chairs.

She handed Frank a glass of heavily sweetened iced tea and Serach a glass of Chardonnay.

"Your efforts have earned you some well-deserved rest," she added. "So just sit still and enjoy yourselves till I call you in."

The Modigliani had been unwrapped and ceremoniously replaced on the special hook in the living room that Paloma had never taken down from the days when it had originally hung there.

The two-dozen jewel-toned Lacoste tee-shirts, the ten pairs of chinos and four pairs of light-weight gray wool pants, the six bespoke suits, the seventeen silky cotton button-down shirts, the six tweedy sports coats in shades ranging from muted cocoa to fog to charcoal, and the two concert tuxedos—plus a host of silk ties and a black pleated satin cummerbund—were carefully re-hung in the mahogany wardrobe that took up half a wall in Frank's bedroom.

The ten cashmere sweaters and the innumerable pairs of underwear and socks were all precisely rolled or folded within the drawers of Frank's bureau.

The twelve pairs of shoes were laid out on the shoe rack from left to right, according to their color (from brown to wine-red to black) and degree of formality.

The hundreds of books and long-playing records had been re-placed on the bookshelves in the hallway outside the living room in an order that only Frank understood, and the four boxes of music were all re-arranged on the shelf behind the Bösendorfer—with the six pieces on which Frank was currently working stacked neatly on the piano itself.

"Tell him what you're making," Serach said before Paloma could duck back into the kitchen.

"Sole meuniere—and yes, it is genuine Dover sole," Paloma said, smiling seductively. "A whole lovely fish apiece, lightly floured and pan-fried in butter and then drowned in even more melted butter along with capers, lemon juice, and parsley. Asparagus steamed just to the point of emerald-green crispness. Saffron rice with dill and pine nuts."

She looked straight at Frank and smiled even more deeply.

"Then, for dessert, we are having everything that you love best. Raspberry sorbet topped with freshly whipped cream and—as if that were not enough—a plate full of sand tarts from your very favorite bakery."

She caught Frank's look of open longing and grinned.

"I'll be back," she said.

"Dining room, Frank," Serach called out, when Paloma finally reappeared in the doorway and Frank began instinctively heading toward the kitchen. "Paloma has truly done it up right for this particular welcome home party."

Entering the dining room, Frank couldn't help it. His eyes filled with tears as he beheld it all.

The cobalt blue and gold Limoges dinner plates that the opera diva, Judith Skollar, had bequeathed to Paloma so many years before were set out on the cream linen tablecloth, while the silverware—each heavy piece etched with a huge baroque "JS"—rested on matching napkins. Crystal water goblets (and matching wine glasses for Serach and Paloma) stood to the left of each place setting.

A buttery fish already lay temptingly on each plate, while piles of green-flecked golden rice and of brightly-hued asparagus gleamed from their serving dishes.

At the center of the table was an enormous silver vase overflowing with yellow, purple, and orange chrysanthemums and white baby's breath—an identical bouquet to the one that Paloma had placed in a similar vase on Frank's bureau.

"I absolutely feel that we must say grace," said Frank, sitting down and gazing around.

"Yes of course, Frank—lead away," said Serach.

"For that which we are about to receive," he chanted in his best altar boy intonations, "may the Lord make us truly thankful."

"Well!" said Paloma. "Thank you for making it short and sweet—you know how I feel about all that religious stuff. Anyway, the main thing for which we are thankful is that you are back home with us, Frank. Now let's toast to that and dig in."

They ate and drank in happy silence for a good long time. Paloma cleared the table, brought out the sorbet in three little cut-glass bowls—along with a bowl of stiff-peaked whipped cream and a handful of silver teaspoons—and set the plate of sand-tarts right in front of Frank.

"Before we end this incredible meal, I want to say a few more things," Frank eventually announced, wiping the last bit of sorbet from his lips. "That is... I want to elaborate a bit more on the reasons for my gratitude. I've finally had a few hours of sanity in which to sort everything out in my head and it would be wrong not to share what I've come up with."

Serach smiled at him benevolently.

"First of all, of course," he continued, "I am grateful for the voluptuously generous welcome that I've received from you two ladies today. Totally above and beyond. I mean that."

He took a breath.

"Then, of course, I am grateful for the assistance that you gave me in the packing and hauling and unpacking and repositioning of all my possessions. I could never have managed any of that by myself. Never. I was far too traumatized to even contemplate it."

He shut his eyes.

"Third, let me repeat how grateful I am for the feast that we've enjoyed tonight—and not just to the Lord who is the Ultimate Provider. To you, Paloma, the most heavenly of all chefs. I had almost forgotten what real food tasted like—I've been living on Grubhub for almost four months, I swear it. Kae-Dang went totally on strike on that front as well. I wasn't asking him to keep sleeping with me for God's sake. I would never have dreamt of doing that once he made it clear that... well, never mind. But couldn't he at least have kept on doing the cooking for me?"

Paloma looked away. *Sweet Jesus—now that we've opened the floodgates, are we going to be inundated with every trial and tribulation of this man's break-up?*

Frank, however, thankfully caught himself in time.

"Well, enough. That's all history. It's over."

His eyes welled up again.

"But what I'm perhaps the most grateful for is that... all three of us seem to have survived the worst tolls of the pandemic nightmare, relatively unscathed. All our faculties have seemingly remained intact. We have all retained our sense of smell and taste—as evidenced by our robust consumption of this sumptuous meal. None of us has lost anyone we loved..."

He sighed dramatically.

"Now, if that isn't cause for thanksgiving..."

Paloma stood up and began swiftly clearing the table of the dessert dishes.

"Paloma—wait! Sit down! I wasn't finished speaking. And I was planning to have a few more of those divine cookies."

Paloma put the plate back down on the table in front of him.

"Help yourself, Frank," she said. "Do you want some more sorbet as well?"

"No, dear, but..."

Frank turned to Serach as Paloma swiftly exited.

"Dear me. Prickly, prickly. What did I say wrong?"

Serach sighed. How was she going to get through to the most self-centered person that she knew? She loved Frank dearly. But there were limits.

He kept looking at her, waiting for her response. He genuinely didn't realize what he had said.

"Frank," she finally began. "First of all, Paloma hardly got through this pandemic nightmare 'relatively unscathed.' She's a nurse, Frank! She was right there on the front lines, living through some of the worst of it. You clearly have no idea, but she suffered tremendously."

Frank blanched.

"More to the point, how could you say that none of us lost anyone? Don't you remember that Paloma's brother died just last month? Sure, it wasn't from COVID—he had a heart attack. But it was a terrible death for her, nonetheless. Or didn't she tell you about that either?"

"Yes, of course she did. Well, in passing, almost. She mentioned that she'd gone to his funeral and that his youngest son made a scene right there in middle of the cemetery. But she didn't dwell on any of it. Plus—as you say—it wasn't COVID that killed him, now, was it?"

He looked briefly away.

"She was very... matter-of-fact about the whole thing, really. Macho, almost."

"Yes, she can be that way," Serach sighed, before turning to look at him, hard. "You have to learn to read between the lines."

She paused for a moment and then posed the question that she couldn't avoid.

"But Frank, I'm baffled," she said. "You and Paloma spoke all the time over the past months, as far as I know. What did you talk about? You didn't tell her about Kae-Dang. She didn't tell you how incredibly hard it was to be working in a hospital where people were dying all around her. She didn't as much as hint at how much she suffered about losing Manny. What have you been...? I mean..."

Frank looked up at the ceiling.

"We talked piffle, Serach. Lots and lots of piffle. Evidently, that's what we both needed most during all those infinitely trying times."

"Well, perhaps. But now that you've finally made it through the worst of it, as you say, you need to be a little bit more tuned into one another's sensitive spots. I would suggest that you begin by going into the kitchen and apologizing to your very best friend for having been so totally clueless about the impact of her brother's death."

Frank hung his head.

"I suppose you are right. But before I do so, let me ask you something: Is there anything else that I should know about, so that I don't..."

"Make some other royal mess of things?"

He continued to look down while finishing off the last of the sand tarts, one by one. He wasn't going to let them go to waste, after all. Not when Paloma had gone all the way to William Greenberg Jr. on the Upper East Side to retrieve them.

"Well, is there?" he asked, swallowing the last crumbs and draining his water goblet.

"Yes," said Serach.

"Oh Lord, I was hoping you wouldn't say that."

"Well, unfortunately, there is one other terrible thing looming ahead for our poor Paloma. It would probably be better for her to tell you about it herself, but then again— knowing how you two seem to operate—that might never happen. So I guess it's up to me."

Frank blinked. "All right. Tell me."

"In two weeks' time, Paloma will be driving up to some forsaken corner of New York State with her nephew Roberto to tell her mother that Manny—that mother's only son—is dead."

"The mother doesn't know yet?"

"No. It's a rather... difficult family."

"I'll say," said Frank, primly. "I didn't know that Paloma even had a mother. Not that Paloma and I have ever spent much time regaling one another with tales of our childhoods."

"Well, she does have a mother. Of sorts. But she hasn't seen that mother—or spoken to her—in nearly twenty-five years. So the first words that she and that mother will be exchanging in more than two decades will be about Manny's death."

"Dear Lord."

Frank picked up the plate that the cookies had been on, turned it over to check that it really was Limoges, and then set it down again.

"So... what do you suggest that I say to her about all that?"

"Well, you probably shouldn't say a thing. As far as she knows, you know nothing at all about any of it."

She pointed toward the kitchen.

"But enough. Go in there and do what you need to do. Acknowledge your startling lack of tact about everything else that she has been going through and say that you are sorry."

He didn't move.

"Go on. It doesn't have to be a long, complicated apology."

"Of course not," said Frank, sighing and turning toward the doorway. "Paloma doesn't like 'long and complicated.' She's too..."

"Yes, I know," said Serach. "*Macho.*"

November 2021: Brooklyn, Rock Point, the Bronx, Brooklyn

- 8 -

Frank was not exaggerating when he remarked that he and Paloma didn't generally chat about their early histories. Paloma had no idea what forces might have blasted her best friend out of his Kentucky Catholic childhood into New York City without so much as a single backward glance. Or what family dynamics might have contributed to his seemingly bottomless need for an audience—and for applause. Or what past terrors might be associated with enjoying a single glass of wine.

She was, therefore, thoroughly unprepared for what he volunteered, as he cupped his hands around his mug of perfectly-brewed coffee on the Sunday morning of her journey to Dolores' house.

"I have a tip for you, darling," he said, catching her eye and then looking swiftly away.

"Yes?"

"On the occasions on which I have been obliged by circumstance to interact with relatives with whom my relationship has been…less than ideal," he drawled, continuing to gaze elsewhere, "I have found it useful to imagine them as characters in a story. A story of interest to me, perhaps, but definitely someone else's story. It helps me to react to them more appropriately than I might otherwise be inclined to do."

He took a small sip of the coffee and put the mug down again. He then reached for one of the freshly-baked croissants that Paloma had fetched for him earlier that morning from the new bakery on Cortelyou Road, split it in half, lengthwise, and applied himself to spreading an even layer of black cherry jam over its two cut surfaces.

"I might advise you to do the same, today," he eventually added.

Paloma regarded him for a moment before walking directly behind him, ruffling his hair briefly, smoothing it out again, and bending to kiss the top of his head.

"You're a dear, Frank," she murmured, as she considered the fact that his hair had become significantly grayer and thinner since she'd last surveyed it from that vantagepoint. "And a very good friend. I don't know exactly what you are talking about, but you're a dear."

She then slipped out of the room before either of them was forced to admit anything more about what they knew or didn't know about one another.

"Do you mind if we listen to some music?" Gordito asked as they sped upstate in his little blue Prius. The company pick-up truck, he'd explained, wouldn't be permitted on the parkways they were going to follow. Besides, the Prius was so much more comfortable. Not to mention his pride and joy— the one great luxury in his life.

"No, I'd like it. Anything but country."

"Okay, we'll listen to Gregorio Uribe."

"Never heard of him."

"Papito used to play him a lot after he stopped going into the shop."

Paloma gave a sideways glance at the shift in her nephew's voice, but his face remained stoic as he began talking again.

"I turned a bunch of Uribe's You-tubes into a playlist for him," he said, "and then I transferred all that from his phone to mine. I've got it all right here."

He swerved into the fast lane.

"Uribe is from Colombia. Maybe that's why Papito kept listening to him," he concluded.

"Do you like it? Do you like the way Uribe plays?" he asked after they had listened to the first piece, and then he kept going without waiting for an answer. "He's, like, this really great accordion player and he uses lots of drums—you can hear that, right? It's kind of like *cumbia* with *vallenato* and some funk traditional stuff. Plus, some—like—things he picked up from Big Band music."

He waited a moment before adding: "When I hear him, I remember Papito."

"Maybe it's what the priest should have played at the burial," said Paloma, after her own pause.

Gordito shrugged.

"No one asked me what to play."

The road continued stretching out before them, and the landscape outside Paloma's window began to tax her patience. Bare trees, small snow patches, rocks, gray sky, other cars. Nothing remotely stimulating enough to distract her from the barrage of acid thoughts that had begun pouring into her mind as soon as Gordito stopped talking.

Eventually, however, Frank's breakfast advice popped into her head, and she determinedly shoved aside the thoughts to begin spinning out a plot line for her mother's story.

She went back to the beginning and pictured the little two-story house in Santa Fe de Antioquia, Colombia in which she knew Dolores had grown up—and in which she, herself, had lived for two years. She conjured up the musty, once-grand furniture that stood in the living room. The huge replica of Leonardo's Last Supper that dominated the dining room. The two tiny bedrooms up the rickety flight of stairs in which her mother and grandparents had slept. The third, locked bedroom that periodically housed a gigantic statue of Jesus Christ.

She immersed herself in the recollected sights and smells of that starkly grim dwelling—so suffocating a place for any young girl to spend her days, whether she was born into it or exiled into it as a teen.

Paloma! You have no idea whether your mother found it oppressive! This is her story—not yours! Siphon yourself out of the narrative—that's the whole point of this exercise.

She visualized the way the sidewalk ended, several short yards to the east of the front door. She pictured the riotous mass of tropical vegetation and the looming range of blue-hued mountains that took over the vista just beyond the street's dead end. She imagined her mother exiting the house as a young teen, peering out into the wilderness, and plotting ways to machete her way through it all to reach a freer world beyond.

There you go again. That's how you felt about it. Couldn't it be that your mother loved being in that stifling little house in that boring little town?

She evoked the Cathedral that sat on the main town square—the Cathedral whose priest had seduced her mother in a confession stall at the age of fifteen. She pictured the sleaziness of that priest, the pomposity—the way that she, herself, had cringed as she watched him conduct the Mass, even before she knew what he had done.

She conjured up the tough blocks of the South Bronx and the convent into which her mother had been shipped, in all her pregnant shame—and within which she remained until she managed to seduce the convent's handyman, Joe, into whisking her away into a new life, along with her newborn son, Manny, and (eventually) Paloma herself.

She thought of her mother working all night in a dark bar on a dimly lit street and then sleeping all day while Paloma trudged through parochial school and prepared the family's meals. She thought of her mother's reaction to Paloma suddenly blossoming into her own sexuality—how her mother had concluded that everything would be a whole lot easier if she simply sent Paloma off to live with her grandmother in Colombia, and—

Paloma gave up. What Frank had suggested was futile. And impossible. Had he, himself, ever really succeeded in creating a story line for his parents without scenes of his own life insistently splicing themselves in? Unlikely.

At that moment, however, she was shaken out of her thoughts by Gordito's voice.

"We're here," he announced, as he steered the car off the main parkway, around a few hairpin turns and into a landscape that was even bleaker than the miles of road. "We're in Rock Point."

"Rock Point?"

"Yes. Rock Point. It's where Abuela lives."

"Good Lord. I never knew the name. Your father always called it 'East Bumblefuck.'"

Gordito nodded sheepishly.

"Yeah. He did. It wasn't so nice of him. This place isn't so bad."

Paloma held her breath as her nephew navigated the car down a street of identical, moth-colored mobile homes, each one perched on its own little platform on its own small, short-grassed plot of land.

"She lives in one of these little shoebox houses?"

"Mnnn hmnnn. She lives in this one. Right here."

He deftly parked the car, exited, ran around to the trunk, pulled out his tool chest and walked around to the passenger door to help Paloma out.

"Papito bought it for her a few years ago," he said, extending one large, square brown hand to his aunt. "Now I help her keep it up."

Papito bought it for her!

Paloma suddenly found that she didn't have the wherewithal to get angry yet again at the brother who had so blatantly lied about his ongoing relationship with their mother. There is no future in rage, as Serach would say. Anyway, Manny was dead.

Manny was dead. Manny was dead.

She took the proffered hand and allowed Gordito to lead her forward. They mounted the platform to reach the front door. Gordito pressed the doorbell and after several long moments the door opened.

"Oh, it's you. You sure took your time."

Gordito bent his head.

"Traffic," he mumbled as they stood in the doorway.

"I thought maybe it was because you were fooling around with your girlfriend instead of driving," said his grandmother, taking a step beyond her door.

She jerked a thumb at Paloma without as much as glancing at where she was pointing.

"Is this her?" she asked.

Gordito's eyes opened wide, his mouth opened as well, and he shook his head strenuously back and forth.

"I'll go and, um, do the vents," he said, turning briskly away from his grandmother and his aunt. He ran into the house, retrieved a step ladder, and sped around the back, ladder in one hand and toolbox in the other.

Paloma took a breath and surveyed her mother, up and down. The gray hair. The deflated mouth. The shrunken frame, clothed in a bathrobe that might once have been pink. The hard pot belly (it looked like a basketball) protruding from that otherwise unremitting skinniness.

Ascites, Paloma immediately thought—ever the nurse. My mother, the drinker.

She shut her eyes for a moment and took a step backward.

"I asked a question," said Dolores, still looking elsewhere. "Are you the girlfriend?"

Paloma yanked off the mask that she had automatically donned as they approached the house.

"No," she said. "I'm the aunt. I'm your daughter."

Dolores swung around, gazed hard at Paloma's unmasked face, and felt a huge tremor go down her spine.

"You look just like me."

Paloma's reaction was swift and hot. *No, I do not! I don't look anything like you. Perhaps we looked alike, once. Perhaps I was even proud of it. But no more. God forbid.*

Dolores' eyes narrowed briefly, watching the horror on Paloma's face, but she remained silent for a long moment.

"Gordito!" she finally called out, craning her head around Paloma's shoulder. "It's not just the vents that need help—it's the toilet, too. Then check out the freezer. It's been acting up."

Gordito responded with something unintelligible.

"Mama, we need to talk."

Dolores turned back to Paloma.

"Why talk after all this time?" she asked, and suddenly began to cough. It was a nasty cough—a profound cough. Dolores bent over with it, covered her mouth, then uncovered it again and let the cough rip.

Paloma felt herself slipping again. Did she really have to do this? Couldn't she just turn on her heel, run away, and leave her two-pack-a-day mother to cough herself to death?

No. No, she couldn't. Not if it meant leaving Gordito stuck there all alone to mop up everything after her—along with fixing the vents and the toilet and the freezer. She stood up straighter and took a breath.

"Mama," she repeated. "Like I said. We need to talk. Can we go inside?"

Her mother stood up straighter as well, turned around, and marched through the still-open door. Paloma walked in behind her, pulled the door shut, and absorbed the surroundings.

The trailer's doll-house-sized interior was laid out with remarkable efficiency. The living and dining spaces were combined, with a sink and set of basic kitchen appliances plastered against one wall and a small table and two chairs placed in front of the appliances. Two small windows on the wall opposite the entrance looked out on the identical neighboring house. The bedrooms and bathrooms were evidently off to the sides, hidden from sight.

The furniture of the living area was spare and utilitarian. It included a Formica-covered coffee table, a lime-green couch, a single matching armchair, and— could it be? Yes, it was! —Joe's old Barcalounger.

Paloma swallowed hard.

Her mother had somehow managed—somehow wanted— to hang onto the tan, vinyl-covered reclining chair in which her Puerto Rican boyfriend had sat every evening, listening to Latin Big Band records on that blasted phonograph with a copy of the *Daily News* on his lap, a cigar in his fingers, and a beer can within close reach.

Paloma's head began to pound at those thoughts. The sights before her were blinding and the smell was overpowering— stale cigarette smoke, spilled drinks, and something much worse.

"Mama, I need a glass of water."

Dolores shrugged, reached for the pack of mentholated Newports in one of her bathrobe pockets, found a book of matches in the other, and lit one up.

"Help yourself."

Paloma walked to the kitchen sink—it was filled with dirty dishes—and watched a parade of tiny black ants march across the sink's back edge. She yanked open a cabinet door, pulled out a glass, squirted it with detergent and scrubbed it with her fingers (the sponge was too slimy to even contemplate using). She then rinsed it, filled it with water from the tap, made her way back into the living room area and sat down.

Her mother was already seated, puffing away, an ashtray in her free hand.

"You have ants, Mama!"

"I like them. They keep me company. And they remind me of myself. Small. Dark. Tough."

Had her mother developed a sense of humor? Had she always had one?

They sat in silence as Paloma sipped at the water and Dolores smoked. Paloma found that she was having trouble swallowing.

"It feels so strange to be speaking to you in English," she finally ventured. "You always made me use Spanish when I was growing up."

"English is what I speak, now. My boyfriend is American— no more Puerto Ricans for me."

Paloma stopped herself from pointing out that Puerto Ricans are American, too. She was much more interested in the other half of her mother's sentence. My boyfriend? Was her mother involved with yet another man? In her current condition? Was that man here right now, tucked away in one of the bedrooms?

She glanced surreptitiously around her.

"Jeff's not here, today," said Dolores, smiling at Paloma's clear confusion. "He comes and he goes. Mostly he comes when he wants something."

She gave out a cackle.

"Men all want the same thing."

She began coughing again. It lasted for several moments. Paloma closed her eyes.

How was she going to deliver her grim, grim message to this shattered woman, when all she wanted to do was either run away from her entirely or take that small, gray, shabby head into her hands and plead with the Virgin to save her?

"Vents all done, Abuela," said Gordito, suddenly pushing the door open to enter a room that looked far too small to contain his bulk.

"Now the toilet," said Dolores, without as much as looking up. "The one in the bathroom by my bedroom. The other one still works."

"Okay." He ducked away to do it.

"Mama," Paloma began again, "the reason I'm here is because we need to talk. I have something to tell you."

"Oh? What is it that you could possibly have to tell me? It's me who needs to tell you something. I've been thinking about it for a long time."

"What?"

"How come Miss Big Shot Nurse—and yes, Manny told me you were a nurse—didn't as much as call to see if I'd made it through all the COVID *mierda* that we've all been through for the last couple of years? Hmmn? Miss Big Shot Nurse?"

"Let's not start throwing accusations at one another, Mama," Paloma said, very softly. "Because if we do, I have a few of my own to throw."

Dolores looked up at her and said nothing. She took a long drag on her cigarette and let it out again, very slowly.

"I'm not going to get into any of that, however," Paloma continued, "because..."

Gordito re-entered the room.

"It's real easy to fix when that happens, Abuela. I could show you how so you could do it yourself the next time or... Jeff could do it for you."

Jeff! So Gordito even knows the boyfriend! Did my brother know him too? Did they all sit around drinking beer together like one happy little family, while I was completely shunted off to the side? How much more do I have to take of all this? How can I even begin to bear it?

"Another time, Gordito," said Dolores.

"No, Abuela—let me just explain it to you. Then you won't have to live with all that... stuff anymore. Look. You just pick up the top of the tank and—see—sometimes the chain comes off inside so you need to re-attach it. I could show you if...."

"Never mind, Gordito. Why don't you go take care of the freezer?"

Gordito plodded off to the refrigerator, right across from where they were standing.

Damn! Paloma brought her lips together tight. *I wanted him totally out of the way for this. Well, I guess he'll have to hear me say it—and to witness her reaction.*

"Mama, I'm here because I have to tell you something," Paloma began one last time.

She stole a look at the tiny woman sitting opposite her, very straight and staring back at her with eyes that hadn't changed at all from how she remembered them, despite the ruin that had overtaken the rest of her. They were still the same black, snapping eyes that she had always had. The same eyes that Paloma herself possessed.

"Mama. Manny got very sick this year."

Dolores' eyes stayed fixed on Paloma's face while her body remained perfectly still. The cigarette burned perilously near her fingers, but she didn't seem to notice.

"Really sick. His heart gave out. He died this past September."

Dolores remained motionless for one long moment more before grinding the still-smoldering butt into the ashtray and tossing the ashtray down onto the coffee table. She then pushed her face into her hands. She made a huge noise. Was she crying? No, she was coughing. It went on and on until suddenly it stopped. Gordito closed the freezer door, ran up to his grandmother, bent down, and put his arms around her.

"It's okay, Abuela. It's okay. It was God's will about Papito. God's will."

Paloma looked away.

Why couldn't I hold her, too? Why couldn't she hold me? Why couldn't we all cry together?

Dolores pushed him away and eventually he stood up.

"Why did this have to happen to me?" was all that Dolores said.

Paloma waited. Gordito waited. Then Paloma turned to Gordito and said: "I think that's it, Gordito. I think we'd better be going."

"Abuela?"

Dolores looked up at her grandson.

"Everything is fixed, now. The freezer... you just needed to move some stuff around. It was too crowded. The cold air couldn't get out. I'll come back in the spring and check it all out for you again. If something else happens before then, you can just call me, and I'll..."

Dolores walked up to Gordito and gave him a brief hug.

"That's right, Gordito. You're the big man around here, now."

She seemed to be finished until she suddenly spun around to face Paloma.

"And you—Miss Big Nurse. Tell me one last thing about Manny's death. Tell me why you couldn't save him. Tell me why you couldn't save my son when he was so sick."

Then she turned her back on the two of them and disappeared into the bedroom.

Paloma and Gordito drove in total silence for a good half hour until Gordito reached around and yanked out a bag of donuts from the back seat. He rested it on his lap, opened it up expertly with one hand, fished out a substantial-sized glazed donut, and shoved a good half of it into his mouth in a single bite.

"Want one?" he asked, as he chewed.

"God forbid. I might throw up."

"Well, I kind of need..."

"Of course you do, Gordito. You have to keep up your strength."

In almost no time he had emptied the bag, balled it up and tossed it back behind him, and wiped his hand on his pants. Then he cleared his throat.

"Yes, Gordito? You want to say something?"

He breathed out heavily.

"Are you angry, Tía?" he finally ventured. "Are you angry at me because I take care of things for Abuela?"

Paloma looked at him curiously. How much more did this young man understand than he seemed to let on?

"I mean, Papito did tell me that she..."

"That she treated me like crap when I was a girl? Like she did just now?"

He shrugged.

"No, Gordito," Paloma sighed. "Of course I'm not angry at you. You're doing the right thing. Your father would want you to do it."

Did Gordito heave a sigh of relief? It certainly sounded that way.

Paloma waited a moment.

"There are, however, a couple of things you could do that would make it a little easier for me, right now."

"Sure, Tía. Whatever."

"First of all, you could put the music back on. This silence is making me crazy."

Gordito reached for his phone and brought Gregorio Uribe back into the car, full blast.

"Then, do you think that before you take me home you could possibly drive us to the Church of St. Nicholas of Tolentine? Up on Fordham Road? I've always hated that place, but there's something that I need to do there."

"Sure, Tía."

Neither one breathed another word until they were approaching the right exit, at which point Gordito said: "There are no more Masses, today. I hope we can get in."

"Drive around the block. There's bound to be an entrance open somewhere."

As they circled the premises, however, it looked absolutely locked up tight.

"Just let me off here in front, then. I'll find a way in," said Paloma. "And I won't be long—I promise. If you can keep circling around a bit, I'll meet you back where you dropped me off."

"Are you sure you'll be able to...?"

"Yes. I'm sure."

He waited for a beat.

"And, um, Tía?"

"Yes?"

"Why do you want to go in there?"

"I need a word with the Virgin," said Paloma. "And the first Virgin I ever really spoke to happens to be in this particular church."

Gordito smiled. He loved the Virgin, too.

"Okay, Tía. I'll see you when you come out again."

"You're an angel."

Paloma scurried out of the car and began searching out the various side doors that she remembered. She rang each of their bells (several times) and finally, a door on the north side opened and a small Asian man came out. Oh, yes. Paloma had read that the church now hosted the biggest Vietnamese re-settlement program in the city.

"I'm the sexton," said the man. "What do you want at this hour?"

"I need to get inside."

"The church is closed. There are no more Masses. It's late."

"I don't need a Mass. I just need to say a few prayers. Please? I won't be but a minute. Please let me in! Please!"

The man took a long look at the gorgeous woman with the heartbroken face.

"Okay, miss. But only for a minute. And I'll have to stay with you while you do it."

"Sure, of course. Whatever. Thank you."

He stepped aside and she ran in and found her way easily down the corridor, up the stairway and in through the back to the main sanctuary. As a girl she had rooted out all the church's secret passageways—though it was generally to make a quick exit, not to get inside.

She passed by the altar to the side wall where her favorite Virgin Mary statue stood. It was a statue with an uncommonly kind face and robes of a particularly beautiful blue. She dropped a quarter into the box beside the altar, reached for a candle and placed it in one of the cups lined up in rows beneath the statue, took a taper from the half-burnt cluster to the side of the cups, used it to transfer a flame from an already-lit candle to her own little offering, and knelt.

"Why did you put me through all that?" she pleaded, as she gazed upward at the statue. "Why didn't you let me save my brother when he was so sick? Why did you let him shut down to me like that? And why—oh why—couldn't you melt my mother's heart? Just this once? Just this once!"

She put down her head and wept briefly. The statue remained mute.

"Why have you deserted me?"

Paloma rose from her knees, wiped her nose on her jacket sleeve and walked slowly to the back.

"Done?" asked the sexton. How beautiful she looked in the dim light of the church! That lovely, tragic face—those cascades of lustrous hair. Like the Virgin herself.

"Definitely done. Totally done."

She walked wearily down the corridor, down the staircase, and back to the door through which she had entered, the sexton trailing helplessly behind her.

She reached for the handle, opened it, remembered herself, and turned to face him.

"Hey," she said, watching him light up at the small smile that she managed. "Thanks for letting me in. I know it was a little out of the ordinary."

As promised, Gordito continued circling around till he finally found Paloma standing on the sidewalk, head lifted and face firmly set. They didn't say anything to one another until they arrived back in Brooklyn, at her door—at which point she turned to him and pulled him close.

"Don't you be a stranger now, Gordito. Hear me? Come visit us, soon," she said. She raised her face and kissed her nephew's fat cheek. "And may God repay you. For everything."

Then she let go of him, slid out of the car, walked up the path and up the porch steps, and let herself into her big, fancy house.

Brooklyn

- 9 -

Paloma had switched off her phone's ringer and had not called home for all the hours she was away. She could not have borne discussing the day's events as they were unfolding. Nor did she have any desire to recap them now that they were over.

She unlocked and pushed the front door open, strode across the entryway, traversed the living room, and followed the hall to the rear of the house—carefully and gratefully negotiating the silence and darkness within.

Thank God Serach and Frank seem to be safely upstairs, she sighed. Or out. Or anywhere other than right here, right now. I can just slip into the kitchen, sit down, drink a glass of water, and totally blank my mind for a while.

Once she rounded the corner, however, all hopes for that much-craved bit of respite evaporated. Every kitchen light was blazing and there was Serach, sitting at the table with her spine as straight as always and her gaze fixed on the back door.

"Good heavens!" she exclaimed, whirling around as she sensed Paloma's approach. "You startled me! You never come in through the front! How are you doing, my love? I've heard nothing from you all day long. I've been worried half to death."

She stood and ran toward Paloma. Paloma held up one hand.

"Serach, please! I need to breathe."

Serach brought her arms back down to her sides—the ache to draw Paloma close suddenly eclipsed by the shock of what she was seeing.

In the fierce illumination of all those kitchen lights, Paloma's normal blast of beauty was nowhere in evidence. Her cheeks looked creased rather than dimpled. The laugh lines at the corners of her eyes—rather than telegraphing her years of past mischief—now conveyed only deep weariness and the inexorable passage of time.

"Okay, Paloma," said Serach, stepping back. "Just come sit down, then. Let me get you a glass of wine."

"No wine."

"Really? You're always up for a glass of wine."

Paloma shook her head and Serach gave her a gentle look.

"Okay," she repeated. "But there is something else here, waiting for you, that you cannot possibly refuse."

Paloma closed her eyes.

"No, Paloma—you can't! It's way too special. Frayda brought it here at lunchtime so you could enjoy it after your long, hard day."

Serach reached behind her to transfer the familiar red-and-green plaid picnic basket from the counter to the center of the table. Paloma opened her eyes again, glanced down, and sighed.

"Frayda should only know how long and hard it was," she said, pulling out her chair and sinking slowly into it.

"Well, this should help," Serach continued. "Let me open it up and serve it to you."

"I couldn't eat a thing right now, Serach. Really."

"Oh, but you must! Frayda says that it's the meal that you loved the best from that time when she was here, taking care of me and cooking for both of us."

Paloma couldn't help herself. She gave Serach a small grin.

"Her famous roast chicken?"

"And her famous noodle *kugel* with *schmaltz*. And her famous spinach *kugel*..."

"Man. Frayda is too much. But..."

"No buts, Paloma. She prepared it specially for you last night after I told her what you were facing today. Then she petitioned her boss for an extra-long lunch hour so she could warm it up, pack it up, and get it over here. True devotion, given how seriously she takes her job."

Paloma closed her eyes.

"That's all very nice," she said, sadly. "But I still don't think that I can..."

"Hush! You have to."

Serach paused, desperately searching for some sweet phrase—some light-hearted remark—that might lift Paloma out of the depths of her sorrow, if only for a moment. Well, discussing Frayda's food practices had always amused her partner. Maybe it would work now.

"Frayda didn't just leave the food for you, you know" she began. "She left detailed instructions on how to present and to consume it. She announced that she'd arranged everything on one of her beautiful stoneware plates, and that that's where it should stay. That she'd included a setting of her finest silverware, and that that's what you had to use to eat it. That she'd wrapped it all up tightly in tin foil so that—between the basket's insulation, the quality of the stoneware, and the thickness of the foil—it would stay perfectly warm and you wouldn't need to re-heat it."

No reaction.

"She even went so far as to say that I also shouldn't bother washing anything when you were done—that I should just put everything back into the basket and zip it all up tight again."

Nothing.

"Of course," Serach continued—desperately scanning Paloma's face for any sign that she was listening. "What she was doing with all those exhortations wasn't just making sure that everything would be nice for you—or easy for me to manage. She was ensuring that everything would stay kosher. That the food would stay that way by keeping it on one of her own plates. That the plate would stay that way by keeping it away from our silverware. That everything would then stay that way by keeping it far from our microwave or our sink."

No use. Paloma was clearly someplace unreachable. Someplace that Serach had never been and couldn't even visualize. How could she possibly know what had gone on in Gordito's little blue Prius, when she had rarely paid attention to Paloma's interactions with the quietest, least-demanding of their nephews? Or what Paloma could have seen in that Upstate wilderness into which she, herself, had never so much as set foot? What did she know of that mother, herself, when Paloma had never offered more than a few brief, bitter comments during moments of rare, sad weakness? What did she actually know of daughters and their mothers?

Serach leaned forward to place her hand softly on her partner's wrist.

"My darling, I'm sorry it was so rough for you today."

Paloma contemplated Serach's long slim fingers, absent-mindedly noticed a hangnail, looked away again.

"Don't worry," she eventually muttered. "I'll survive. Just let me be a bit, can't you?"

But then—glancing up just long enough to finally register the degree of Serach's own pain—she managed the approximation of a smile.

"Okay, Babe," she said. "You win. Let's open that basket and see what Frayda has prepared."

Serach leaned over eagerly to unzip it, fished out the plate, and removed the tinfoil wrapping. Paloma gave it all a brief look and instinctively reached out two fingers to test its temperature.

"Not exactly what I would call warm," she said, and then—before Serach could do anything to stop her—she grabbed the plate, popped it into the microwave, and turned it on.

"Paloma! Didn't you hear anything I said before? You've just—"

"Just what?" asked Paloma, not turning around.

"You've just *de-kashered* Frayda's plate!"

Paloma spun on her heel to give Serach an uncomprehending look.

"I just finished telling you," said Serach—her voice rising upward several few notes— "that putting Frayda's plate inside our microwave renders it completely un-kosher! Now I won't be able to give it back to her!"

"Oh, sweet Jesus!" said Paloma. "I am surrounded by crazy people."

She reached over and turned the microwave off again.

"That won't help," said Serach. "The damage has been done."

"Yes, I suppose it has."

Paloma walked up to the sink and poured a glass of water.

"Well then, if you don't mind," she said—downing the water and putting the glass in the sink— "I'm going to let you deal with the mess and go upstairs to take a hot shower."

She grimaced.

"There's a lot of stuff that I need to wash away."

"Of course."

"I wasn't hungry anyway," Paloma added. "Like I said."

Serach looked down. When she finally lifted her head, Paloma was halfway out the door.

"Paloma—wait!"

"Yes?"

"Please remember that I'm here for you whenever you feel ready to talk about it."

"I know," said Paloma.

She exited and Serach closed her eyes in sadness for her partner, for her partner's mother, for Manny, for the unbridgeable gulf between kosher and not kosher—and for everything else that she was helpless to explain or repair. She then walked over to the microwave, opened the door, and reached inside for the food.

It looked good. It smelled delicious.

I might as well eat it, myself, she sighed. I can't let all Frayda's efforts go to waste.

I'll hide the plate away when I'm done and then—first thing in the morning—I'll speed off to Continental Table Settings on 14th Avenue and find a replacement. Luckily, it's always been a popular pattern in our community—the store is bound to have it in stock. And luckily, it's stoneware—no need to carry out all the extra kashering that is mandated for a new plate made of porcelain.

Frayda will never know that I've made the switch. She will never know that her act of kindness didn't land in quite the way she intended.

Paloma will never tell. I certainly won't.

In this one small respect, at least, I can make things right.

INTERLUDE ONE: The Sukkashlo

*"Before the great sage Rabba began his lecture, he would
make some humorous comment, the rabbis would laugh,
and then he would sit down with awe and reverence and
begin his lecture."*

Pesachim 117a

September 2022: Jerusalem

When it came to mastering the art of speech—in fact when it came to mastering just about everything—Shmuely' first-born child, Asher, proceeded at his own pace. Placid and keg-shaped ("he must take after Ruchel's people," sniffed his Aunt Mierle, the first time she saw him), he felt no need to push himself, even as his younger sister Shoshanna began gleefully picking up words (whole sentences, even) in all three tongues (English, Hebrew, and Yiddish) that regularly swirled around their house.

Shmuely couldn't understand how his own beloved son could be so blasé about acquiring the skill that separates man from the animals. He found it hard to maintain equanimity in the face of Asher's ongoing verbal vagueness ("What is he saying, Ruchel?") or of his marked indifference to the intriguing connections between the spoken and the written word. He devised imaginative strategies for stimulating Asher's interest and bolstering his performance.

Every evening when he came home from teaching, he would sit Asher down on his lap, shuffle a set of Hebrew flash cards under his round nose, and explain the marvels that they contained.

"Shin is for '*shokolad*,' Asher," he would say, gesticulating enticingly at the letter and the picture. "See the shin? See its two pretty loops? See the chocolate? Can you say 'shin'? Would you like to have a chocolate? Can you ask for it by forming a complete sentence?"

At bedtime, he would tuck Asher in with a story from Rabbi Noam Schneiderman's *Biblical Tales for Torah-loving Tots*—a book whose lively depictions of floods and towers, ladders and angels, fierce battles and treks through the desert were so perfectly geared toward igniting a Jewish boy's imagination and provoking his thoughtful questions.

All to no avail.

Asher would smile benevolently up at his father and gently pry the chocolate out of Shmuely's hand while ignoring the flash cards. He would turn away from Rabbi Schneiderman's book, mid-story, to bury his face in his pillow and peek back at Shmuely with one eye.

Ultimately, Shmuely would sigh, put away the cards or the book, bless his son, and leave the room. Until the next time.

Asher's mother Ruchel knew better. She had spent a lot of time with the children of her siblings and her friends. She knew that boys weren't always so quick in the language department—that they had more important things on their minds. She knew that her Asher would catch up nicely when the spirit finally moved him.

For goodness' sake, he was only three-and-a-half years old!

She never pestered her son with unnecessary questions. She dispensed mid-afternoon chocolates into his chubby hands without asking him to earn them. She responded to his most unintelligible utterances as if she understood them perfectly, even though (truth to tell) much of the time she was just as baffled as Shmuely.

Today, however, when Asher strolled into the kitchen to say: "Shoshi's in Tatteh's *sukkashlo!*" Ruchel had no doubts about the meaning of his message. Or about its urgency.

Shoshanna—Asher's spitfire of a two-and-a-half-year-old younger sister—had somehow managed to slip past their housekeeper Dalisay's eagle eye, barge into her father's study, and put herself right into the crosshairs of Shmuely's potential paternal ire.

Shmuely, normally the gentlest of parents, had one uncrossable red line. Without a formal invitation, no child was permitted to breach the boundary that separated his study from the rest of the house. To enter the room that he called (not entirely ironically) his "*sukkat sh'lomecha*" or "shelter of peace"—and that Asher managed to mangle into "*sukkashlo*".

Even Ruchel hesitated to knock on that door once it closed behind her husband—and would never enter without first being told that it was all right. When Shmuely—when the great Rav Gottesman—was cosseted away in his private oasis, he was not to be disturbed for any cause short of fire or flood.

The sole time that Asher had inexplicably decided to turn the doorknob, meander in, and stand in the center of the room looking amiably around, Shmuely had abruptly broken with all past practices and yelled unrestrainedly at his eldest child. It was a dressing down that Asher was not likely to forget. Nor was his mother. It had taken Ruchel a full two hours to resettle the desperately weeping toddler.

And now, evidently, Shoshana was about to suffer the same fate.

There was no time to lose. As soon as she heard Asher's pronouncement, Ruchel flung down the spoonful of drippings with which she had been basting the evening's brisket and bolted out of the room. The swiftness of her departure left Asher dazed and gratified. He plopped himself down on the kitchen floor, stuck a fat thumb in his mouth, and contentedly pondered the magnitude of the reaction he had elicited.

Once Ruchel reached the study door, however, she forcibly calmed herself down. Hysteria never worked with her husband. Quite the contrary. She knocked quietly but decisively and—receiving no answer—pushed the door open a crack.

"Shmuely?"

Something like a small squeal from within.

Had he just hit Shoshanna, *chas v'cholileh*? Had it come to that?

Forsaking all caution, Ruchel shoved the door fully open and peered inside. There in the shadows of the far-left corner of the room, in an armchair tucked between two towering bookcases and illuminated by a single standing lamp, sat her husband.

A big book open to a swirling mass of colorful Hebrew letters was balanced on one of his knees. On the other—bright blond curls nearly obscuring her face as she peered down at that page—perched their daughter, Shoshanna.

"Shmuely?"

Shmuely finally looked up, and Ruchel glimpsed an expression of joy fiercer than any she had ever beheld on her husband's thin face. Joy deeper than he'd let shine from his features since he'd sat on his own big sister Serach's lap, poring over a text under her tender guidance, so many years before.

His turquoise eyes were narrowed into bare slits—that's how deeply he was smiling.

And Shoshanna? When she too finally lifted her gray eyes to greet her mother, they were even merrier than Shmuely's.

"We're learning, Mama!" she squealed again, one hand banging on the book and the other one resting happily on her father's arm. "Me and Tatteh! We're learning!"

PART TWO: The Lunch Trays

"Fortunate is the man who has not walked in the counsel of the wicked, nor stood in the path of sinners, nor sat in the company of scoffers."

Psalm 1:1

Fall 2022: Brooklyn

-1-

"Frayda wants to come for dinner on Thursday night," said Serach as she knelt behind Paloma, drawing a brush through her partner's hair in a series of well-practiced strokes. "She called late this afternoon to ask whether she could, and I said: 'sure.' I hope you don't mind..."

"Mind? I'd love it. It's been forever since I've seen her."

"But now I'm worried. Why would she ask to do such a thing, just like that? She's never done something like that, before."

"Good Lord, Serach. There's no mystery about why she asked. She's been missing me. She gets to eat lunch with you once a month, but the only way she can count on seeing me is to come here for dinner."

Paloma smoothed the comforter out around her hips and tilted her head back, the better to luxuriate in Serach's attentions.

"It will be great—just like old times," she continued. "She'll bring her own food in a hermetically-sealed container. She and I will discuss new trends in dentistry's use of prophylactic antibiotics for patients with heart conditions—there's a lot of new research—"

"But it won't be like that at all," interrupted Serach, softly. "It won't be anything like what it used to be."

"What are you talking about? Why on earth not?"

"Because it won't be just us on that night," answered Serach, as close to petulant as she ever got. "Frank will be eating here, too. He's begun venturing out again at last, as you know. But he's a total creature of habit and his going out is never on a Thursday night. Never."

Paloma laughed.

"Ah yes. Silly me. Well, that opens all sorts of interesting new possibilities, doesn't it?"

Serach put down the brush and began fiddling with a particularly stubborn knot in Paloma's hair with her fingers. Paloma looked slyly back over her shoulder.

"Hey. What's the worry? Just because they're the two most difficult people we know..."

Serach cringed.

"Come on," Paloma said, turning to face front again. "It'll be just fine. What evidence do you have that it won't be? It's not as if there's some long history of explosions between them. They've never even met each other." She paused. "Or have they?"

"Well..." murmured Serach. "Not technically."

Not technically! My partner, the accountant.

"Serach! What aren't you telling me? What's up?"

Serach shook out her head.

"It's because of something that happened today," she began slowly. "Something really out of the ordinary."

"Yes?"

Serach bit her lip.

 "See," she finally continued, "Frank has this routine that ensures that he gets away from the keyboard for at least part of the day. Keeps him sane, he says. He speeds out the front door at precisely ten-to-twelve to treat himself to a pimento-cheese sandwich at the Cortelyou Road Diner—he insists that there's this Southern Black chef there who makes them almost as well as his favorite aunt used to do. Then, he goes for brisk hour's walk in Prospect Park, rain or shine—he calls it his 'daily constitutional'—before he comes home again."

She gave a half-smile.

"Those practices have pretty much insured that he's stayed completely unaware of Frayda's lunchtime visits. And—also—that she's never run into him when she's here. Which is probably all for the good, given... well, given who they are."

She took a breath before going on.

"Today, however—just after Frayda walked in and began unpacking our sandwiches—there was this huge burst of music from the living room. Evidently, for the first time that I can remember, Frank decided to cut short his constitutional, slipped in through the front door without a sound, and launched into his afternoon practice session way earlier than usual."

She gathered Paloma's hair into one hand, contemplated its dark silkiness for a moment, let it billow back out again, and then went back to brushing.

"The fact that he'd chosen to rush back like that didn't surprise me all that much—you know how obsessed he's been about his upcoming recital. But it had to have been a rude shock for Frayda to hear that explosion of notes coming out of nowhere, with no warning. And sure enough, when I turned to look at her, she was sitting bolt upright in her chair with this expression of—Paloma, it looked like agony—on her face."

"Frayda always looks pained."

"Not like this. I quickly explained—I mean, I had to—that it was our housemate Frank, preparing for a concert, and asked whether she wanted me to close the kitchen door to muffle the sound. But she just waved her hand and kept listening, ramrod straight—her features twisted into that terrible grimace. She stayed that way for a good ten minutes before suddenly getting to her feet, shoving the unopened sandwiches back into the basket, zipping it shut, and scuttling out the back door without a word.

"Bizarre," murmured Paloma. "Though, of course, Frayda does all sorts of strange things."

She thought for a moment and grinned.

"For all we know, her flight may have had absolutely nothing to do with Frank's playing. Maybe she suddenly remembered a patient file that she'd left out on her desk and now who knows who might rifle through it to learn all about Reb Moishe's denture issues. So off she dashed to put it back where it belongs."

"Paloma, you're not being helpful."

Paloma stopped smiling.

"Have you been worrying about this incident all day, Babe?"

"Well truthfully, I didn't think about it very much at all, at first. As you say, Frayda often behaves bizarrely—rudely, even—for reasons that no one can fathom."

She stopped brushing.

"I didn't even worry when she called to invite herself over. Or think it had anything to do with Frank's playing. I don't know—I guess I just assumed that she was trying to 'make nice' after taking off with the sandwiches like that."

Paloma snorted.

"Frayda doesn't 'make nice,' Serach."

"Well, no. She doesn't. Which is why—once I started telling you about her wanting to come over—everything suddenly fell into place and all these red flags began waving."

She contemplated the brush for a long moment before starting to use it again.

"It's not as if I've kept Frank a secret from her or anything. She knows that he's this famous concert pianist and that you and he have been friends for years and that he used to live here. She even knows that he's moved back in. I mean—I wouldn't do anything actively deceptive with her—so I know I had to have mentioned it when it first happened."

She paused in her brushing again.

"Still, I'm certain that my account of his move here was very brief and that I never mentioned our living situation again. And that she never inquired into it any further, either."

"But why not? I thought she was a total busybody."

Serach gave a tiny, private smile.

"Because doing so might uncover something that would make her uncomfortable. Might lead us to quarrel. Or worse. She'd never risk that. She holds my friendship too dear."

"Of course she does," Paloma said, smiling as well. "Mine, too. But I still don't get why it would be such a problem. Frayda's very cool, in her way. Just look at how she accepts us!"

"Yes, Paloma, but I suspect that it's only because she's researched every aspect of the topic and found the three obscure rabbinic texts that argue that we're not technically breaking any law."

She paused.

"But Frank's being here with us is... something else entirely."

She drew a breath.

"Paloma—just think what our household must look like to someone who lives in a world in which every possible interaction among and between the genders is strictly prescribed. Here is this totally unrelated man of unspecified but dubious sexuality sleeping in the bedroom right next to ours, sharing bathrooms with us, coming and going as he pleases—perhaps bringing other men in with him. The possibilities for sin are exponential. Frayda didn't even want to join our pod when she thought that Frank might be part of it. I'm sure the only way she's been able to deal with our living situation is by compartmentalizing it away."

She sighed.

"But then with him arriving today and making all that commotion? How could she go on ignoring it?"

"Serach, even if you're right—even if Frayda totally disapproves of Frank's being our best buddy and live-in housemate—why would she invite herself over exactly at a time when she knows he'll be here? You'd think she'd do everything she could to prevent such a thing."

"But that's the whole point," Serach answered miserably, putting the brush down again. "I think that after spending all afternoon thinking about Frank living here, she decided she needed to do something about it. Like announcing right at the dinner table—with everybody present—that what we're doing is wrong."

"That's the most ridiculous thing I've ever heard."

"No, it's not. You didn't see her face this afternoon."

"No. Fortunately, I was spared that. But look, Serach. No need to worry twice. We'll find out what she's up to soon enough. In the meantime, please either brush my hair or don't brush my hair. Leave off all this starting-and-stopping business. It's driving me nuts."

Serach went back to brushing at a steady pace.

"By the way, which piece was Frank playing?" asked Paloma, after a small pause.

"The Beethoven. Not the whole thing. Just the section that causes him such *tsoris*."

"Was he playing it over and over again?"

"Mnnn hmnnn."

"Then maybe that's your answer—maybe that's why Frayda looked so appalled. Ten minutes of that and anyone would go crazy. I do, regularly."

"I don't know ...."

"Or maybe she was just put off by all those late-Beethoven dissonances. They can be totally unnerving for anyone.

Imagine how they might sound to someone who's never heard anything more musically taxing than the folk songs of the *shtetl*."

"Frayda isn't a product of the *shtetl*, Paloma. I'm sure I've told you that. Her parents were refugees from some fancy part of Jewish Berlin. She only became *frum* when she got married."

But Paloma suddenly had enough. She yanked her tresses out from between her partner's fingers, twisted them into an expert knot at the top of her head, and bound it all up with a hair tie.

"Well, then stop fussing, Serach!" she said. "Let's go to sleep."

She paused.

"There is, however, one other question of relevance. Frayda may be aware that Frank will be here, but does Frank know that Frayda is coming?"

"Yes. I told him tonight, just before he took off for dinner with his cellist friend Alyosha."

"And he was okay with it?"

"He seemed pleased, actually. Said that he feels he practically knows her after hearing so much about her all these years."

"Then that settles it. I'll spend part of my day off tomorrow preparing something delicious. Butter Frank up—put him in a good mood. And if Frayda begins telling him to go rent a room somewhere else? Or that a world-renowned pianist should get a piece right the first time, instead of banging it out over and over? Well then, that's a show I wouldn't want to miss!"

"We'll seat them directly across the table from one another," said Paloma once Thursday night arrived. "That way, they'll be stuck gazing right into each other's eyes whenever they speak. No escape."

"Paloma, please! Stop making things worse than they are!" said Serach, handing her the napkins and the silverware. "I'm nervous enough."

"Oh, Serach," Paloma chuckled, as she deftly organized the settings around the table. "Don't you know when I'm teasing you? It will all work out. I promise. Frank is never in a bad mood when eating my version of Julia Child's *Saumon Wellington En Croute*. He'll remain docile as a lamb. Charming, even."

"He's never eaten Julia's salmon with Frayda around."

"Serach—calm yourself!"

"But—"

At that moment, however, Frayda rang the back doorbell. Serach let her in and Frank—almost simultaneously—strode downstairs and into the kitchen. He looked around, pointedly eyed Frayda, pointedly eyed the table, and slid into his seat.

"You've only set places for three people," he said, gesturing grandly toward their guest. "What about Frieda?"

"She brings her own place settings," said Serach, pulling out Frayda's chair and motioning for her to sit down. "And it's 'Frayda,' not 'Frieda.'"

Frayda stepped forward, put her bag down on the table, opened it up, and began emptying out all its contents—place mat, place setting, two-handled silver cup, plastic clamshell of food.

"Frayda?" asked Frank, raising an eyebrow. "So the vowel is pronounced more like the one in 'Freya', as in 'the Norse Goddess of Love, Fertility, War, Childbirth and Magic'—than it is like the one in 'Frida' as in 'Frida Kahlo?'"

"Actually," said Frayda, carefully arranging everything to her liking, "what it started out as—what my parents called me before my husband took over and turned everything into Yiddish—was 'Freude.' Joy. As in the 'Ode to Joy' from Beethoven's Ninth? You're familiar with it?"

She paused for a moment and smiled so briefly that Frank wasn't even sure that he'd seen it.

"You know. *Freude, schöner Götterfunken, tochter aus Elysium?*"

Was there a strong whiff of Beethoven's immortal rhythmic pulse within Frayda's rendition of that quote? Perhaps. What was impossible for Frank to miss, however, was the flawlessness of her German pronunciation. So startling—so incongruous—given the vividly New York inflections that shaped her speech in English.

She paused for a moment, glanced briefly at each of her dinner companions, and then looked away again.

"It was my mother's favorite piece—the Ninth," she said, softly.

She rose before anyone could comment and walked to the sink with her two-handled silver cup, ritually washed her hands and said the appropriate blessing. Once she was finished, she returned to the table, pried open the plastic clamshell, said the appropriate blessing over the roll contained within, and took a small bite. She then walked back to the sink with her plastic glass and filled it with water from the tap.

"There's ice water right here on the table, Frayda," said Paloma, reaching for the pitcher.

Frayda gave her a stony stare.

Paloma smiled innocently back at her, poured water into Frank's glass and white wine into Serach's and her own. She then picked up each of the serving dishes in turn and began walking around the table to fill the three plates with grilled red and yellow peppers, sugar snap peas with mint, candied carrots, and a generous slice of the salmon *en croute* to which Frank had been looking forward all day.

"I can't believe that you are content to eat that pallid tuna salad, that limp cole slaw and that pickle of unmentionable color, while we are sitting here enjoying this incredible repast," Frank intoned, motioning toward Frayda's meal with one elongated hand.

"It's very good tuna salad," Frayda responded, mildly. "It's from Edelman's. Only the best."

The table grew quiet.

"So, Frank," said Paloma brightly, after a long silence. "Why don't you tell Frayda what you are going to be playing at your January Alice Tully Hall recital?"

Frank paused in his eating and pursed his lips.

"It may well be the hardest solo program that I've ever undertaken," he said, primly. "Each piece is more difficult than the last. And more beautiful."

He took a bite of the salmon and savored it before continuing.

"I begin with Bach's Partita Number 6. Fabulously challenging. Glorious. Followed by Prokofiev's Sonata Number 7, with that utterly relentless last movement. You've heard me practice both, I'm sure. "

"Bits of them," said Paloma. "Haven't heard either of them completely, yet."

"In the concert's second half," Frank continued, as he delicately ate a few of the sugar snap peas, "I begin with Beethoven's Sonata in C Minor, Opus 111."

He sighed.

"It is a spectacular piece. A piece that only a madman could possibly have composed. Beethoven was clearly both totally deaf and totally mad at the time—channeling harmonies and rhythms from some future universe."

He gave a small, unmistakably provocative smile to Frayda.

"It was written during the same epoch as the Ninth Symphony."

He took another bite and a small sip of water before beginning to speak again.

"I then finish with back-to-back performances of Ravel's *Le Tombeau de Couperin* and *Gaspard de La Nuit.* Crowd dazzlers. My audiences always eat them up."

He sat quietly with his food for a long while before turning to Frayda once more.

"Ravel was Jewish, you know."

"It's a myth," said Frayda, waving her fork around. "People think that—even other Jews think that—because he wrote all those Jewish songs. But writing Jewish songs does not make a person Jewish. The man was Swiss. And Basque. Father Swiss. Mother Basque."

She took a large bite of her cole slaw and chewed slowly.

"He also wrote Spanish songs. He wasn't Spanish, either. Basque isn't Spanish."

"No, but I've read that..."

"Not Jewish. My grandfather knew people who knew him. Not Jewish."

Frank blinked several times and returned to his food.

"He always dressed very well," Frayda added, after a pause. "Like a dandy. Like you."

What do you reply to that?

"There is chocolate mousse for dessert," announced Paloma into the ensuing silence. "Are we ready for it? And does anyone want espresso or tea?"

When they had scraped the last bit of their dessert course off their plates and Serach had whisked all the dishware into the sink, Frayda suddenly looked straight at Frank and gave him a small, shy smile.

"Now that we're done," she said, "will you play the Beethoven that you are working on for us? From beginning to end? Straight through?"

Her expression conveyed such anguished longing that Serach blushed for her.

"My mother loved that piece, too."

Which is why, six weeks later, the three women once again found themselves seated in the living room, listening attentively as Frank tried out a subset of his upcoming concert pieces. Paloma had suggested—and they had all eagerly fallen into—this new bi-weekly tradition of Thursday evening dinners-and-mini-recitals, and now nothing was going to stop them.

Until the moment on that last fateful Thursday when the front doorbell rang right in the middle of what is probably the most challenging passage in *Gaspard de la Nuit*.

"Good heavens," said Serach. "Who could that possibly be at this hour?"

"Hold that phrase, Frank," said Paloma. "This won't take long—it's probably just a neighbor coming over to borrow some milk."

But Frank removed his hands from the keyboard and definitively closed the piano lid.

"No, I am done," he muttered. "Some interruptions are irrevocable."

"Well, we'll see," said Serach. She strode toward the front hall and—moments later—a mighty din exploded from out of that space.

"That's not someone asking for milk," Paloma said, springing up and dashing after her partner. She arrived to find Serach with her arms wound tightly around a frantic

Anteojitos and Gordito standing sheepishly and silently by—an overstuffed re-usable Stop & Shop grocery bag in each hand.

"Papito is gone—and now they took away my room!" Anteojitos was shouting as he flailed around in his aunt's embrace.

"What is it that you're saying?" asked Paloma.

"Papito is gone—and now they took away my room!" he yelled again. "So I've come to live with my Tías!"

- 2 -

"Okay, Gordito, spit it out!" said Paloma, once Frank had scuttled up to his bedroom, she and Serach had settled Anteojitos in the guest room with two melatonin gummies and a cup of hot cocoa, and Serach had nudged Frayda into her car to drive her back to Boro Park. "What the hell has been going on!"

"Can I have something to eat first?"

"Jesus, Gordito!"

But he looked so sad and hungry that she relented.

"Okay, okay. You want some of tonight's leftover spinach and mushroom quiche? No, huh? Well, I think I may have an individual pepperoni pizza somewhere in the freezer. I sometimes get a yen for one myself."

"And a beer?"

"And a beer."

She popped the pizza into the microwave, turned it on for the prescribed time, pulled out a bottle of Corona Premier from the inside shelf of the refrigerator door, found the bottle opener, and placed everything in front of her nephew.

"Okay, Gordito. That's it. No more excuses. *¡Hablame!*"

"Well," he said taking an enormous bite of the pizza and swallowing it down without seeming to chew it at all. "You know how Negrito has this really great new start-up computer programming business?"

"Mnnn."

"And how he's been living with his girlfriend Gloria in this rental apartment in Ridgewood?"

"Mnnn."

"Well, see... Gloria has this start-up business, too, but it's a different type. I mean, I think it's, like—in fashion or something? So, all their money has been going into those start-ups but they also want to buy an apartment somewhere—a, like, bigger place—because what they had was really small and, like, not convenient and they need to save some money so they can get something better and maybe start a family?"

"Gordito, for God's sake, are you ever going to get to the point?"

"Mnnn hmnnn," he said, and took another bite. "So on Tuesday, last week, see, they—like—decided to move in with us for a while."

"What do you mean by 'a while'?"

"Well, yeah, a long while I guess. I mean, housing prices are pretty high now and—like I say—all their money is going into their businesses. They're going to have to save a lot."

"Jesus. They'll be living with your mama forever."

"Yeah," said Gordito, finishing off the pizza in two additional bites and then opening and downing the beer. "Probably. Is there anything else to eat?"

Paloma pushed the serving dish with the quiche toward him.

"This is the only other thing there is, Gordito. Frank will be desolate if you swallow it all down and he doesn't have any leftovers to pick at. But blood wins out. Go ahead."

Gordito gave the remnants of the quiche a puzzled glance, but then shrugged and took a tentative bite.

"Mnnn," he said as he chewed. He swallowed and then reached for his beer bottle. "And can I have some more...?"

Paloma pulled out a second bottle and put it in front of him.

"Okay, Gordito—but that's it. I'm not giving you another thing till you finish your story."

He gave a mini-shrug.

"But there's nothing else, Tía. That's it."

"Nonsense. You haven't told me what happened once they moved in. What does Anteojitos mean by 'now they took away my room' ?"

"Oh. Yeah. Well, see—Mama moved Gloria and Negrito into the bedroom that Anteojitos and me were sharing, and—"

"Jesus! So now you and Anteojitos are sleeping...?"

"Me on the living room couch."

He took a big bite of the quiche.

"Hey, this stuff is *real* good!"

"Yes, I know. Finish it off if you want. Frank will survive. But stop interrupting yourself! You're sleeping on the couch and Anteojitos...?"

"On the couch cushions, on the floor."

"Jesus Christ."

"Yeah, well. Yeah."

He took the last bite of the quiche.

"It hasn't been so terrible for me. I mean—I'm always working or else out with the guys. And the couch is pretty comfortable. Even without its cushions. But Anteojitos...."

"But Anteojitos is home all day, doing nothing—and now is exiled from his room and sleeping on the floor. It's got to be rough."

Gordito nodded.

"Yeah. Plus," he added wisely, "Anteojitos hates any kind of change."

He sighed.

"He cried a lot at first. Then he stopped eating for a couple of days."

Paloma massaged her temples.

"What about his saying that he was coming to live with us? When did that start? And why? Is Negrito bullying him again?"

"No. Gloria wouldn't let that happen. Gloria is… real nice."

"So…?"

"Well, it's funny. By Saturday, Anteojitos was kind of getting better. He wasn't crying so much. Eating some stuff. On Sunday morning, Gloria and Negrito and me and him even went out to IHOP and he ate a bunch of pancakes."

Gordito took a long swig of his beer.

"But then," he continued, "later that afternoon he gets this call from that house parent at the school he used to be at? The guy he really liked?"

"André?"

"Uh huh. André. When he calls, it's usually a good thing. Makes Anteojitos feel better. But this time it, like, really charged him up. That's when he began saying—well, like he was saying tonight—all those things about how Papito is gone and how he lost his room and how he's going to go live with his Tías. Every day, as soon as I got home, he would start in on it, and he wouldn't stop till he fell asleep. Tonight, I finally said: 'You want to go there now?' and he said: 'Yeah.' So I helped him pack up and brought him."

Gordito took a deep breath, lifted the bottle to his lips and drank deeply.

"You never even considered that Serach and I might say 'no' to his moving in?" asked Paloma, shaking her head. "It never occurred to you that we might have just told you to turn around and take him back? You never even thought to call us first to see if it was okay with us?"

Gordito gave her a puzzled look.

"No."

He downed the rest of the beer in a single gulp.

"So anyway," he said. "That's what happened."

Paloma raked her hands fiercely through her hair a few times.

"Do you think it was André who told him he should come here?"

Gordito shrugged.

"It's logical, isn't it? He didn't start saying that part till after André called."

It's logical. Sometimes Gordito is really surprising.

"Well, André sure has some explaining to do."

All that would have to wait, however.

"And what has your mother been saying to all this? Was she upset that Anteojitos was so messed up? That he wasn't eating? That he began saying all that stuff about coming here?"

"She didn't really see all that. She's, like… at work most of the time."

"Well, what about his actual packing up and leaving? Was she upset about that? Did she try to stop you from bringing him?"

"Um, she doesn't… know about that yet. She was out when that all happened, too. I guess she'll find out about it when I get home and he's not with me."

"Do you think she'll explode?"

"She and Anteojitos," he began. "They don't… I mean, they don't fight or anything. But—"

"Yes, of course. She may actually be relieved when she learns that he's left."

Gordito shrugged again.

"Not to mention pleased that it's me and Serach who are now stuck with him. Serves us right since we've always tried to interfere with how she's raised him."

They fell silent for a moment.

"And how did she feel about Negrito moving back in with you like that?"

"Oh, she gets along fine with Negrito. I mean, she gave him our room and everything, didn't she?"

"She's also fine with Gloria being there?"

"Um... well, Gloria is real nice. Like I said. She can really..."

"Handle your mother?"

Gordito shrugged yet again.

"I see."

"Well," said Gordito, getting to his feet. "I guess that's it."

He scratched his cheek a few times and looked sideways at his aunt.

"So, um, good luck with Anteojitos and everything."

Paloma burst out laughing. What else could she do?

"Yeah," she said. "Thanks for bringing him."

Then she gave her middle nephew a hug, told him that she loved him, and walked him out the door.

- 3 -

"Serach!"

Serach spun around on the big green ball that she always sat on while she worked, and what she saw truly surprised her. Frank had never before ventured up into her space, yet there he was, perched in the doorway of her study. Things must really be grim.

"Serach, now that Paloma is off somewhere with her friend Etha, and The Fat One has taken The Creature out for the day, you and I need to talk!"

"Yes, Frank. I suppose we do. Shall we go downstairs and chat in a civilized manner, over a cup of something hot?"

Frank pursed his lips.

"I thought for a moment you were going to say 'over a stiff drink.'"

"Silly man. I would never do that. Come. I'll make you an espresso and myself a cup of tea, and we'll have this all out. It's been a week. I've been waiting for the other shoe to drop."

Frank turned and sped down the two flights of stairs, Serach close on his heels.

They settled in at the kitchen table and Serach put up the kettle, fiddled expertly with Paloma's espresso maker, opened the tin in which Paloma kept her stock of homemade cookies, and emptied a half-dozen of them onto a plate in front of him.

"But Frank," she said as she bustled about. "You must not call Ramon 'The Creature.' I won't tolerate it."

Frank drew a breath.

"Well, perhaps once we have had this out, I won't have to call him anything, anymore."

"I wouldn't count on it."

The kettle whistled and Serach poured boiling water into her teacup, along with some sugar and milk. The espresso maker streamed its precious liquid into the Limoges cup that Frank claimed for his own. Serach brought everything to the table and Frank took a sip of the espresso, closed his eyes, and seemed to relax a notch.

"You may be wondering why I've chosen to have this out with you and not with Paloma."

"Yes."

"It's because Paloma has absolutely no influence over... her nephew. Whereas you do."

"No, I don't. Not really."

"Yes really, Serach. He idolizes you. When you are in the room, he becomes like one of those Renaissance portraits whose eyes follow you everywhere you go."

Serach shrugged.

"Well, I guess he and I have an understanding," she said. "He knows that I love him and that it is unconditional. But I don't think it goes any farther than that. He's kind of his own man."

"Serach, it goes much farther than that. He hangs onto your every word. It's you who were his first teacher, after all. The one who taught him everything he knows—if Paloma is to be believed, and why would she have any reason to say so if it weren't true?"

Serach shrugged again.

"He learned quite a bit when he got to Excelsior, as well."

"Irrelevant. One's first teacher.... my first piano teacher, for example... well, never mind. The point is, you are the one who is foremost in his heart, so if anyone is going to be able to deal with this horrific situation, you are the one best suited to do so."

Serach took a small sip of her tea.

"Okay, Frank. Be that as it may. Go on."

"Well, as you say, it has been a week, now, of all this. A full, long, exhausting, intolerable week. I have tried—Lord knows, I have tried—to be accommodating. I have eaten out every night, because dining with you all means sitting with someone who has the table manners of a two-year-old. I have retired early every evening, rather than staying for a cozy little post-prandial chat with you and Paloma in the living room, as I used to cherish doing, because that would mean remaining in the company of someone who is utterly without social graces—and who has the voice of a foghorn."

Serach nodded. She could not deny any of that.

"Nonetheless, there are limits to my ability to cope. I have reached them."

Serach gave him an intense glance over the top of her teacup.

"Serach—hear me out. I am having a nervous breakdown, here."

"I'm not saying a word, Frank."

He took a breath.

"Look, I know there are things that are beyond his control. Developmental issues, mental issues—whatever. I know, moreover, that he grew up within a primitive cultural environment."

Serach colored visibly and Frank pretended not to notice.

"Some people, however," he continued, "manage to overcome the limitations of their roots. Paloma, for example..."

"Frank, enough! Get back to the point, please."

Frank looked back at her briefly.

"I think I might have been able to adjust to staying away at suppertime and even into the evening," he said slowly. "Or we could have worked out some other compromise."

"Probably."

"But... I cannot—I absolutely cannot tolerate his presence here during the day."

Frank shut his eyes.

"Serach, he lurks in the doorway when I practice. He stands there in that ratty black sweatshirt and those appalling jeans and that hangdog face and just stares at me while I am playing."

Serach nodded. She had seen Anteojitos do that a couple of times, herself. It was definitely unnerving.

"But even that—even that—isn't the worst. I have, on occasion, seen people in my own audiences who look even more unhinged than he does, and yet I am forced to go on. Concert goers are definitely not what they once were."

He ruffled his hands though his hair and Serach was struck by how young he suddenly looked. Like a lost little boy about to cry, almost. Her heart yielded. She resolved to listen with an open mind.

"But the last straw—the absolute last straw," he continued, "occurred on Monday, when I was giving my bi-weekly lesson to... perhaps the best student I have ever had. To the next Yuja Wang, I swear it. I've never seen more talent in a young pianist. And right there, in the middle of our lesson, I look up and there is that... Young Man, leaning against the doorway, and leering at her. And he was barefoot! He was actually barefoot! My poor student—my poor Yan-Xiu—was being forced to play Rachmaninoff's Fifth Prelude with those two large naked feet in plain view!"

Frank put his face in his hands.

"Serach, it is That Creature or me. I swear, if you cannot control him, I will walk out of this house and... oh, sweet Jesus, I don't know what I will do or where I will go!"

"Okay, Frank. It's okay. You will not end up in the street, I promise you. But neither will Ramon. So let's try to work this out. Talk to me. What exactly can you put up with and what absolutely needs to change?"

"I can put up with the concept of his being here," said Frank, breathing out slowly. "I can deal with the idea of him enjoying the manifold pleasures of living in Judith's splendid home and partaking of Paloma's incomparable cooking. Of him benefiting—however obliquely—from the money that I contribute every week to the household expenses without contributing a penny himself. I am resigned to all that."

Serach refrained from saying a word.

"I am willing to take myself out to dinner or eat here on my own after you all are finished. It won't be such a sacrifice. I've always considered it barbaric to be dining at seven, the way that you ladies insist on doing. No one else in the civilized world does that, you know."

Serach looked away. She considered starting dinner after seven o'clock to be totally unhealthy. Too close to bedtime. Not enough time to properly digest.

"But he cannot be anywhere in this house at any point between nine-thirty a.m. when first I sit down at the piano and six o'clock p.m. when I shut down for the day," Frank was continuing. "There can be no further chance that he will be hovering in the doorway while I am practicing, or unexpectedly home from my lunch break or—God forbid— giving a lesson. He has to find a daytime purpose in life, and that purpose has to be elsewhere than in my presence."

He paused.

"He can hang around here on Saturdays. On Saturdays, I have promised myself to start socializing again in earnest. To go into Manhattan and begin picking up where I was pre-pandemic, and... pre-Kae-Dang."

Serach averted her gaze to escape his stricken look.

"Once a month, on Sundays, he can also be here in the mornings," he continued. "Paloma has been saying how she wants to resume having the three nephews over here for those monthly brunches of hers. I can manage to disappear on those occasions."

He paused.

"But on all the other Sundays—and on every Sunday afternoon—I will need to return to practicing without that boy being anywhere in the vicinity. And on Thursday evenings... well, we'll have to wait and see what happens with our little soirées with Frayda, won't we? But I hope we can go back to them without his being here, ogling us as I play."

Serach looked away again, but this time it was to hide the breadth of her smile. *Frank really likes Frayda! He really likes playing for her. He looks forward to those soirées with her. Who could possibly have predicted that?*

"We'll work it all out, Frank. I promise. I see what you've been going through and you're right. It hasn't been fair. You were here first. This is your home. Ramon will have to adapt."

Frank looked at her with something approaching awe.

"Then you understand?"

"Yes, Frank, of course I do. Moreover, I'm grateful to you for providing the nudge that I've needed for a long time. I've been utterly negligent with regard to Ramon. I did nothing to get him into doing something constructive when he first left school because he was so distraught that no one could do anything with him. I did nothing for him after his father got sick because—well—because everything fell into chaos. But it's been ages since all of that happened and I still haven't done anything. Shame on me. It's no better for him to be doing nothing but watch you play piano than it is for you to have to put up with that."

She paused.

"But the hour has finally come. I'm on the case. It will all change. And very soon. No fears."

Frank found himself smiling for the first time in a week.

"I have never had any fears where you are concerned, Serach. When you say you will do something, you do it. You are the most determined—the most capable—person that I know. Don't think that those qualities have been lost on me."

Serach blushed.

"Good heavens, Frank. I've hardly done anything to deserve such a compliment."

"But it's true."

She looked up at him and smiled.

"Well, be that as it may," she said, "in this case I can, in fact, assure you that your confidence is not misplaced. You see, I have just had a very interesting idea. And I have a secret weapon with which to execute it. Give me another week or two."

January 2023

- 4 -

Shprintza was deeply skeptical when Frayda first brought Anteojitos into her office at the *B'Sevah Tovah* Assisted Living Facility, despite the transformation that Serach had wrought in his appearance through the purchase of four pairs of black pants, seven long-sleeved white Oxford shirts, ten pairs of black socks, a neat pair of black sneakers, a new black sweatshirt, a black down jacket, and a black Yankees baseball cap that he had immediately donned and hadn't taken off since.

"He doesn't seem to be all there," she remarked to Frayda when Anteojitos stepped out briefly to use the men's room. "Are you sure he can handle it?"

"He can handle it."

"You know, it's a very complicated routine. He'll have to keep track of which rooms get which trays, and what they get on those trays, and it changes all the time. There are those who can't get to the dining room because they are temporarily ill but then they get better and can go back. There are those who are chronic and always need trays. There are those who can't eat salt because of their pressure and those who can't have sweets because of their sugar. There are the lactose-intolerant and the glucose-intolerant."

She paused to catch her breath.

"He'll have to stay on top of all that."

"He's some kind of mathematical genius, Shprintza. With a little guidance, he'll keep track of everything just fine. You'll make him a chart at the beginning of each week. On one of those big whiteboards that you write on with one of those— what are they called? Magic markers? Eventually, he'll be able to fill in the chart himself. Make improvements to your system, even."

"What about his reliability? Will he always be here when he says he will? Will he always be ready to work? Will he always see the job through? Our residents get completely *farmisht* if they don't get their food on time, you know."

Anteojitos suddenly re-appeared in the doorway.

"Come on in, Ramon—come sit down with us again," said Frayda. "Mrs. Bernshteyn was just asking whether you are reliable."

"I am reliable," Anteojitos said, emphatically. "I am very reliable—"

"You see, Shprintza? I told you—"

"I was the best worker they ever had at the Excelsior School. They always told me that. The students used to cheer when I brought them their trays. I always got the trays right."

"Does he know how to get here on his own from wherever it is that he lives?" asked Shprintza, blinking a bit at Anteojitos' volume.

"Both by bus and on foot," said Frayda, nodding. "You practiced it, didn't you, Ramon?"

"Yes. Tía Serach and I practiced it four times, back and forth. She showed me how to get to work on the bus and then back home on foot, to work on foot and then back home on the bus, to work and back both times on foot—"

"That's great, Ramon," said Shprintza.

Anteojitos narrowed his eyes. He hadn't finished.

"—and to work and back both times by bus."

He nodded to himself.

"It is a thirty-two-minute trip for me to get here on foot," he said, glancing at Shprintza and then glancing away. "Always. Because I always walk at the same speed."

He paused.

"On the bus, it is three minutes' walk to the bus stop, two minutes waiting. Generally. Then thirteen minutes on the bus and four minutes' walk here. Twenty-two-minutes in all. Generally."

He looked up at the ceiling for a moment.

"But there is always the chance," he added, "that the wait for the bus will be longer. One time when we were practicing, it was a seven-minute wait. It could happen again. Or worse."

He drew a breath.

"I plan to get here on foot every day, since I know just how long that will take. On the way home I will take the bus—and if it is raining or snowing when I leave home, I will also take the bus. But on those days, I will leave enough time for if the bus is late."

He took another breath.

"Like it was on that day, when..."

"Okay, Ramon," Frayda said, before he could start in again. "I think Mrs. Bernshteyn now knows that you can get here—"

Anteojitos shook his head. This was important. If this woman—this Mrs. Bernshteyn—didn't see how well he knew how to get there, she might not hire him.

"To get here by bus," he began again, in an even louder tone, "first I walk up Marlborough Road to Church Avenue. Then I cross Church Avenue and turn left to get to the bus stop between Rugby Road and Argyle Road, and then—"

"Ramon!" Frayda finally bellowed. "That is absolutely enough!"

He closed his eyes tightly, bit down on his lip, and stopped talking.

"Can you handle sudden changes in your daily routine?" interjected Shprintza. "Changes in the rooms to which you will be delivering the trays? Changes in who gets which tray? Our residents get very upset if they get the wrong tray."

"I don't like changes," said Anteojitos, shaking his head.

"Yes, Ramon—" said Frayda, speaking loudly and slowly. "But if someone explains those changes to you carefully beforehand? If they help you to make a big chart showing who gets which trays on which days, so you know what is happening ahead of time and can see exactly what the changes will be and can plan for them? Will you be able to handle the changes then?"

"Yes. I can handle changes if I have a chart," said Anteojitos, now nodding vigorously. "They made me a chart every week at the Excelsior School. For when there were changes. There were changes there, too. I like charts. They put everything in order so you can know what to do. Even when there are changes."

"You see?" said Frayda. "Ramon likes charts."

"What kind of name is Ramon?" Shprintza turned to Ramon after a moment's silence.

"It's my name."

"I mean where does it come from?"

"It's a Spanish name, Shprintza," said Frayda. "He comes from a very good Spanish family. They raised him very well and they named him very well."

"Hmnnn."

"It's a family that truly respects work. Isn't that right, Ramon?"

Anteojitos blinked and swallowed.

"Yes. Papito loved to work."

He swallowed again.

"But he's gone now. My mother loves to work, and my brother Negrito loves to work, and his girlfriend Gloria loves to work, and my brother Gordito loves to work, and my Tía Paloma loves to work, and my Tía Serach loves to work. I was the best worker they ever had at the Excelsior School. They used to—"

"Yes, Ramon. They used to cheer for you. Shprintza, what else do we need to do before you can hire this wonderful, hardworking young man?"

Shprintza looked hard at Frayda and then hard at Frayda's young charge.

"We will need to fill out some forms. I assume you have a Social Security card, Ramon?"

"It's in the works, Shprintza..."

"My Tía Serach took me to the Social Security Office last Friday," interrupted Anteojitos, freeing Frayda from the task of explaining why his family had never attended to such a vital matter before this. "She took me to the office, where they make things official about the Social Security card. It takes two weeks to get the card, but my Tía Serach..."

"He will have it in two weeks, Shprintza, and in the meantime, you can begin training him. Set up the chart for delivering the trays during the first week that he will be responsible for them. Show him around. Are we in agreement?"

"Yes, Frayda. We are in agreement."

She looked hard at Anteojitos.

"I will see you here tomorrow at ten o'clock a.m. sharp, Ramon," she continued. "I will take you to the kitchen so you can learn how the meals are prepared and how they are set out on the trays. I will then take you around and personally introduce you to all the people that you will be serving, so that you will know what to expect and they will know whom to expect. Then, over the next week or so, you will go around from room to room with the worker who has been handling the trays up till now, so you can see exactly how he does it and learn from it."

Anteojitos began rumbling in his throat. Something was bothering him.

"Who—" he finally managed to blurt out. "Who is that? Who has been handling the trays up till now?"

Shprintza looked up sharply. She really needed to wrap this meeting up.

"One of the kitchen workers, Ramon. As soon as he finishes filling the trays in the kitchen, he loads them up on the cart and takes them around."

"Will he be angry at me for taking away his job? Will he not want to show me what to do?"

"Goodness, no. He hates doing tray duty. It was never part of his original job description. It's just that we've had no one else to do it for the past couple of years. We've had to be a bit creative about work assignments since all this COVID *meshugas* began."

Shprintza shook her head.

"It has not been the best arrangement—I can tell you. Not only does that kitchen worker dislike doing it, but he doesn't speak any English. Which the residents don't like. Our residents want to be able to ask questions about their trays. They want to be able to get answers. Real answers. Not garbling."

"Ramon speaks both Spanish and English, don't you, Ramon?"

Anteojitos licked his lips.

"I can speak in Spanish, some. Not like my mother. Or like ... Papito. Did. But more than my brothers. My brothers don't like speaking in Spanish at all."

He rubbed his eyes behind their thick lenses.

"That will all be a great help for you, won't it, Shprintza?" said Frayda. "Ramon can speak English to the residents and Spanish to the kitchen workers. He can maybe even assist Penina, the kitchen supervisor—help her make things clearer to those workers. You're always saying how she has trouble with that."

Shprintza nodded despite herself and Anteojitos began to rumble again.

"I have another question."

Shprintza looked at Frayda and Frayda shrugged.

"He has another question."

"Yes, Ramon? What?" said Shprintza. This meeting had definitely been going on for far too long. She needed to check out the credentials of that new security guard and reprimand the janitor who had made such a mess of the showerhead crisis in Room 22, earlier that morning.

"Who does the tray shift at breakfast time?" asked Anteojitos.

"The night attendant," said Shprintza, standing up and beginning to walk toward the door. "It's the last thing he does before he leaves the facility in the morning. He is a Romanian—he speaks English. And morning tray duty has always been part of his job—since he was first hired. So we have never had any problems with any of that."

Frayda caught Shprintza's expression, stood up from her chair and began motioning vehemently to Anteojitos to do the same.

"But he's probably very tired when he does it, if it is the last thing that he does before going home," Anteojitos continued, turning his head to watch Shprintza walk but making no move to stand, himself. "Maybe I should do that shift, too. I can come in earlier."

"There will be no need for that," said Frayda at top volume. "And we are done here, Ramon. Mrs. Bernshteyn is holding the door open so we can leave. Stand up! Let's go!"

Anteojitos slowly got to his feet and Frayda led him out of the room before he could say anything else. Anything that might make Shprintza change her mind about the whole thing, chas v'cholileh.

Anteojitos, however, was feeling very happy. Once he and Frayda were back out on the sidewalk, he turned to her and gave her a big grin.

"It was a very good interview," he said, nodding briskly to himself. "I got the job."

"Yes, Ramon," said Frayda. "You did."

- 6 -

"You are a miracle worker, Serach," said Frank. "I am forever in your debt. Beyond crossing paths with your nephew in the kitchen when I'm finishing breakfast or when you all are finishing dinner, my life has been blessedly interaction-free since last Tuesday. In fact, this morning, he was nowhere in sight by the time I reached the kitchen."

Frank had made himself two slices of toast and was now fussing with the espresso maker.

"It's Frayda who did all that," replied Serach, as she strode to the stove and began fixing the second cup of tea of her morning. "Not me. But yes, Frank. Ramon will now be reliably absent during all the hours that you requested. What's more—once he finishes his training period and is officially on the job—he'll be gone for even longer, since they've agreed to give him breakfast every morning and dinner every night as part of his compensation."

She gave Frank a small, mischievous look.

"Which means that you can safely return to having supper with us, as well. That is, if you are willing to put up with eating at such an uncivilized hour."

Frank sighed.

"I might be persuadable. It is so expensive to always eat out."

He looked away.

"And so tedious to always eat alone. Lunch is one thing. Dinner is quite another."

Frank poured himself his espresso, walked to the refrigerator, rummaged around for the butter dish and marmalade jar, and brought everything to the table.

"So, is the boy happy in this new situation? Excited about his job? Pleased at his new surroundings?"

"He's absolutely delighted, actually."

"What exactly is he doing?"

"He's working at an assisted living facility for older men in the Boro Park neighborhood, right near where I grew up. He's bringing trays of food to all the room-bound and bed-ridden residents. It's what he used to do at his old school. It's a perfect job for him."

She paused and smiled.

"He likes the people. He likes the work."

Frank raised both his eyebrows.

"It boggles the mind, all this progress."

"No it doesn't. He just needed the right environment in which to blossom."

"That part boggles the mind even further. Who could possibly blossom among all those peculiar people with their preposterous costumes and their eccentric ways?"

Serach looked down and smiled again.

"The people among whom Ramon is blossoming are my people, Frank."

Frank raised an eyebrow and Serach looked up, her cheeks evolving from alabaster to blush.

"Well, yes. I may have left Boro Park, but it's still where I come from. Where I still feel some deep connections. Some pull. Does anybody ever really escape their roots? Don't you still have a pimento-cheese sandwich every single day, because it reminds you of home?"

Frank flushed as red as she was.

"Does the boy know all about your past?" he asked, after a short pause.

"Not that I know of. There's been no need to tell him. He doesn't even know how I know Frayda. He's not curious in that way, you know. He just kind of accepts things. It's part of why I love him."

She paused.

"I'll be honest with him if he ever asks, of course. But for now, I think it's best for him to explore what he's getting into with a completely open mind. I don't want him liking it just because I was raised there—or rejecting it because I left. He has the right to decide things for himself."

She waited for a beat.

"Still," she finally added. "It seems very fitting that he should be there—and that he should be happy in that environment. I've always felt a deep bond with him, you know. Almost as if we knew one another in some past place or past time. As if we were already family, long before we met."

She paused and looked away for a moment.

"So there is something, somehow, very... appropriate in all this."

· 7 ·

After decades of unquestioned authority over his household, his study group, his *shul*, his once-flourishing printing business, and his own sturdy little body, Reb Avram Bernshteyn had yet to adjust to life in Room 39 at the far end of the third-floor corridor of his eldest son's flagship assisted living facility.

The sorrow that had first engulfed him at his wife's untimely passing had inexorably deepened into bitterness. How could the woman he had trusted to support him in his declining years have failed him so thoroughly? How could she have just abandoned him to this fate?

The disappointment he felt as each of his six younger children, in turn, had settled far away from him—in Cleveland, in Houston, in the Holy Land—had hardened into rock-solid resentment. What kind of offspring would leave a father so totally beholden to the one son with whom he had never gotten along?

His frustration at the behavior of his fellow residents had steadily soured into scorn. What did he have in common with men who preferred jabbering about their ailments to parsing the meanings hidden in each daily page of Talmud—or unearthing the surprising links between certain key Scriptural passages and certain key mathematical principles? How had his son managed to gather so many *dummkopfs* into a single place?

Even the prayer services offered in *B'Sevah Tovah's* Assembly Room offered little in the way of consolation.

Yes, of course, the rabbi whom his son had hired to lead those services was perfectly competent. It was just that he was incapable of providing anything resembling enlightenment or inspiration. ("He was available when we needed someone," his son had shrugged when Reb Avram had voiced his concerns. "This COVID thing has made it impossible to be choosy. His credentials are fine, he's here every day without fail, what are you *kvetching* about, Tatteh?")

Finally, there was the matter of the attendant who wheeled him back and forth to the Assembly Room and assisted him in standing and sitting at the right times during prayers. Yes, that attendant always showed up on time. Yes, he knew exactly when to grip Reb Avram's arm and lift him to his feet. But did he have to do it so roughly, so rudely—with no regard for the shame that a once-vigorous man might feel in requiring help at all?

Reb Avram had actually begun dreading the points in the service when he knew he would need a hand. Not that he would ever complain about it. Not after experiencing his son's indifference to his reservations about the rabbi. No use banging your head against the wall.

Ultimately, moreover, Reb Avram knew that—despite the indignities that he suffered—he possessed certain advantages over everyone else living in the facility.

He had been given one of the facility's rare single rooms (there were only two per floor), for example, rather than having to share close quarters with anyone else, *chas v'cholileh*. He had been allowed to outfit that room exactly as he chose, rather than having to put up with the sterile blond furniture allotted to everyone else.

His formidable daughter-in-law, Shprintza, was committed to supporting his personal hygiene and comfort. Thanks to the air-tight control that she maintained over all housekeeping functions, he had never had to wait for his daily bathroom cleaning or for fresh and neatly folded laundry. He could count on the shower attendant arriving every other day at ten o'clock sharp. Best of all—thanks to Shprintza's eagle eye and unparalleled supervisory capacities—he was spared the ever-present threat of theft facing Jewish widowers who remain home at the mercy of *goyishe* care attendants.

He had much, in short, for which to be grateful.

Nonetheless, it must be said that there were many mornings when—awakening in his little bed in that third-floor private room—Reb Avram struggled to greet the dawn with the words of thanks that are the obligatory first daily utterance of any faithful Jew.

"We are about to meet Reb Avram Bernshteyn, my father-in-law," Shprintza announced, as she glanced back at Anteojitos over her shoulder. She marched briskly forward to Reb Avram's door, knocked, and then opened it wide in a single fluid motion.

"No salt, decaffeinated tea, a dish of prunes and a soft roll with every meal," she added, confidentially, before bringing her voice back to its usual mega-decibel level.

"Reb Avram!" she called into the room. "Shprintza, here. I've come to introduce you to our newest staff member."

Room 39 was markedly larger than the handful of other single rooms that Anteojitos had visited that day. It was even larger than some of the double rooms.

It had two big catty-corner windows—one facing the avenue, the other facing the street.

Late morning sunshine was pouring in through both those windows as they entered, and each window offered an unimpeded view of the neighborhood beneath.

You could spend a whole day watching the world go by, if you had windows like that.

Room 39 was also furnished differently than any of the other rooms that Anteojitos had seen. Yes, the wheelchair in which the room's tiny, white-bearded, black-clothed resident was sitting—face buried in a book—was just like all the other wheelchairs that he had observed. Yes, the bed was just like all the other beds—metal-frame, side bars, crank at the head and crank at the foot.

Everything else, however, was distinctive.

Rather than the confusing sameness of chairs and tables and lamps and floor coverings that dominated every other room (and that made Anteojitos fear that he might mix up whose room was whose once he began making his daily rounds) everything here was colorful and beautiful.

It was all, in fact, highly reminiscent of the furnishings to be found in the house of Tía Paloma and Tía Serach.

The chair by the window was upholstered in the same kind of wonderful, knobbly material as the little chair that sat against the far wall of their living room. ("Needlepoint," Tía Paloma had once called it—though when Anteojitos had surreptitiously run his hand up and down its surface there had been nothing pointy lurking beneath.)

The legs of the wooden table under the window were carved with little balls and curlicues in much the same way as the legs of Tía Paloma's dining room table. The two big bookcases dominating the room's longest side were filled top-to-bottom with books sheathed in dark brown leather— just like the books on several shelves in his aunts' expansive library.

Even the floor looked comfortingly familiar. It was covered, wall to wall, with a wine-red rug bordered in flowers and squiggles—so like the rug in front of his aunts' sofa. The rug on which he had been known to walk around and around for hours when he was younger, carefully tracing the path of all those interesting squiggles with his feet.

In fact, the only major difference between the décor of this room and that of his aunts' house was the total absence of anything that could possibly be called a painting. The resident of Room 39 clearly had no desire to be surrounded by gold-leaf-encrusted portraits of the Virgin Mary like those that Tía Paloma loved so dearly. Or by paintings of naked ladies like the ones that he, himself, liked to inspect when he thought neither of his aunts was looking.

No, the only thing adorning those four walls was a single black-and-white print hanging over the little sink in the far corner of the room—a humble, simply-framed object that would have been dwarfed and ignored had it had to compete for attention with the paintings in Paloma's house. In this setting, however, it was vivid and attention-getting, and—once Anteojitos spotted it—nothing else in the room mattered.

For one long moment, he merely leaned forward on his toes to squint at it from afar. But then his curiosity grew too great to bear. He elbowed Shprintza aside and careened right up to the sink to get a better look.

"Ramon! What are you thinking? You can't just barge right into someone else's space like that!" said Shprintza in her loudest voice. "You haven't been invited in yet! You haven't even been properly introduced!"

Anteojitos couldn't begin to explain that the only thing that he cared about right then was inspecting that entrancing little picture at closer range—was verifying whether it was what he thought it was.

It turned out that such an explanation was not necessary, however.

"It's all right, Shprintza," Rev Avram called out in a voice of surprising resonance, emanating as it did from such a shrunken frame. "Let the boy look."

- 8 -

Anteojitos had spent much of his life learning to decode the hierarchy of power in any given situation. Over time—as the repeated target of bullying—he had developed a nearly flawless capacity to sense who was best equipped to hurt him and who to protect him.

He therefore quickly recognized that the control center in Room 39 had just shifted from Mrs. Bernshteyn to the little man sitting in the wheelchair. The little man who had just given him permission to stand in front of that intriguing black-and-white print for as long as he pleased.

For several long minutes, he stood and inspected and thought about what he was seeing there. Eventually, however, he spun around and posed the question that was top on his mind.

"Why is that Fibonacci spiral made up of all those groups of funny symbols?" he asked, turning his gaze from the print to its owner.

"That is a very good question," said Reb Avram, surveying the tall, clumsy youth with great interest. "But before we get to it, you must tell me why you are so sure that what you are seeing is a Fibonacci spiral."

Anteojitos shrugged his shoulders.

"I don't know," he said. "I just am."

"Well then," said Reb Avram. "At least tell me what you know about Fibonacci spirals."

Anteojitos brightened up. That he could do. He took a deep breath.

"They are spirals," he said, "that are based on the Fibonacci series. Which is a series of numbers in which every number is the sum of itself and the number before it."

"Yes. Go on."

"Some people start counting the series with 'zero' and some with 'one,'" Anteojitos continued, screwing up his eyes and shifting back and forth between his feet. "Fibonacci himself started it from 'one and two.'"

He opened his eyes and glanced toward Rev Avram.

"I like starting it from zero."

"So do I," said Reb Avram. "Go on."

Anteojitos took an even deeper breath and closed his eyes tight again.

"The series the way I like to say it," he said in a loud and totally uninflected voice, "goes: Zero, one, one, two, three, five, eight, thirteen, twenty-one, thirty-four, fifty-five, eighty-nine, one hundred forty-four, two hundred thirty-three, three hundred seventy-seven..."

He opened his eyes, looked up at the ceiling, took another breath and continued.

"... six hundred ten," he said, "nine hundred eighty-seven, one thousand five hundred ninety-seven, four thousand one hundred eighty-one..."

"Dear me, young man!"

"... six thousand seven hundred sixty-five, ten thousand nine hundred forty-six, seventeen thousand..."

"Yes, yes—I see!" Reb Avram broke in again. "I see very well. You needn't go any further."

"But I can!" said Anteojitos, nodding vehemently to himself. "I can keep going for the first hundred and seven numbers. The record—the record for memorizing the series is much higher than that, but I am working toward it, and one day—"

"I am seriously impressed," said Rev Avram, raising his own voice to reach the volume with which he had earlier silenced Shprintza. "But—really—we must leave all that for another time."

For a short, tense moment Anteojitos looked as if he were going to explode. But he had recognized that this man was the person in charge in this room, and he fell reluctantly silent.

"It is remarkable that you have memorized such a long list," Reb Avram continued. "How have you managed to do it?"

Anteojitos shrugged.

"There must be a trick to it."

Anteojitos shrugged again.

"I see it all in color," he said, after a long moment. "Every number has a color. I see the patterns."

"Fascinating!"

Anteojitos shrugged for a third time.

"I can also recite the digits of 'pi'," he said, suddenly perking up again. "Up to two hundred places. I am working to go further with that as well. Some people have memorized it up to a thousand places. Some even more. I am hoping to surpass them all, someday."

"No need to show us right now," said Reb Avram, kindly. "Instead, why don't you return to trying to explain how you know that my spiral is a Fibonacci spiral? I would love to know."

Anteojitos was about to shrug yet again but then he stopped himself. He breathed deeply, in and out. He peered at the picture, looked up at the ceiling and then down at the floor. He stood first on one foot and then on the other.

"I know!" he finally said, in a voice full of awe, "I know how I know it! It is because once you have seen that shape, you can never forget it. You can never mistake it for anything else. It is the most beautiful shape—the most perfect shape—in the whole universe."

Rev Avram beamed.

"Yes, it is my son. Yes, it is."

He leaned forward in his wheelchair and perused Anteojitos's face.

"So tell me," he finally said. "Where else in the universe can you find this perfect shape?"

"You can find it everywhere! In seashells, in sunflowers, in the galaxies!"

"Interesting. Almost as if it were all planned that way."

"God did plan it that way," Anteojitos suddenly raised his voice. "Tía Serach says that the Fibonacci spiral is God's favorite shape."

He marched right up to Reb Avram and bellowed even louder.

"But you still haven't told me why the Fibonacci spiral on your wall is made up of all those groups of funny symbols. Why is that? What are those funny symbols?"

"Those are not groups of funny symbols," said Reb Avram, shrinking back in his chair a bit.

Anteojitos narrowed his eyes.

"Well yes, of course, they are groups of symbols—you are right about that," Reb Avram finally resumed, once he had swallowed hard and stroked his beard for a moment. "But they are far from funny. What they are is meaningful. In fact, they are the most *meaningful* symbols in the whole of that universe of which you speak with such appropriate reverence."

Anteojitos continued staring at him, but his eyes lost a bit of their squint.

"They are groups of letters, my son. Hebrew letters. Hebrew letters that fit together to form words. My Fibonacci spiral is made up of seventy-two Hebrew words, strung side by side. Or—more precisely—it is made up of seventy-two Hebrew names, strung side by side."

He leaned back in his wheelchair, closed his own eyes, and smiled.

"To be the most precise of all, it is made up of the seventy-two names of God. Or—as we Jews prefer to say—the seventy-two names of 'Ha-Shem.' A word which, in itself, simply means: 'The Name.'"

"God doesn't have seventy-two names," said Anteojitos, shaking his head. "God has only three names. The Father, the son—"

"No," said Rev Avram, as sharply as he could. "He has seventy-two names."

Anteojitos began to make the rumbling sound in his throat that his aunts knew only too well.

"No. God only has..."

"God has seventy-two names. Trust me. I will explain it to you another time."

But Rev Avram's stern expression suddenly melted as he regarded the youth before him. The youth who was the first person in the three years that he had been at *B'Sevah Tovah* who had shown any interest at all in these deep and important matters.

"What is more," he continued, after a pause, sliding into the sing-song voice of a yeshiva teacher, "you should be very glad that God has those seventy-two names. Because seventy-two is very special number."

Anteojitos nodded. He knew just how special seventy-two was. It was made up of twelve factors, and one of those factors was twelve itself. No other integer could claim that distinction.

Reb Avram, however, had other ideas about why seventy-two holds a special place among all integers.

"It is special," he continued, "because it spells out the word 'kindness.'"

Anteojitos gave him a perplexed stare.

"You see, the way that we express integers in Hebrew is by pairing them with the letters of the alphabet," Reb Avram continued. "And the letters that happen to be paired with the number 'seventy-two' also happen to spell out the word 'kindness.' Which, as you must know, is one of the most important words in any language. Right up there with 'justice.'"

Anteojitos began to say something, but Reb Avram suddenly placed a white, gnarled finger on his bearded bottom lip.

"There are lots of other things that we can discuss related to this topic," he said, "but I fear that any further discussion will have to wait. For I have just caught sight of the face of my good daughter-in-law, Shprintza, and I can see that she has reached the end of her patience. She no longer wishes to hear us talking about anything. She has something to say herself, and we must defer to her wishes. For the moment."

His voice was so confident—and so strong—that Anteojitos managed to keep himself from protesting. He shifted back and forth on his feet, but he didn't say a word.

"We will talk once again—I promise!" said Rev Avram. "But for now, I fear we must yield the floor to your employer. Shprintza—you came here for a reason. We have interfered with that reason. We apologize. Please—say whatever it is that you came to say."

Shprintza let out a long and beleaguered breath of air.

"Reb Avram," she said, "this young man, as you call him, is named Ramon Rodriguez. He is going to be bringing you both your lunch and your dinner from now on, on all the days on which you don't feel up to going to the dining room."

"I never feel up to going to the dining room anymore," Reb Avram sighed, waving one hand around in the air. "Very unappealing. Bunch of *dummkopfs* at every meal."

He gave a small, sad grin.

"Nonetheless," he continued, "the prospect of this young man bringing me my food—and of pursuing further conversations with him—is a very appealing one, indeed."

He paused, took off his glasses, blew on them briefly, and began wiping them with the handkerchief that suddenly materialized in his hand.

"In fact, I will implore you to please arrange this young man's schedule in such a way that I am the last person whom he serves at lunchtime. That way, we will have a good stretch of time in front of us in which to enjoy a nice long chat."

He gave another smile that then quickly disappeared into his beard.

"You would like that, Ramon, wouldn't you?"

Anteojitos nodded vehemently—up and down and up and down.

"So, no worries, Ramon. Be assured that if anyone can make such a thing come to pass, it is our good Shprintza. So we will leave it all in her capable hands, knowing it is as good as done."

Reb Avram bent his head down to smile once again into his beard and then he lifted it up again.

"So when does Ramon start in on this new enterprise?"

"He will start delivering trays as soon as his social security card comes through. Ten days? Two weeks? You can never tell with this government of ours. Till then, he'll just be in training."

"Well then, Ramon, we may have to wait a bit before embarking upon our mealtime discussions of mathematics and linguistics and theology," said Reb Avram, with a final, wistful smile. "At least... officially. But it is something to look forward to, is it not?"

He then dropped his head down again to stare at the book that he had been reading when Shprintza and Anteojitos had first entered. His lips began to move as he read.

Anteojitos opened his own mouth to say something, but Shprintza lurched so near to him and waved her hands so frantically that he was forced to reclose it.

"That's it, Ramon," she said in her loudest voice. "It is time to go."

Anteojitos knew that he had no choice. The power dynamic in the room had shifted back again. He gave one last longing look back to the Fibonacci spiral over Reb Avram's sink and shuffled out of the room behind his boss.

- 9 -

Shprintza had made it clear to Anteojitos that—until his training was completed—his interactions with *B'Sevah Tovah's* residents were to be limited to nodding when he trailed into their rooms behind the kitchen worker he was shadowing and then nodding again when he left.

("We do not bother the residents. We do not harass them. We are here only to serve them.")

Nothing, however, was going to keep Anteojitos from seeking out something more substantial than a nod exchange with the wonderful man who lived in Room 39. What is more, he suspected—with all the fine-tuned accuracy of his survival antennae—that Room 39's occupant would not consider such a thing to be harassment.

He thus found a way to sneak in regularly as soon as he had helped to clean up the last of the breakfast detritus and organize the lunch trays. He would bound up to the third floor, look right and left to make sure that no one was around, and then knock on Reb Avram's door.

"Come in!"

Grinning broadly, he would scuttle inside, and then he and Reb Avram would spend fifteen blissful minutes discussing numbers and letters and colors and their relationship to God.

Of course, when Anteojitos would arrive again at Reb Avram's door later in the day—trailing the kitchen worker who was showing him the ropes—he would have to pretend that he hadn't been there at an earlier point. He would have to press his lips together to keep from saying something. He would have to screw up his eyes. He would have to twist his hands together. It was not easy.

But the need for all that stressful subterfuge finally came to an end on the last, icy-cold Wednesday of January, when Anteojitos—too excited to even knock—burst into Room 39 and announced that he was now the official tray deliverer for all the room-bound patients at *B'Sevah Tovah* and that Mrs. Bernshteyn had arranged it so that Reb Avram would always be his last lunchtime stop.

"Every single day, we can talk for a whole half hour—maybe even forty minutes—till I have to return all the trays to the kitchen for cleaning!" he yelled.

"Well, well, well, this is an excellent development, Ramon," Reb Avram had replied as he surveyed the flushed and grinning youth.

Anteojitos placed Reb Avram's tray on the little table, pushed the table to Reb Avram's wheelchair, yanked the needlepoint chair right next to it and plopped himself down on it.

"So let's talk!"

"Patience, my son. Patience. First, I must see about this lunch. It seems that—for once—I am very hungry. It must be your presence that is inspiring my appetite."

He smiled slyly at Anteojitos.

"What is more—because it is Wednesday—I assume that this is actually my very favorite meal. Blintzes. Am I right?"

"Yes, you are right!"

"Wonderful. So before we begin to converse, let me go over to the sink, wash my hands, say all the proper blessings, and then launch into this feast."

Ramon stood up obediently, moved the table out of Reb Avram's way again, and watched as Reb Avram wheeled himself over to the sink with surprising ease and reached for the little two-handled cup that rested on the sink's edge.

"May I ask you for yet another favor, Ramon?" Reb Avram asked, looking back over his shoulder.

"Yes! You may!"

"It is perfectly permissible for me to carry out the ritual of washing my hands while I am seated," Reb Avram began, holding the cup firmly in his hands. "Nonetheless, I would feel much better if I could do it in the way that it should really be done—namely, standing up."

He sighed.

"The problem is," he continued, "that it is very hard for me to get up and down from my wheelchair without support. I am always afraid that it will roll away from me while I am doing so, regardless of what the wheelchair manufacturers promise about the security of the brake mechanism."

"I can help you to stand up," said Anteojitos, excitedly. "And also to sit down again."

He swallowed and was silent for a moment before continuing.

"When Papito got so sick," he finally said, "It was me who always helped him get up and down from his chair."

Anteojitos walked up to Reb Avram, tucked his hands confidently under his armpits, lifted him to his feet and carefully held him there while Reb Avram filled the cup with water, poured it over each of his hands in turn, made the appropriate blessings, and dried them on the towel that was hanging by the sink. Anteojitos then lowered Reb Avram back down into the chair again and wheeled him back to the table with his food.

How light he is compared to Papito, he thought, blinking.

How gentle this boy is, Reb Avram thought—blinking as well.

Once they were back at Reb Avram's table, Anteojitos whipped the silver dome off the food with a flourish to display a small plate with two blintzes, a smaller plate with a roll and a pat of butter, a small saucer containing four prunes, a small carton of cranberry juice with a straw taped to its side, a cup with a decaffeinated tea bag lying on its saucer, a tiny pot of hot water, two little individual dairy creamers, and all the appropriate accompanying tableware.

"Here is your lunch, Reb Avram!" he said, beaming.

Reb Avram picked up the bread and blessed it and then picked up every other item and scrupulously inspected it.

"This is all very nice," he said after a moment, with a deep sigh. "But once again, they have not included a *kichel*."

Anteojitos looked at him anxiously.

"It's not as if I haven't asked," Reb Avram continued. "I explained to the last person who brought me my meals that I am not a diabetic. That I can have a *kichel* with my blintzes. When they give me mushroom barley soup, they give me a *kichel*. When they give me tuna fish salad, they give me a *kichel*. Would it be so terrible to humor an old man and also give me a *kichel* with my blintzes, sweet as those blintzes may be?"

Anteojitos brought his eyebrows together hard.

"What is a *kichel*?"

"'What is a *kichel*?' he asks? Oh, Ramon, you have not lived till you have eaten a *kichel*. It's this little light bowtie of dough, all crispy and nice, with just a little sprinkle of sugar on the top. It's the extra sugar they object to, I suppose, but there is never very much of it."

"I didn't know about the *kichel*. I didn't know they were supposed to give you a *kichel*. I would have asked for it."

"Of course you would have, my son. But then, how could you possibly have known such a thing? Would they have told you that I always asked for it? Would they have remembered my request? No of course not. They are not nice, those kitchen workers."

Anteojitos began to rumble. The kitchen workers had been treating him very well.

"Yes, they are, too! They are too very nice."

"Then why would they deny an old man his *kichel*?"

"Maybe they didn't understand what you asked."

Reb Avram shrugged.

"I'll go down and fix it," said Anteojitos, standing up and shaking out his shoulders.

"How are you going to fix it, if they have refused up till now?"

"I'll ask them for it in Spanish."

"It's an interesting idea."

Anteojitos made a face of resolve.

"I'll be right back."

When he returned with not one but two *kichels*, it took Reb Avram less than thirty seconds to fully comprehend what a wonderful gift *Ha-Shem* had sent him in the shape of this tall young man with his black baseball cap and his thick glasses and his hidden talents. It took him less than ten additional seconds to see that he would be acting ungratefully indeed if he didn't make the most of such a gift.

First, however, he handed one of the two *kichels* to Anteojitos.

"Here, my son," he said. "One of these is for you."

Anteojitos took it, took a bite, chewed it thoughtfully, and swallowed. *Not bad.*

"And now you must listen very carefully," Reb Avram was continuing. "For I have just had an idea about something else we might do together. Something that will keep you busy when you aren't doing kitchen duty. Something that will keep you learning new things. You'd like that, wouldn't you?"

April 2023

- 10 -

"Hey, watch out!" shouted Paloma as Anteojitos barreled right in front of her—dressed for the unusually cool spring weather in his big black sweatshirt and black baseball cap. He grabbed the refrigerator door handle, yanked it open, and pulled out a container of orange juice.

"And what are you doing raiding our refrigerator like that?" Paloma added, scowling at him. "Isn't it part of the deal of your job that they feed you breakfast?"

"Yes, but that is not until nine o'clock, and I'm thirsty now," he said—untwisting the cap and downing a few large gulps straight from the container.

Paloma's mouth dropped.

"Good Lord!" she yelled. "Use a glass, *Muchacho!*"

Anteojitos shrugged.

"Meanwhile," she sputtered. "Why are you even up at this hour? I'm not usually up now either, of course, but I have this special staff training to run today. What's your excuse?"

"I am up because I have a new assignment at work that starts at seven o'clock," Anteojitos replied, nodding to himself. "I've been doing it since the second week of February. You just never noticed because you never come downstairs so early. Like you said. Frank hasn't noticed, either, because he comes downstairs even later than you do. Even Tía Serach—who wakes up the earliest of everybody—hasn't noticed because she has to finish all her morning exercises before she eats anything and she does many different exercises."

He stood up straighter.

"But if any of you had been coming down to the kitchen at this time, you'd know that I always drink juice before I leave, so I can do this new part of my job without being thirsty."

"Huh," Paloma said, looking him up and down with new interest, despite herself. "Well, fine then. I guess. But there's still no excuse for slobbering down juice without a glass. Look, give me that container and I'll write your name on it and then I'll buy a totally new one for Serach and Frank and me to drink from. We'll start keeping one for you and one for us."

"You don't have to write my name on this one, Tía Paloma," Anteojitos said, taking one last emphatic gulp. "Because the juice is now all finished."

He gave a swift glance toward the open trash can at the other end of the room and pitched the empty container right into it with a single fluid nonchalant motion.

Paloma narrowed her eyes. What other surprises did her nephew have in store for her? Still, if he was being given new responsibilities at his job, that was a good thing.

"So, what are you doing at seven o'clock, anyway?" she continued, after a moment. "Have they started you in on delivering breakfasts, too?"

"No. It is something more important than that. I take Reb Avram down to morning prayer services and help him to stand up and sit down at all the right times. I can't help him during afternoon services because I'm cleaning up the lunch trays—or during evening services because I'm setting up the trays for dinner. But Reb Avram says doing it just in the mornings is fine."

"My goodness, Ramon!" said a new voice in the room. "That is truly interesting news. Like your Aunt Paloma, I had no idea you were doing all that. Tell us more! Tell us at what points in the service you help Reb Avram to stand."

Anteojitos and Paloma whirled around to see Serach leaning against the doorway in her gym shorts and tee-shirt, with an expression on her face that hovered between amazement and delight.

"I help him to stand just before this special prayer that they call the '*Borchu*' and just before this special prayer that they call the '*Amidah*,'" Anteojitos answered, nodding happily at his aunt. "At first, Reb Avram had to tell me when those prayers were coming, but now I recognize the pages and can do it without his asking. He is very proud of me."

He paused for a moment and beamed even harder.

"I also help him to take the three steps backward and the three steps forward that you have to do at the beginning of that special *Amidah* prayer."

"Did he tell you that the word '*Amidah*' means 'standing?'"

"Yes, he told me that. Wow, Tía Serach, you know everything about everything!"

"Hardly."

"So are you enjoying this new part of the job?" asked Paloma, looking at Anteojitos with an expression that hovered between amazement and horror.

"Yes. I like to go to morning prayer services. Everyone puts on their *tefillin*, which are these leather boxes with Bible passages that they attach to their foreheads. They look very funny when they do that but no one minds. They also wrap up their left arms with those leather straps and wear big hats and black and white shawls, just like the shawl on the piano in the living room! They all have to stand and sit at the same time, which is why I have to help Reb Avram."

He drew a deep breath.

"I like that they all dress and all pray together like that. I like that they all always know what to do and when to do it."

Serach snapped herself out of the trance into which she had begun drifting at Anteojitos' words. She walked up to him and placed a soft hand on his shoulder.

"I think you'd better be going, Ramon," she said in a voice that was hoarser than usual. "You can't afford to make Reb Avram late. He has to say the '*Sh'ma*' prayer at a very particular point in time, too."

"That's just what he says!"

"Yes, I'm sure he does. But really, Ramon—no more *schmoozing*. You need to go!"

Anteojitos nodded, zipped up his sweatshirt, adjusted his cap, and bolted through the door.

"So Serach," said Paloma, gathering up her own bag and heading for the door, so that she wouldn't be late for her meeting, either. "How long do you think it will be before he converts?"

"Oh, he won't convert."

"Why not?"

"He would need to be circumcised. Which is an absolutely terrifying procedure for an adult. I mean, I presume he would need to be circumcised. I presume that he isn't, already."

"Damn straight, he isn't. My brother would have punched anyone out for even suggesting that the supremely precious organ of his supremely precious offspring be mutilated like that. It's not a Latino thing."

"That's what I figured. So, you see. No danger. You will still only have one Jew to contend with in this house."

Serach smiled.

"Nonetheless, it makes me happy that he is enjoying his work so much. When have you ever seen him so excited? So purposeful? So proud of himself? Don't you see how much we've given him? Doesn't that make you happy, too?"

Paloma bowed her head for a moment. Then she put her bag back down on the counter, strode over to her partner, took her in her arms, and gave her a kiss that they both would recall with a shiver of pleasure for the rest of the day.

"What I mostly see," murmured Paloma as they finally drew apart, "is how much you have given him. You, Serach. Not me. You."

May 2023

- 12 -

"We have yet to celebrate Paloma's promotion," announced Frank, as he marched into the living room, music tucked under his arm, to find Serach energetically vacuuming the rug.

"Hold on! I can't hear a thing you are saying with this machine going!" Serach muttered as she leaned over to shove the nozzle into the area underneath the sofa. She was scrupulous about scheduling her housekeeping chores in such a way as to avoid infringing upon Frank's practice times. What was he doing, showing up fifteen minutes early, today? He would have to wait.

"Let me just finish up," she added, shaking her head, "and then the living room is all yours."

She continued pursuing dust bunnies till she was sure they had all been seized and disposed of and then gave everything a few last swipes of the nozzle, just to make sure. Then she switched off the machine, unplugged it, and marched off to the front hall closet to put it away.

When she returned, she found Frank sitting the wrong way around on the piano bench, his long narrow legs and long narrow feet extending out into the middle of the room.

"Okay," she said. "I'm done. You can turn the right way again and begin practicing."

"I am not here to practice yet, Serach," he said, primly. "I am here to discuss what we're going to do about Paloma. How we're going to celebrate that major promotion that she keeps pooh-poohing. How best to show her that—as untypically modest as she's being about this whole thing—we think that it's as special as special can be."

Serach smiled and sat herself down in a chair across from him.

"That's a very nice thought, Frank."

"Of course, it is," said Frank. "And not just nice. Necessary. We can't let her get away with treating this whole thing as if it doesn't matter. It's not every day that someone gets asked to supervise all her peers in the fanciest oncological treatment center in the city. That kind of plum assignment—not to mention the major raise that goes along with it—generally requires all sorts of extra degrees. All Paloma had to do was just do her job better than anyone else and they plucked her out of the crowd and elevated her to a management position."

Serach nodded, looking at him with approval. It also wasn't every day that Frank showed such appreciation for someone else's achievements.

"So what kind of celebration did you have in mind?" she asked.

"I think we should all go out for a big Saturday night dinner in a fabulous restaurant with everyone all dressed up."

He waited for a beat.

"And I do mean everyone," he added. "Not just you, me, and her. I want to invite the nephews, too. And the girlfriend who is now, evidently, joined at the hip to one of those nephews."

"Good heavens, Frank," said Serach, gazing at her housemate with amazement. "That's a truly startling idea, given what you think of them all. Are you sure you could bear sitting at the same table as that crew for a whole long, fancy meal?"

Frank raised his chin.

"I admit it will be a challenge," he said. "But it is one I am willing to accept. It would mean a great deal to Paloma to have them all there, don't you think?"

"Oh, definitely." Serach smiled.

"What is more," Frank continued. "I am proposing to foot the entire bill."

Serach beamed.

"Goodness, Frank. Now, that's a truly lovely thought. It will make the whole thing even more special for her. Show her that you finally accept everyone."

"I'm not sure I would go that far," he said. "Still, it's only fair that I should play the host here. I owe Paloma a lot."

Serach nodded. He did.

"Plus, there is very little I wouldn't do to try to propel her out of this incomprehensible mood of hers," he added, after a moment. "She's been absolutely impossible about this whole thing, don't you think?"

Serach nodded again, this time unwillingly. It was something on which she had preferred not to dwell.

"Have you any idea as to why she's been behaving this way?" Frank persisted. "I don't even know how to describe her reaction. Upset about it all, almost."

Serach sighed. It was as good a description as any.

"Do you have any insights to offer? Have you asked her about it?"

"I haven't had to ask," Serach replied softly. "She's told me. Directly. She says that she doesn't deserve this promotion. That she won't be good at it. That the only reason she got it is because she's gotten so bad at providing hands-on patient care. 'I'm being kicked upstairs,' is how she put it. Nearly broke my heart to hear her."

Frank shook his head.

"I hope you've been disabusing her of all that nonsense."

"I've been trying," said Serach, sadly. "For all the good that it's done. I've told her that the powers-that-be at Manhattan East would never give her a top management position if they didn't think she was up to handling it. That she's outrageously good at getting people to do what she wants without them realizing that she's twisting them around her little finger. I don't know what to call what she does, but... I've frequently felt its effects."

"Seductive bludgeoning," said Frank, looking pointedly away. Paloma had used that skill on him often enough, as well.

Serach nodded.

"But how could she possibly think that she's lost her touch with her patients?" Frank began again, after a long moment. "Things like that don't just disappear."

"No, of course they don't," Serach said, sighing. "But her self-confidence suffered a real blow during COVID when so many of those patients died. Then, of course, when Manny passed away ...."

"Good heavens! People were dropping like flies from that hideous disease, no matter what anyone did. And as far as Manny is concerned, from what little she managed to tell me the poor fool didn't want to be saved. Who in his right mind refuses to go to a hospital after suffering a major heart attack?"

"I know."

Serach took a breath.

"Paloma had finally begun surfacing from the depths," she continued, slowly. "Putting all those losses behind her. Getting back some of her old electricity. But this promotion seems to have thrown her off balance again. Proven that everyone knows her true gift is gone."

"Well," Frank murmured. "Then we'll just have to wine and dine her till she stops feeling so sorry for herself. I can't believe that my favorite diva will stay utterly impervious to a standing ovation from her entire clan."

Serach smiled.

"Perhaps not. I hope so."

"The only question left is where we should take her," Frank added. "I was thinking about *La-di-Da*, in Park Slope."

Serach didn't respond.

"What? You don't think so?"

"Oh, I know *La-di-Da* has quite the reputation," she said, averting her eyes from Frank's stricken face. "But consider your audience. Picture Ramon and Roberto puzzling over what to do with those huge, odd-shaped plates of mini-zucchinis surrounded by little dots of pesto."

Frank pouted.

"Even Paloma is someone who likes her pasta best when it's covered with red sauce—despite the haute cuisine that she regularly whips up when you're around."

She smiled at him, warmly.

"She only makes those elaborate dishes for your sake, you know," she added. "Because she knows that you love them so. And because she loves you so."

She took in the brief flush that her words brought to Frank's cheeks.

"So what alternative venue would you suggest, my dear?" he said, once he collected himself.

"I think," she said, "that we should go to some big family-style Italian-American restaurant in Sheepshead Bay."

"Sheepshead Bay?" Frank murmured. "Goodness me, what an unappetizing name!"

Serach smiled again.

"I agree that the name isn't all that appealing. But the neighborhood is. Have you never heard of it?"

Frank shook his head.

"Well, it's right here in Brooklyn, somewhat to the south of us. It's perched on the water—there are lovely views. Paloma really liked it, the couple of times that we've been there."

"Do you have a particular restaurant in mind? One that you can... vouch for?"

"Yes. *Stelle di Mare*. Stars of the..."

"I do speak Italian, Serach."

He looked at her hard.

"You're absolutely certain that that's what will please her best?"

"Positive. Her nephews, too. Maybe not the girlfriend— whom I understand is pretty fancy, herself. But she'll have to learn to cope if she wants to join this family."

"Well, I suppose that you know best," Frank sighed. "Will you handle all the logistics, being that this is all rather foreign terrain for me? Coordinate the schedules? Make the reservations?"

"Yes, Frank. As long as you pick up the bill. This crowd can really eat."

"I am prepared."

"Dear, dear me, I swear I've been air-lifted back to the 'sixties," Frank stage-whispered, as he trailed the hostess through the main dining room and onto an enclosed verandah—its windows dramatically swathed in pink satin curtains. "They even managed to have Frank Sinatra immediately launch into *Strangers in the Night* as we arrived. I love it!"

"Dear, dear me," mouthed Negrito, a few steps behind them—wiggling his hips as he walked. "I swear we've managed to impress Paloma's very best friend, Frank! He loves it!"

"Oscar!" hissed Gloria, close beside him. "Don't be a *pendejo*!"

After some initial awkwardness, the group managed to arrange itself at the table that Serach had reserved for them earlier that week. Negrito, Gordito and Anteojitos took their seats on one side—Anteojitos nearest the foot of the table, right by the windows, with the lights of the Bay winking just over his left shoulder. Paloma, Gloria, and Serach made their way to the other side, with Serach just across from Anteojitos. Frank claimed the seat at the table's head.

No sooner had they assumed their places than the head waiter appeared—tall, trim, silver-haired, and decked out in a full tuxedo.

"Good evening, everyone," he said, parlaying his twenty-five years of professional experience into determining who was who and what was what and then planting himself directly at Frank's side. "My name is Giulio and I will be your server tonight. You'll be starting with a bottle of something festive, I presume?"

Frank sighed.

"I think someone besides me should handle that decision. Paloma?"

"Yes, we'll start with a bottle of your best red," said Negrito before his aunt could open her mouth. "What would you recommend?"

"I would suggest the 2016 *Castello di Ama San Lorenzo*" said Giulio, shifting his attention to the darkly handsome young man. "It's a flawless Chianti blend. Savory and classic."

"Perfect," said Negrito. "And a Shirley Temple for the boy at the far end."

"Oh, please, Negrito. Can't Anteojitos have a glass of wine, just for tonight?" said Paloma. "No one will ask him for an ID. No one will care."

"I care," said Negrito. "You would not believe what happened the last time we allowed him to drink. The nonsense he came out with! And no, Tía, I am not being mean—I am being wise. Besides—you love your Shirley Temples, don't you Anteojitos?"

He smiled winningly at his brother.

"He's tall, but he's underage," he added as an aside to Giulio.

"Just sparkling water for me," said Frank, as he took in Negrito's slicked-back ebony hair, his flawlessly pressed black shirt, his gorgeously chiseled face, his commanding voice. *Such a dangerous specimen. As arrogant as a Rhode Island Red Rooster in a Kentucky hen yard, but unmistakably, undeniably—killingly—attractive.*

"How about everyone else?" Giulio continued. "Sparkling water or tap?"

"Tap," said Gloria. "We don't need any more plastic contaminating the ocean."

"Tap? Tap, everyone?"

"Sure," said Serach. "Tap."

Giulio came back carrying a tray with the wine, the water, the Shirley Temple, and a big green plastic bottle of Perrier for Frank. He offered Negrito the first taste of the wine and Negrito sipped it, considered it for a moment, and nodded authoritatively. Giulio filled his glass and then went around the table, carefully serving everyone else. When he had finished and had discreetly withdrawn, Negrito clinked his spoon against his glass.

"Time for a toast," he said. "I will begin."

He stood up and lifted his drink.

"I want to toast my wonderful aunt, Paloma, who has just been promoted to the position of boss-of-all nurses in her super-dope hospital."

He flashed his splendid grin at Paloma, while she muttered: "It's not the whole hospital, Negrito. It's just the Adult Department."

"My Tía Paloma," he continued, ignoring her words, "couldn't deserve this position more. She is the Queen of Swagger, the Empress of 'Don't Give Me Any of Your Shit,' and the Biggest Bad-Ass in all of New York City."

He lifted his glass higher.

"She's going to whip all those nurses into shape," he concluded. "So let's drink to that!"

He sat down again, while Paloma walked over to him, gave him an audible kiss on the cheek and returned to her place.

"Bravo, Oscar. You do have a way with words," said Frank. "Anyone else?"

Gordito stood up. He was wearing the same ill-fitting black suit that he had worn to his father's burial, but this time he had paired it with a salmon pink shirt and a turquoise blue tie.

"Tía Paloma," he said, clearing his throat. "My Tía Paloma. I want to congratulate you."

He paused, lifted his glass, took a gulp, and put it down again. He then pushed his chair out of the way, walked over to his aunt, and smothered her in a mammoth hug.

"I love you too, Gordito," she said to him.

He hung on to her for a long minute before walking back to his seat, his face steadily reddening as he went.

"That was lovely, Roberto," said Serach, quietly reaching across the table to put her small white hand on top of his large brown one.

"Anyone else?" said Frank.

Anteojitos stayed silent, sucking steadily on the maraschino cherry from his Shirley Temple.

Gloria shook her head softly. Serach looked around her and stood.

"Then I guess it's my turn," she said. "I don't generally make speeches, but tonight is special."

She smiled at Paloma—her face suddenly alight.

"Paloma already knows just how proud I am of her," she said. "But—as Frank so wisely pointed out to me—sometimes these things need to be said out loud. So let me say it."

She looked down for a moment, as everyone gazed at her small frame, neatly clad in the black pants and white shirt that constituted her invariable uniform when she wasn't in tee shirts and blue jeans or gym shorts.

"I would also like to offer an appeal to everyone," she continued, looking back up again, and taking in each of the faces around her, in turn. "As you all know, Paloma is someone who—when she takes something on—does it all the way. She's also someone who does everything she can for anyone who needs it. So, for a while at least, let's not ask her to do anything that we can do for ourselves. Let's ask what we can do for her."

She tilted her wine glass toward her partner.

"*Mazel tov*, my dearest. We all love you. We're all here for you. Every step of the way."

She sat down again and Frank got to his feet.

"Well, I guess it's finally time for me to say a few words," he said, looking pointedly at Negrito. Didn't that cocky young man know that it is the host who should lead off the toasts?

"Some of you have known Paloma longer than I have," he began. "I mean, you three fellows have been acquainted with her since you were in diapers, as far as I can tell."

Negrito brought his eyebrows together. Paloma caught him and kicked him under the table.

"¡*Suave—suave!*" she mouthed.

"But I would warrant that I've seen sides of her that no one else here has."

He took a breath.

"I met Paloma back in the early 'aughts' when I was living with Judith Skollar—the late, great opera star of the Metropolitan and of *Teatro La Scala in Milan*. I was Judith's devoted accompanist and closest friend. Paloma came on board as Judith's home health aide."

He paused to take a sip of his Perrier.

"The sixteen-year-old Paloma whom I first encountered was—as Oscar so eloquently put it—already the Queen of Swagger. Plus, as drop-dead gorgeous as she is today, if a little less... tastefully dressed. I didn't assume the role of arbiter of her fashion choices till much later."

Paloma shook her head and Gloria gave Frank a long, appraising look and decided that his claim to being a style influencer was warranted. His perfectly tailored cashmere jacket, summer-weight wool pants, Sea Island cotton shirt, and thinly striped silk tie—not to mention the gleaming Italian monk-strap shoes that she had already thoroughly scrutinized as he preceded her onto the verandah—all went together impeccably. Plus, he wore the whole ensemble with the aplomb of a runway model.

"Paloma was the original worker bee—as well as being a truly magnificent chef," Frank was continuing. "Even at that tender age. But what she was most of all," he added, "was a healer the likes of which rarely comes around on this good earth."

He paused to take another small sip.

"Judith was not at all well when Paloma began to tend to her. Paloma burst into our lives like an angel from heaven and took over all aspects of Judith's care. She couldn't have saved Judith—nobody could have. But she gave Judith the best last eighteen months of life that anyone could ever want."

He looked down, his eyes glistening suspiciously.

"So, yes, Paloma. You will be—what kind of supervisor did you call her, Oscar?"

"Bad-Ass."

"Yes, that. But don't ever forget that you are—first and foremost—a healer. A divinely inspired healer."

Serach—eyes fastened on her partner like a mother hawk—saw Paloma give a shiver of something that looked suspiciously like pain at Frank's words. Gloria—eyes darting back and forth from Frank to Paloma—caught it as well.

"So," Frank concluded. "Here's to your success in all aspects of your calling. I know that you will go from triumph to triumph."

He raised his glass in her direction and then sat down again.

Paloma looked all around her, saw that no one else was making a move to speak, and realized that she needed to respond.

"Thank you, Frank," she said, standing up. "Thank you, everybody."

Then she just remained there, looking around her without another word.

"Tía Paloma, you're actually speechless!" said Negrito, after the pause went on for far too long. "What's up with that?"

Paloma threw him a look that he would have preferred not to receive, but quickly turned it into an approximation of her usual megawatt smile.

"Shut up, Negrito," she said. "I'm just gathering my thoughts."

How totally alluring she is for someone approaching middle age, thought Gloria, as she regarded Paloma top to toe. *The wrap-front dress that she's wearing clearly came off a rack, but it is perfect for her voluptuous figure, neither emphasizing nor obscuring it. And that deep wine color makes everything about her pop—from the velvety dark skin to the vivid red lips, to the jet-black eyes, to that lustrous hair just beginning to streak with gray. The gray may become a problem in time, but for now it adds just the touch of authority that she will need to project.*

"All I really want to tell everyone," Paloma was finally saying, "is that I'm grateful that you are all here. I love you all so much. And Frank—how the hell did you know that this is one of my favorite restaurants in the whole world? I don't think I've ever told you that."

"No, you never have, dear. But don't forget that we've been friends forever. I know your style."

"I'll never tell," said Serach. Gordito chuckled. Negrito cocked his head appraisingly at their host. Maybe he wasn't as clueless as he seemed.

"Well, it definitely is the right choice," Paloma added. "Do you know that they have the best linguine with scampi in all of New York City? They've won awards. And did you know that linguine with scampi is my absolute favorite dish? But, of course, that's why you picked this spot—isn't it?"

She paused again, and Gordito and Negrito again exchanged smiles.

"Serach always says that no speech should go on for more than a few short minutes, and—as you all know—Serach is always right. So I'll wrap up by just saying: 'Thank you,' once again. And also: 'Where's our waiter?' I'm totally ready for some of those fabulous scampi!"

"I don't know, Paloma." said Negrito, leaning back in his chair. "You don't sound so tough to me today. You'd better go back to sharpening your street creds before you try bossing all those nurses around."

"Oh, Negrito," said Paloma—her eyes briefly registering their old blaze. "You know what the rappers say these days. Street creds only go so far. They don't pay the family bills."

Negrito snapped his fingers at her. She grinned back at him, took her seat, and everyone began talking all at once. The noise level grew so loud that—when Gloria unexpectedly got to her feet—it took Frank several seconds of banging his spoon against his glass before everyone finally piped down again.

"I wasn't going to say anything because… well, because I can't say that I know you very well yet, Paloma," Gloria began, once she had everyone's full attention. "After all, this is only the second time I've ever met you. And the first time was in a graveyard. In the pouring rain. Not the best place for making a good initial impression."

She smiled and shook her head.

"Nonetheless," she continued, "your presence—your aura—it was all unmistakable, even under those unfortunate circumstances. You exude such strength and poise and purpose. I know you'll be a wonderful supervisor, a superb role model, a leader—a change agent. And as such, you will have so much greater impact than you could as a plain old bedside nurse.

She smiled at Paloma warmly.

"We women should be running things," she concluded, before resuming her seat. "Not just constantly trying to patch things up."

Paloma gave Gloria a brief, pained nod of acknowledgement and then looked away.

"So, what is it that *you* do, Gloria?" Frank said, after a moment of looking back and forth between Paloma's sober face and Gloria's glowing one. Gloria had said exactly the wrong thing, of course, but there was nothing more he could do about it. Paloma would just have to come to terms with her evolving role. Meanwhile, Gloria was turning out to be an interesting specimen in her own right. *That flawlessly fitting, electric-blue dress. That perfect chignon. The looks of admiration that Oscar kept throwing at her as she spoke. Worth a bit of exploration.*

"I'm the founder and CEO of a new non-profit," she answered, turning to give Frank her full attention. "It's called: *Alta Costura—Alta Ambición*. High Fashion—High Ambition. It's a collective run by a group of women of color who have worked in the city's sweatshops. Instead of doing piece work for pennies, they are getting the chance to earn a fair living, build solid business skills, and design and market their own fashion creations. We're just a start-up right now, but we intend to go far. To inspire. To organize. To influence. Our long-term vision is the total dismantling of the sweatshop economy and the elevation of the women on whose backs it runs."

"What sorts of things do you-all design and market?"

"For now, we are sticking to small items that sell easily. Hair wraps, place mats and napkins, cushion covers, tote bags—using Fair Trade African, Indian and Caribbean fabrics. In the first few months of the pandemic, we made customized masks, which literally flew off the shelves. We've stopped doing that, however, now that China is flooding the market with K-95s."

"Have you cultivated any major investors willing to... take a chance on your fashion chops?"

"Not yet. We're still pretty much dependent on small foundation grants."

She gave Frank a swift, sweet glance.

"Would you like to be our first?"

"I'd have to inspect some of your hair wraps, first. See if they suit me. But do tell: was it one of those former sweatshop workers who designed and executed the exquisitely cut dress that you're wearing this evening? The dress that practically shouts 'be-spoke.'"

"No, Frank, it was Gloria herself who designed it," said Negrito, slipping out of his seat and striding to her side. "As well as executing every seam. She wouldn't be teaching other people how to do all that if she couldn't do it perfectly herself."

He put his hand possessively on her shoulder. She glanced briefly up at him and allowed the hand to remain.

"She's an amazing person, my Gloria. Rocketed out of Texas at the age of seventeen to enter the Fashion Institute of Technology on a full scholarship. Won a year's apprenticeship with Tracy Reese—Michele Obama's favorite designer—in Detroit. Earned a master's degree in public administration at N.Y.U.—also on full scholarship. Founded her amazing non-profit."

He paused to flash the group a smile. He briefly caught Frank's eye, and Frank gave him a brief chivalrous nod in return. He had been right. Gloria was definitely turning out to be a dazzler.

"And, best of all," Negrito concluded—nodding gracefully back at Frank, "she was smart enough to choose me."

Gloria looked as if she really needed to say something, but—before she could—Giulio re-appeared at Frank's side.

"Are you ready to hear about today's specials?" he asked the assembled crew.

"No need," said Negrito, walking back to his seat and waving his hand. "We all know what Stelle di Mare is best known for, don't we?"

"Scampi!" yelled Gordito.

Negrito smiled at his brother and turned to Giulio.

"Yes, scampi. We'll each take a plate of linguine with scampi."

Frank raised an eyebrow.

"I haven't even looked at the menu, Oscar," he said.

"Trust me, Frank, you won't regret it." He turned back to Giulio. "So, like I said, seven plates of linguine with scampi. With red sauce, of course, all of them."

"Seven plates of linguine with scampi," Giulio repeated. "Marinara—not *aglio-olio*."

"No, wait! Please. Sorry!" came a voice from one end of the table. "Not seven. Just six."

Giulio spun around to see Serach lifting her head up from the menu that she'd been carefully and quietly perusing on her own.

"Six plates of linguine with scampi," she said, softly but distinctly, "and one order of broiled snapper. Please—"

"And some garlic bread to start!" yelled Gordito, cutting her off. "Two big baskets of it! Plus, two big appetizer platters—one of stuffed mushrooms and one of stuffed clams!"

"And another bottle of wine," added Negrito.

Giulio nodded again.

"Two baskets of garlic bread, two platters—one apiece of stuffed clams and stuffed mushrooms—six plates of linguine with scampi alla marinara (those all come with salad, by the way), one broiled snapper (which also comes with salad, or you can have a side order of pasta if you wish) and one more bottle of wine. Is that it?"

"For now," said Negrito.

"For now."

Giulio nodded one last time and departed, while Frank—with great effort—kept silent.

I am clearly trapped in a crowd that has no sense of decorum, he sighed. *No sense of who deserves to take charge and who to fall in behind. Yet, I will not fuss. I will not ruin Paloma's special day.*

"Why don't you want the scampi, Tía Serach?" asked Gordito, after a moment. "Tía Paloma says it's the best dish here."

"Well, Gordito, I'm sure that's true," Serach responded, smiling gently at him. "But although I'm far less timid in my eating habits than I once was—thanks to your aunt—there are still certain limits for me. And shellfish is one of them. If

I ever as much as attempted to eat a shrimp, I suspect that my fork would simply halt midway to my mouth of its own volition and then return to the plate, its contents uneaten."

"But why?"

"Because Jews aren't allowed to eat shellfish, and some habits are too deeply ingrained to break. I have let go of following many of the rules that we observe, over the years, but I do still seem to draw a line at shrimp."

Gloria, whipped around to focus fully on Serach for the first time since they had all sat down.

"I didn't know that you were Jewish, Serach!" she said.

"Does it make a difference?" asked Paloma, a little too quickly.

"No!" said Gloria—also, a bit too quickly. "Of course not. No difference at all. Still—why did no one ever tell me?"

"It isn't something that we talk about very much, Gloria," said Negrito, after a pause. "Tía Serach is just... Tía Serach, as far as we are concerned. No one cares what she is."

"Your mother cared," Paloma said drily. "And she made sure we all knew about it."

"Yeah. Well. We all know that Mama's a bigot," Negrito said with a sheepish grin. "In fact—"

But at that moment, there was a loud cry from the end of the table.

"What, Anteojitos?" asked Paloma, hoping against hope that her youngest nephew wasn't about to launch into a defense of his blasted mother. "What are you yelling about, now?"

Anteojitos rose to his feet, practically shaking with excitement. He downed the last drops of his Shirley Temple with an enormous slurping sound. Paloma winced. What was he going to say?

"Tía Serach is Jewish?" he finally managed to sputter. "My Tía Serach is Jewish?"

Paloma smiled in relief and nodded.

"Yes, Anteojitos," she said. "She is."

He looked around the table, grinning wildly.

"My Tía Serach is Jewish?" he said. "My own Tía Serach? Wait till I tell Reb Avram! He's going to be so happy!"

- 13 -

Frayda's morning was rolling out nicely. She gazed around her domain with satisfaction, reviewing all the things that she'd already dispensed with, and planning how she would carry out the day's remaining tasks.

Reb Lazer was thoroughly bibbed, anaesthetized and seated in the dental chair in preparation for his root canal, and since it was only a bottom incisor—not one of those inevitably-far-more-complex top molars—Dr. Pessin could easily finish it all up without her. Nor would she have to do any immediate preparatory work for Reb Chaim's cleaning or Reb Heschel's gum work, since Dr. Pessin wouldn't want her to set them up till he was almost finished with Reb Lazer.

Meanwhile, Reb Issur may have barged into the office as soon as the doors opened that morning, but that wasn't her problem. His X-rays were not scheduled until eleven o'clock. He could wait.

All of which meant that she had a good half-hour free from direct patient interactions—thirty nice long minutes in which to finally begin tackling the stack of charts that had been piling up so irritatingly on her desk.

She picked up the first chart, made all the necessary annotations, and strode with it to the filing cabinet. She had just opened the bottom drawer and begun sliding it back into its proper place when the doorbell rang. Three times in quick succession.

No one else is scheduled for an appointment till after lunch, she bristled. *Why do people think they can just appear* on my doorstep and have me squeeze them into Dr. Pessin's busy schedule? And who rings the doorbell three times when once is more than enough?

She walked wearily back to her desk to buzz the person in. She then had just enough time to sprint out of the way before the intruder flung the door open, threw himself down on her desk, and began to howl.

The three men seated in the reception area spun around in tandem. Reb Chaim and Reb Heschel merely gaped in silence. Reb Issur—a man who believed that action is always better than inaction—grasped his walker firmly, got to his feet, and took three steps forward.

"Who is this?" he trumpeted. "And what does he think he is doing?"

"It is nothing, Reb Issur," countered Frayda, swiftly regaining her equilibrium. "Leave it all to me. I will have this entire situation under control in just one moment."

She marched back to her desk and gave a good whack to its left side with her right palm.

"Stop yelling this instant, Ramon!" she commanded.

Anteojitos lifted his head up to give her one startled glance and then put it back down again to begin bawling more fiercely than ever.

"Stop it, I said! And get yourself up from my desk! You cannot just burst in here like this and drape yourself all over my papers like a piece of lox on a bagel. Up! Now!"

Anteojitos remained prone, but he drew one last sobbing breath and fell silent.

Frayda shook her head. One thing at a time. She spun back to the three men, pointed a finger at them, and issued an order.

"All of you need to leave immediately," she said. "Reb Chaim and Reb Issur, both of your procedures are strictly routine. No tragedy if we postpone them for a couple of days. There should be some time available for you on Wednesday, let me check."

She yanked her date book out from underneath Anteojitos' torso and looked within.

"Yes. Wednesday. Ten o'clock for you, Reb Chaim. Three o'clock for you, Reb Issur."

She scribbled in the appointments and then looked hard at Reb Heschel.

"With you, Reb Heschel, it is a different story. We cannot just let your gums bleed. Come back here at two forty-five and Dr. Pessin will see what he can do for you. As he always does."

She fixed him with her sternest look.

"But Reb Heschel—we cannot keep doing this. You need to change your hygienic practices, once and for all. You don't floss regularly—your gums are going to bleed."

She then looked from one man to the other and waved them away decisively.

"All right, that's it—all of you! Depart! As you can see, I have pressing matters to handle."

Reb Chaim and Reb Heschel seized their canes, stood up, and made their way to the door as hastily as they could. Reb Issur paused mid-route to cast a curious glance back over his shoulder, but Frayda gave him another brisk wave and he tightened his grip on his walker and scuttled out best as he could.

The door shut behind them and Frayda whirled around to face Anteojitos.

"Now, you! Stand up! This minute! Explain to me what you think you are doing!"

Anteojitos rose slowly to his feet.

"Speak!"

He wiped his nose on the sleeve of his shirt.

"Reb Avram—" he began. "Reb Avram says that I am—" and here he began to sob again.

"Ramon, I cannot understand a word you are saying with you *fonfedik-ing* away like that!"

He gave one last shudder and then stopped.

"Reb Avram says that I am living in a house of sin!" he yelled.

"Reb Avram says what?"

"He says that Tía Serach and Tía Paloma are sinful women and their house is full of sin!"

Frayda put her fingertips up to her well-kerchiefed brow and shook her head back and forth.

"He says that I am a sinner, too, because I am living with them," Anteojitos continued at top volume. "He says that he cannot associate with me anymore unless I move out!"

He returned to full-fledged sobbing.

Frayda removed her hands from her head and slammed them resoundingly down on the desk. "Ramon, enough! Be a *mensch*. And tell me: How does Reb Avram even know anything about your aunts? What have you been telling him? Don't you know that it is wrong to share personal stories with someone when you are serving him his lunch?"

And didn't my good friend Serach know to warn this poor shlemiel to keep his mouth shut about her and Paloma? Where is that girl's brain—she who is supposedly so smart?

"I don't just serve Reb Avram his lunch!"

"What?"

"I don't just serve Reb Avram his lunch—I also serve him his dinner! And I take him to services."

Anteojitos hiccupped.

"And we talk about all sorts of things, Reb Avram and me! We talk about math! We talk about Hebrew! We talk about the Torah portions that they read at the Monday and Thursday services."

His face crumpled.

"He calls me 'son' when we talk! He calls me 'son'!"

He wiped his nose on his sleeve again.

"But now he thinks I am a sinner and he doesn't want to talk to me anymore or have me serve him or take him to services, or—"

"Ramon, stop babbling. Begin at the beginning! What did you say to Reb Avram about your living situation that set him off like that!"

Anteojitos drew a breath.

"I told him that one of the two aunts that I live with—Tía Serach, not Tía Paloma—doesn't eat shrimp because she is Jewish!" he began. "Just like him! I was so excited! I thought he would be so excited, too."

He began to tear up again and Frayda handed him a tissue from the box on her desk.

"But he wasn't excited!" Anteojitos continued, blowing his nose hard, balling up the tissue, and pitching it easily into the wastepaper basket on the other side of the room. "He started asking me questions. He asked: 'How can one aunt be Jewish and the other not, if they are sisters?'"

Frayda drew in a big breath.

"To which you answered...?"

"I answered that they aren't sisters. So he asked: 'Well, then, what are they?'"

Frayda closed her eyes.

"So I said they were just... Tía Serach and Tía Paloma. That they lived together. That they always have."

"And then?"

"Then he asked me where they slept."

"Oy."

"So I told him that they have this big, beautiful bedroom and that their bed has a big soft pink comforter on it. That it's on the second floor, right down the hall from Frank's bedroom, and…"

Frayda gasped.

"You told Reb Avram about Frank?"

"Yes, I told him how Frank lives with us and plays the piano so beautifully and how he gives piano lessons and how he is Tía Paloma's friend—and also Tía Serach's friend. That's when Reb Avram got really angry and started saying how I am living with sinners and that I have to leave my Tías or he can't see me anymore."

Anteojitos looked straight at Frayda and his nose began to run again.

"What will I do? How can I leave my Tías? I have nowhere else to go!"

Despite the weepy mess that Anteojitos was making all over himself and her desk, Frayda was impressed at how well he was now speaking. Clearly, this was Reb Avram's doing. Clearly, talking with him was making a difference for the boy. Well, Rev Avram was a German Jew, just like she was. He had more culture and a better education than most.

"Ramon—stop bellyaching! Pay attention! I have a few important questions for you."

Anteojitos looked back at her and slowly stood up straighter. Yes, he had definitely evolved since he had first arrived at *B'Sevah Tovah*—despite his red-blotched face and tear-fogged glasses. Had he grown taller? More mature somehow? Something was better.

"Ramon, tell me," she said, sighing. "Do you like this job and this place—and having Reb Avram in your life—as much as you seem to do?"

"Yes!" he answered loudly. "I do. I like everything here a lot. I like bringing the residents their meals. I am very good at it. I never mess up. I like the other kitchen workers. They speak Spanish to me and they are my friends. I like Reb Avram best of all. He calls me 'son'!"

Frayda took in everything he was saying for a moment and then looked at him hard.

"Yes, but do you like all that enough to give up living with your aunts? To give up living in that nice house, and being with them every day, and having them care for you so nicely?"

Anteojitos closed his eyes tight. It took him a long moment, but then he spoke.

"They don't want me there," he said. "They yell at me. Well, Tía Paloma does. Not Tía Serach. Maybe she wants me. But Tía Paloma doesn't. And Frank doesn't. He says bad things about me. He calls me names. I've heard him."

He began to choke up again.

"Reb Avram wants me. Except that now he doesn't. Now he is yelling at me, too! Now he is calling me names. He says that I am a sinner. That I am a sinner because I live with my aunts!"

He began babbling unintelligibly.

Frayda handed him another tissue and waited till he had blown his nose into it, balled it up, and tossed it into the wastepaper basket as casually and accurately as the first time.

"Do *you* believe that you are a sinner, Ramon?" she finally asked, swallowing hard. "Do you believe that you are a sinner because you live with your aunts?"

Anteojitos closed his eyes again. Then he shrugged.

"No. Yes. I don't know."

"You are not a sinner, Ramon," she said, forcefully. "You must never think that. Ever."

"Yes, but Reb Avram thinks it, and he knows so much about everything and he reads about God all day and he knows what God wants and then tells me about it."

Frayda sighed. Yes, she mused. Reb Avram believes he has a direct line to Ha-Shem.

"I don't want Reb Avram to think that I'm a sinner," Anteojitos was continuing. "I want him to keep calling me 'son.' I want to keep bringing him his trays and talking with him and going to services with him. It feels good when I am with him. It feels good to be at those services where everyone dresses the same and prays the same and does the same things. It feels..."

He struggled for a long moment to find the word. Then it came to him.

"It feels safe," he concluded.

So, Frayda thought. It's clear. This boy knows what he wants and what he wants is what he's found here at *B'Sevah Tovah*. So—given that I'm the one who brought him here—I am the one who needs to make it work for him.

"All right, Ramon," she said. "I have a solution."

Anteojitos grasped the desk in front of him with both hands and looked up at her.

"But first you need to understand certain things."

Anteojitos nodded, and she paused—her face unreadable, her hands twisting. How could she say this? She had never put anything like this into words before.

"First, you need to understand that the people with whom you live do care about you. A lot. Well, maybe not Frank. But your aunts do. Even if your Aunt Paloma sometimes yells at you. That's just how she is. She has a big mouth."

She took a breath.

"You also need to understand that it isn't for you to judge your aunts. It isn't for Reb Avram to do so, either. Only *Ha-Shem* is our judge. Only God."

He looked at her steadily—neither agreeing nor disagreeing. She took a breath.

"Finally, you need to understand what it means to be part of this community. Reb Avram will ask you to do more than just move out of your aunts' house. He will ask you to 'build a fence' around that move. To have no more contact with your aunts at all. That is the way that Reb Avram is, that is the way he thinks, and he isn't going to change or bend from it."

She looked hard at Anteojitos and watched his face contort.

"And, Ramon, you should not even *mention* your aunts to anyone after this."

She looked away.

"Except with me. With me, you can always talk about them."

She looked back

"But if anyone else besides me asks about them—or says anything about them—you must say that such talking is gossip and that you do not engage in gossip. Then you must not say another word. Gossip, in this community, is also a sin."

She paused.

"It is a lot to ask. It is a lot to give up. Are you really willing to do all that? *Can* you do it?"

Anteojitos looked at her for a moment, his face still twisted in pain. But then he nodded.

"All right," she said. "Then I am going to go interrupt Reb Lazer's root canal to tell Dr. Pessin that I've changed his morning schedule around and that I will be stepping out for a bit. After which we will go see Reb Avram and straighten everything out."

They exited the dental clinic—Frayda first and Anteojitos right behind her—and swiftly climbed the two flights of stairs to arrive at the third floor. Before they reached Room 39, however, she again turned around to face her young charge.

"I am going to knock on Reb Avram's door and go in, leaving the door ajar," she said. "You, meanwhile, are going to stay in the corridor, ten paces away, and wait till I call for you. You cannot be eavesdropping on what we are discussing and Reb Avram cannot see that you are here till everything is all settled. Are we clear?"

Anteojitos nodded and backed up exactly ten paces. He counted them.

Frayda waited till he had gone the proper distance and then knocked.

"Reb Avram, it is me—Frayda Goldblatt. I need to talk with you."

Frayda Goldblatt? Who is Frayda Goldblatt?Well, I suppose I had better find out. "Come in," he said.

"We have a problem," said Frayda, striding into the room and leaving the door swinging wide open behind her. "A large one."

Reb Avram looked up at Frayda for a long moment, trying to place her. Suddenly it came to him. *The dental assistant.* He waved his hand at her briefly and returned to the book on his lap.

"I had my check-up with Dr. Pessin a month ago, and everything was just fine," he mumbled. "Including the billing for all those extra procedures. If it is the billing that is a problem, it is my son who handles all that. It is my son that you should talk to."

"This has nothing to do with your teeth," said Frayda. "Or the extra procedures. Or the bill."

Reb Avram slowly raised his head.

"So what is your concern? What is the purpose of this visit?"

"My concern relates to the young man who delivers your meals to you and takes you to services in the morning. My concern is Ramon Rodriguez."

"Oh, I see," said Reb Avram, suddenly animated. "So you have heard about his situation! Such a fine, upstanding young man—to be living in Sodom and Gomorra like that!"

Frayda held her breath, waiting for the questions about how she had learned about Ramon's living situation, and how she was connected to it, and what exactly she knew.

Nothing. Reb Avram was clearly uninterested in either the extent of her knowledge or in how she had managed to obtain it. Women's chatter.

"It is totally unacceptable, that living situation," was all that he repeated. "A total *shanda*. I let him know all that in no uncertain terms. I am sure that he will leave it far behind him, now."

He then returned to reading his book. Matter closed.

Frayda drew herself up to her full five-foot-ten-inches of height and shot him a look that would have crushed a man twice Reb Avram's size.

"Leave all that behind and go where?" she asked.

Reb Avram shrugged, still buried in the tome on his lap. "Elsewhere."

"The real *shanda* in this situation, Reb Avram," Frayda continued, in a tone that yanked his eyes—in fact his entire head—out of his book, "is that you—a man Ramon trusts like a father, a man he treats like a father—are essentially forcing him to leave his current home without a single thought as to what his options are or as to how leaving his home might affect his wellbeing."

Reb Avram blinked.

"I am thinking of nothing but his wellbeing. I am thinking of his soul."

"Well, give a few thoughts to his day-to-day survival, Reb Avram. You have made it impossible for him to continue living where he is—and yet he has nowhere else to go."

Reb Avram looked back down at his book. He started to shrug again but thought better of it.

"So," said Frayda, after waiting less than a beat. "What are you going to do about this situation that you have created?"

"I?" said Reb Avram, looking up again—startled. "What am I going to do about it? I cannot just snap my fingers and create an alternative living situation for the boy. I have saved him from a terrible fate. Made sure he no longer walks in the counsel of the wicked nor stands in the path of sinners. That is surely enough."

"You are not listening to me, Reb Avram. The boy is going to be homeless if he follows your directives. What are you going to do about it?"

Reb Avram looked back down at his book, but it didn't help. He pulled at his beard.

"What can I possibly do?" he finally repeated. "What power do I have?"

"You, Reb Avram, are the father of the owner of the facility into which Ramon has so innocently ventured. The facility—the community—which Ramon has grown to love and serve and to which he has made a deep personal commitment."

Reb Avram looked at her blankly.

"You, Reb Avram, have the power to ask your son to put a roof over the boy's head, right in this very facility, since he has nowhere else to go."

Reb Avram's stare evolved from blankness to incredulity.

"I do not have any such power!"

"Yes you do!"

She glared at him steadily.

"I happen to know," she continued, "that Room 36—the only other single room on this floor—has remained vacant since Reb Yitzhak Tannenbaum, may-he-be-remembered-for-a-blessing, died of the COVID, back in February. You can tell your son—the owner and the director of this facility—to install Ramon in that still-vacant room, as part of his compensation for working here. Plus, continuing to provide him with all his meals, of course, like the rest of the residents. Maybe he could reduce his wages a little, make it all come out even. You'll figure out what to tell him."

"Ach!" said Reb Avram. "I cannot tell that son of mine any of that. I cannot tell him to do anything. We barely... Ach!"

He looked away, looked down at his book—looked anywhere but back at Frayda.

"I do not know anything about my son's finances—or the finances of this place," he finally sputtered. "I do not tell him how to run his business."

"What you do or do not know about your son's business is irrelevant, Reb Avram," sniffed Frayda. "This issue does not relate to business. It relates to justice. A topic which—I am sure—is amply covered in whatever text you happen to have right there in your lap, since everything in our religion relates to justice. We are obliged to house the homeless, Reb Avram, as we read in *shul* every Yom Kippur. We are obliged to act in that manner even if we are not the force behind that homelessness. So just imagine the depths of our obligation if we are—in fact—the primary cause of that homelessness. Which, in this case, is the truth. You will be the cause of Ramon's homelessness."

"I—"

"I will leave you with that thought, Reb Avram, and trust that it will motivate you to speak with your son. That it will motivate you to arrange a roof over the head of the boy who treats you a great deal better than that self-same son does, as far as anyone can tell."

Reb Avram glanced up at her for a millisecond, turned bright red, glanced away, looked back down at his book.

"What is more," she added, "I trust that you will accomplish all that by the end of the day, today, so that Ramon has somewhere to sleep tonight. Call in all the debts your son owes you, Reb Avram. Make it happen."

Reb Avram looked up one last time, looked away, sighed, then slowly nodded.

"Excellent," said Frayda.

She stepped outside and motioned to Anteojitos.

"Come on in Ramon. We have something to tell you."

Anteojitos walked slowly back across the ten paces and stood in the doorway. He then took one small step into the room, while keeping his face determinedly turned away. Was it fear that he was feeling? Was it shame? Was he regretting his decision? Was he crying again?

"Reb Avram is going to arrange for you to move into *B'Sevah Tovah*," Frayda announced, looking straight at Reb Avram, not at Anteojitos. "You will continue to work and to eat here and you will continue to receive a small salary. But now, you will be one of the residents as well. In a room of your own. Just down the hall from Reb Avram, as a matter of fact. Room 36."

Anteojitos took a breath, lifted his head, and looked back and forth, from one to the other.

"I can live here?"

"Yes, Ramon," said Frayda. "You can live here. Plus, you can keep your job. Plus, you can keep your connection with Reb Avram that means so much to you."

Reb Avram finally found his voice.

"Most importantly, you will never again have to associate with sinners. Your aunts..."

Anteojitos stood very tall. He was definitely not crying, now. He looked resolved and relieved. He knew what he had to do.

"You cannot speak to me about my aunts anymore, Reb Avram," he said. "It is gossip."

"Has Serach been crying into her pillow over the disappearance of The Creature?"

"No, Frank," said Paloma, filling his espresso cup and bringing it and her own cup to the table. "That's not typical Serach behavior. As you know."

"Has she been discussing it with you calmly and logically, then?"

"Not exactly."

"Has she said anything about it at all? Shared a single juicy detail? Given you any sense of why her little duckling just up and flew away without as much as a 'Goodbye, it's been real'?"

"Not really," Paloma sighed. "When Frayda first called to tell her, all that Serach reported back to me was: 'Frayda said Ramon won't be living here anymore—he'll be getting room and board at his place of employment from now on.'"

"I can't believe that's all that Frayda said."

"Well, it's all that Serach was willing to tell me. Well, almost all. She also said that Frayda told her to collect all of Ramon's things, bring them to the facility, and drop them off at the front desk as soon as she could manage it."

"Just bring them there and drop them off? Without even seeing the boy? Without being able to ask him why he did what he did? Not that he'd be capable of explaining himself. But still."

"Yes, just drive and drop. Which is exactly what she did. Then she came back home again."

"Lordy! And she didn't say anything when she returned?"

"No," Paloma said, shaking her head. "Whatever else she knows—whatever she may be feeling—she's not sharing."

"Well, haven't you been tempted to pry? To sweeten her up in the way that only you can do and then ask her some probing questions?"

"You don't do that with Serach, Frank. She just gets testier and testier and eventually turns over and says she needs to go to sleep."

"But she must be devastated. And furious. After all she's done for that boy!"

Paloma shook her head.

"The real problem," she finally replied, "is that I don't think that she's feeling sorrow or rage—appropriate as both those things might be. I think that what she's feeling is guilt."

"Guilt? The Creature is the one who should be carrying *mea culpas* on his shoulders."

"Not guilt for anything that she did to Anteojitos, Frank." Paloma replied, softly.

She lifted her cup and drained its contents.

"I suspect that she thinks that Anteojtos's departure is punishment for her having bolted out of her own home without as much as saying goodbye to anyone, so many years ago. That it's '*el dedo de Dios*', as my grandmother would put it. 'God's finger.'"

"I didn't think that Jews thought that way. I figured it was just us Catholics who believe we are forever damned for our every naughtiness unless we immediately 'fess up, say twenty Hail Mary's, and walk a hundred paces backwards on our knees."

"Oh, Jews agonize about wrongdoing and punishment just as much as we do, Frank. In fact, I think the whole 'the finger of God' thing is originally from their Bible. Along with a list of potential wrongdoings and wretched punishments that make ours seem positively reasonable. For them, it's not just touching yourself under the covers that brings on God's wrath. Putting a dish in the wrong microwave is enough to trigger a major blast of Divine ire."

"Lord have mercy!"

"In any event, I'm not about to push Serach any further. Why get her fretting about what mess she might have left behind her when she broke ranks and sailed into my arms?"

She tossed off that last phrase almost nonchalantly, but Frank knew better. Paloma was scared that Serach was regretting the decision that had irrevocably changed so many lives.

"Do those people truly believe that they'll roast in hell for putting a dish in the wrong microwave?" he asked as he strode to the sink and placed his cup inside.

"Something like that."

"Other peoples' religions!" he sniffed and then he left.

INTERLUDE TWO: The Doctor's Visit

"We have heard the report of it;
Our hands are limp.
Anguish has seized us,
Pain as of a woman in childbirth."

Jeremiah: 6:24

August 2023, Jerusalem

Ruchel didn't know how she would get through the morning. Why did everything have to fall apart at once?

Why did her housekeeper Dalisay's mother have to break her hip just when Asher and Shoshana entered the week-long hiatus between summer camp and the start of the school year—leaving Ruchel totally in the lurch while Dalisay sprinted off to Manila to tend to her?

Why did her own mother have to choose exactly the same week for her annual jaunt to the beachside with Ruchel's oldest brother and his family?

Most troubling of all, why was she—herself—beginning to feel the same terrible things that she had felt during the last month of her previous pregnancy? The slightly blurred vision. The shortness of breath. The sensations that made it imperative for her to get herself and her enormous belly to Dr. Botwinick as quickly as possible, both kids in tow. *Baruch Ha-Shem*, Dr. Botwinick had been able to slot her into what was undoubtedly an already overpacked schedule.

She carefully dragged the two car seats out the gate of her house while nudging Asher and Shoshanna forward to the curb where the hired car awaited them. The driver took one look at the approaching group and heaved a major sigh. He trudged out to the pavement, opened the two back doors, lifted the car seats up off the ground, and grumpily began strapping them into his car.

Yes, this lady was paying him very well. Yes, he was guaranteed a return trip plus ample compensation for waiting around till she finished her appointment and was ready to go home again. Still, there had to be better ways to earn a living than carting around rich Jewish ladies and their spoiled offspring.

"Okay Mameleh, here we go" sighed Ruchel, lifting Shoshana into one of the seats, strapping her in and then leading Asher around to the other side where he announced that he could do it himself and climbed in with surprising alacrity. Ruchel fastened his straps, shut his door, ran back to Shoshana's side, and carefully climbed over her daughter to squeeze her own swollen body into the tiny space between the two car seats.

Shoshana neither poked at Ruchel as she passed nor did anything else to remind her that she—Shoshana—was there. What is wrong with that girl today—she who is usually intent on making her presence felt in every possible way?

Once everyone was settled and the car in motion, Ruchel turned to her children with the tone that sometimes worked with them.

"Never talk down to children. Always speak to them like adults," her sister-in-law Beile had always counseled, and Beile had the six best-behaved children Ruchel had ever met.

"I need you both to be *mensches* today when Mama is in with Dr. Botwinick," Ruchel said, without a trace of wheedling in her voice. "I've brought you each a book and expect that you will sit quietly reading in the reception area while Mama is in with him, so he can make sure that everything is going well for Mama and for the little sister in Mama's belly."

"I don't want another little sister," said Asher, whose language skills were finally beginning to fall firmly into place. "I hate little sisters."

Ruchel braced herself for the inevitable retort from the girl who always managed to have the last word, despite all Asher's best attempts to bully her. But Shoshi remained silent, her head leaning quietly back against the car seat, being very, very still.

"I hate little sisters—I hate them!" Asher said more loudly, kicking his feet against the car seat in frustration at Shoshi's silence. He was aching for a good fight.

"He doesn't mean it," Ruchel whispered to her daughter. "He's just teasing you."

Normally, that would provoke a reaction as well. Something along the lines of: "Yes, he does! He's a monster! I hate him, too!" But today, it provoked absolutely nothing.

"What's up, Mameleh?" Ruchel asked softly, rubbing her tired cheek against the silky blond curls at the top of her daughter's head.

Still the silence. This wasn't good.

"Shoshi! Are you okay? *Shefele*—little lamb of mine? Are you alright?"

Shoshi suddenly shook her head back and forth so hard that Ruchel sat straight up again.

"No," Shoshi whispered. "No."

PART THREE: The Rice Pudding Pot

"Blessed is she who believed the Lord would fulfill His promises to her!"
Luke 1:43-45

"The stone that the builders rejected has become the cornerstone."
Psalm 118:22

September 2023, Brooklyn

-1-

Serach sat with her forehead in her hand as her client babbled on. It was the second time that this woman had called to propose sneaking a set of purely personal expenses into the already bloated list of her business deductions. Serach had vetoed the first attempt with relative ease, but the woman had clearly become shrewder in the interim. What she was now outlining might well slip under the IRS radar.

Not, however, over the Serach Gottesman signature.

Serach was just about to launch yet again into her standard speech about the ethical and logistical pitfalls of tax evasion when an unusual flurry of activity on her computer screen wiped out all thoughts of dicey ploys and costly audits.

There was that long-silent Skype ringtone, singing out at her. There was that long-dormant Skype icon twinkling away. There was that familiar message grabbing at her heart.

"Are you there, Serach?"

It had been seven years since her brother had last Skyped her. More than four years since she had seen or heard from him at all.

"I'm going to have to call you back," she murmured distractedly to her client. "Sorry."

She then shut down the call without waiting for an answer and reached for the keyboard.

"Shmuely!" she typed, breathlessly. "Is it really you? Turn on your camera! Turn on your mike! Let me see your face! Let me hear your voice!"

Seconds later, her brother's image materialized and Serach took a quick inventory between blinks of tears. He was in a room filled with towering bookshelves, an unlit standing lamp, and a single window with heavy drawn curtains. He was wearing the long-sleeved white shirt that had been the central element in his daily uniform since earliest childhood—and she could see a sliver of his ever-present black silk yarmulke atop his sandy-gold curls as he glanced momentarily downward.

There was, however, no big black hat and no long black coat in sight.

Where was he sitting that he could ignore the vital protective gravitas and modesty of those additional garments? Certainly not in his yeshiva office. Could he be making this forbidden Skype call from his home, where anyone—from his wife to his kids to his housekeeper—could just barge into the room, see the screen, and begin wondering who was who and what was what?

And—if so—what could be so urgent that he would dare to take such a risk?

Even more troubling: the way he looked! His skin was so ashen! His eyes were so fogged and red! Was it the dim light in that room (wherever it turned out to be) that made him look like that? Or was it something else?

"Shmuely!" she exclaimed, momentarily shoving those questions aside to concentrate on the simple miracle of his presence on her screen. "How I've longed to hear from you! How good it is to see you! How are you? I—"

"Serach! Please!"

Shmuely held up a pale hand and she stopped. For a long moment, her brother looked pointedly away and when he finally turned back to the camera she saw, all-too-plainly, that his disturbing appearance had nothing to do with the poor lighting.

He had been crying. Definitely crying. Probably hard and probably for a long time.

"Serach," he finally repeated, a bit more gently, "my daughter—my three-and-a-half-year-old, my Shoshi—is ill. Very ill. Her doctor thinks she may have the same thing that you had."

"The same thing that I had?" Serach said, turning as pale as he was. "Leukemia?"

Shmuely began to cry in earnest—yarmulke in full view as he bowed his head and shook.

Serach waited till he had collected himself.

"We're traveling to New York, to Maimonides Hospital, for all the tests she needs to confirm it," he finally managed—speaking so rapidly that it took his sister a moment to register what he was saying. "If it turns out she does have... that she does have... cancer, we will remain there for the first round of treatments as well. We are scheduled to arrive at Kennedy Airport first thing Monday morning. The fourth of September. Your Labor Day. We will go straight from the airport to the hospital."

He glanced in Serach's direction, caught the shock on her face and kept barreling forward.

"The doctor says that speed is crucial," he added. "Plus, with the High Holy Days coming, I need to get Shoshi settled in as quickly as possible, so I can *daven* all the services."

"Wait a minute, Shmuely," Serach finally broke in. "Please. One thing at a time. First of all, tell me: why does Shoshi's doctor think that she may have cancer? Based on what?"

"Based on that she's so tired—so terribly tired—and that she bruises so easily. All the time, she bruises."

Serach shivered and nodded. She remembered those parts of the illness.

"I see," she said. "Yes, that's about right. The poor darling. The poor child."

She paused.

"But why are you taking her all the way to New York for the tests and treatment?" she continued. "I thought Israel had some of the best doctors—some of the best medical facilities—in the world. Surely, she can be helped right at home."

"Yes, of course, under normal circumstances that would be true. But we are currently under siege here. A bunch of *mamzers* have been trying to shut down the government and it is the doctors who are the worst of the bunch. Have you not been reading about it? Thousands of them went on strike not so long ago. Even Shoshi's pediatrician—the man we depend on—took part in that *shanda*. For the moment, they have all gone back to work, but who knows when they will decide to walk out again? The protests continue. The country continues to fall apart."

He drew another ragged breath.

"It is safer in New York," he continued, after a pause. "In New York, the doctors are not like they are here. They are not plunging everything into chaos."

Serach could not find a single reasonable thing to respond.

"Plus...," Shmuely began again, after a short pause, "I want Shoshi to be treated in New York—I want her at Maimonides Hospital—because..."

He put his hand to his mouth and whispered between his long fingers.

"... because that is where *you* were healed."

So there it was. The real reason—the reason within the reason—for his plan. But not necessarily the best reason.

They were both silent for a moment, while Serach considered her options. She knew what she needed to do, based on what she had just heard. But she wasn't ready to get into an all-out fight with her brother yet. There were other things to clarify first.

"So, what do you mean when you say 'we'?" she finally ventured. "Is your wife coming with you as well? Is Asher?"

"No. It will be just me and Shoshi. My wife..."

"Yes?"

"Ruchel can't come. She's got her own *tsoris*. She's just nine months pregnant and something is—she has some problem with her pressure. She's not supposed to travel and she may have to deliver early. She has what is called... I can't remember what it is called..."

"Pre-eclampsia?"

"Yes, that. When she was pregnant with Shoshi, she also had it. It is nothing to worry about—it goes away eventually, once the baby is born. But it does mean she can't travel."

"Pre-eclampsia is not nothing to worry about," said Serach. "It is serious. Should you be leaving Ruchel alone when she is dealing with her own serious condition?"

"She is not alone," Shmuely replied, ignoring the expression on his sister's face. "Her mother is there with her."

He sighed.

"Meanwhile, my sister Beile and I will handle everything in New York. She will remain with Shoshi during the day while I stay at her house and *daven* at our old synagogue. I will leave for the hospital once evening services are concluded, to take over the night shift. Beile will then return once again before dawn, so I can make it back to morning services. And so on."

Serach swallowed the pain that came with that first: "my sister Beile." Beile was her sister, too! She waited till Shmuely was finished speaking, focused on the task before her, and posed her next question.

"But how does your wife feel about not being with Shoshi when Shoshi is going through... everything. Beile is a good person. I do remember that. But your wife—" she swallowed, "—your wife is the mother. Doesn't she want to be the one who is there for Shoshi?"

"Yes. Sure. Of course. She made a big fuss at first. But then she calmed down. Realized that I was right. The doctor who she herself is seeing—the obstetrician—is a proper Jew, *Baruch Ha-Shem*. He has no desire to go against this government. But who knows about the rest of them? The doctor who ends up taking care of Shoshi could decide to go out on strike again, right in the middle of a procedure."

He looked at his sister hard.

"So yes," he said. "Ruchel accepts that we have to do it in the way that we are doing it."

"Well," said Serach, taking in the challenge embedded in that look, "what about the cost? I'm not sure a hospital here will accept your insurance coverage."

"Money is not a problem," Shmuely said. "It never is, with Ruchel's family."

He looked at his sister steadily, his expression unreadable.

"Ruchel's father agrees Shoshi should be seen in New York," he said, slowly and deliberately. "He's as nervous about the situation in Israel as I—and prepared to pay all the costs. He's in—"

"Yes, I know. Diamonds."

Serach swallowed.

"But what about the fact that you will probably be away for the birth of your third child?"

"It's just another girl, Serach," Shmuely replied, shrugging. "It is not as if we have to worry about the timing of a *bris*. The naming can wait till I get back, whenever that may be."

Serach shook her head—what could she possibly reply to that?

"Meanwhile," Shmuely continued, "Shoshi's pediatrician has sent me a scan of all her medical records, so I can pass them on to the right doctor at Maimonides. Beile's husband— he has connections at Maimonides—is looking into who that doctor should be."

Serach briefly pressed her lips together. Her brother had just given her the opening that she needed. If she didn't speak up now, she would never be able to do so.

"Shmuely, do you trust me?" she asked.

Shmuely looked away.

"I think you do. If you didn't trust me, you would not have—once again—broken all those iron-clad rules and taboos of yours to get in touch with me today. You would not have, once again, shared your deepest sorrows and fears with me. Sought my comfort. Sought my support."

He gave a small shrug. But he didn't contradict her.

"So. If you trust me, then you need to listen very carefully to what I am going to say next. To the advice that I am going to give you."

"Do not tell me not to bring Shoshi to New York, Serach," Shmuely said, coloring. "I can see that you think that I shouldn't. All the questions you've been asking me tell me that you think that. But you cannot dissuade me. The arrangements are all made, the tickets are all bought. I will not entrust my daughter to the *mamzer* doctors here in Israel, who ...."

"I am not disputing that you should come here, Shmuely," Serach replied softly. "You are right that I had my doubts when you first said it, but you have convinced me. I am also impressed with how you, Ruchel, and Beile have worked so well together to put all the pieces into place. Nonetheless," she took a breath, "if you are taking Shoshi all the way to New York City to get her the best possible care, then you should make sure that she gets the best possible care. Which means taking her not to Maimonides but to the Manhattan East Cancer Research and Treatment Center."

Shmuely opened his mouth, but she held up her hand and kept going.

"Maimonides is a very fine hospital," she said. "It has a very fine oncology department. They healed me, as you say. But these days, Manhattan East is the absolute tops for pediatric oncological care. They have won award after award. They have built the most up-to-date cancer facility in the United States. They are attracting the best doctors and researchers in the nation."

She allowed herself a brief, small grin.

"They have the best-regarded nursing staff."

By that point, Shmuely's face had gone completely crimson. But Serach was on a mission. Plus, she was still his oldest sister. She still knew, better than he did, how the world worked and what needed to be done.

"They will give Shoshi the best possible chance, Shmuely," she concluded, emphatically. "For surviving this nightmare. For getting better. For staying better."

"Serach, it is out of the question," Shmuely finally sputtered. "Everything is all set up at Maimonides. We cannot possibly take Shoshi anywhere else."

"Of course you can. It's not all set. Shoshi's records aren't there yet. The doctor isn't arranged. Nor is the bed. You can still change your plans. You must change your plans."

"Serach, I have never even heard of this place that you are recommending," Shmuely said, his voice rising to a level that it almost never reached. "How do you know that it is so good? And who knows if Shoshi can even get in there? With Maimonides, it is a certainty. As I have said. We have connections. Beile's husband does."

There was a long silence and then Serach spoke softly and slowly.

"I'll address your concerns, each in turn," she began. "Number one: You haven't heard about Manhattan East because why would you be keeping up with the latest pediatric oncological developments in New York? I, on the other hand, have solid reasons to do so. After all, as you say, I once battled the illness myself. I have retained a special interest in it."

She gave him a wistful smile and went on.

"Number two: I know that Shoshi can get into Manhattan East because—just like Beile's husband has connections with Maimonides—I have connections there. Strong connections. I'm a long-time donor and... I know the right people. People in high places."

A mildly impressed look flitted across Shmuely's face, but it was swiftly replaced by the expression that had signaled "no" ever since he was a two-year-old refusing to eat everything that his oldest sister had put on his plate.

"Don't send Shoshi's medical files to Maimonides," Serach continued, undaunted. "Send them to me. I will take it from there. Your daughter will get into Manhattan East, and—once she is there—she will receive exactly the care that she needs. The best care that there is."

Shmuely's face remained unmoved.

"Shmuely, have I ever let you down when you have come to me for my help, for my support—for my blessing?"

They gazed at one another for a long moment, gray eyes to turquoise eyes, across the continents and the oceans and everything else that had separated them for so long.

"All right, Serach," Shmuely finally sighed. "I will e-mail you the scan of Shoshi's records. Let me know when everything is arranged at this hospital that you have so much faith in, so I can tell Ruchel and also tell Beile who will put up such a fuss I don't even want to think about it."

Serach smiled.

"She'll have to take a car service instead of just walking back and forth to the hospital—" he said, shaking his head.

"Your father-in-law will pay," said Serach.

"She'll have to explain it to her husband who has already—"

"He'll live," said Serach.

For the very briefest moment, she and her brother exchanged a grin. How many times had they been co-

conspirators in the ongoing struggle against the band of bossy sisters who had dominated their childhood home?

"*Ha-Shem* led you to contact me, Shmuely," she added softly. "He will continue to lead us."

Shmuely nodded and then signed off before either of them could say anything more about the terrifying path ahead.

Brooklyn and Manhattan

- 2 -

As soon as Shmuely's face vanished from the computer screen, Serach reached for her phone. It would have been fine to wait till that afternoon to get back to the client that she had cut off so abruptly. Even the following morning might have been all right. But she suddenly found herself in strong need of distraction from the maelstrom of her thoughts, and a good brisk argument about tax evasion seemed like just the thing.

Her poor brother! How could she have made so reckless a promise to him? What if she couldn't get Shoshi into Manhattan East? What if, after all that, the doctors couldn't help her?

She punched in her client's number and prepared herself to spar, but apparently it was not to be. Swiftly—startlingly— the client folded at Serach's first objection. What is more, this time her surrender appeared to be final. ("Okay, Gottesman, you win. You are a total pill, but what if the IRS is even worse than you? I can't afford to go through an audit right now. Don't put in those extra expenses. We'll just send it all in as is.")

Nor did Shmuely offer Serach any reprieve from thinking about what she next had to do. Not five minutes after she'd finished the call with the client, the scan of Shoshi's records appeared in her e-mail Inbox.

There was nothing written in the subject line of the message to which it was attached. Nor was there anything written within the body of that message. But then, what did she expect? "Thank you, Serach"? Or "You're the best." Not from her Shmuely.

Okay, Serach thought grimly, as she transferred the scanned records onto a flash drive and stuffed the flash drive into her jeans pocket. No excuses. Get going. If not now, when?

She made her way down the two flights of stairs to the first-floor bathroom where she ran a damp comb through her close-cropped curls, easing them into their fiercest-looking ducktail. She donned the black leather jacket that always made her feel invincible—and the chic reflective Ray-Bans that completed the look. She then strode out the front door and up Marlborough Road to the Church Avenue subway station, where she caught the Q train into the city.

The Manhattan East Cancer Care and Research Center first burst into New York's medical scene in the summer of 2005 as a very small, boutique institution.

It was originally housed in two modest conjoined brownstones on a low-scale side street in Manhattan's far East Sixties. Over the course of the following fifteen years, however, it steadily evolved. It expanded its staff, began garnering kudos for both pioneering research and direct patient care, improved its name (it had originally just been called a "Care and Research Unit") and built its brand. It also carried out the major capital campaign required to create a home better suited to its vaulting ambitions and rapidly ascendant reputation.

The new building, completed in the summer of 2022, now took up two-thirds of the block on which the old facility had stood. Months before the doors even opened, it began racking up coveted architectural awards. LEED Platinum-certified, luminously glass-fronted—with a lush interior garden visible from every patient room—it singlehandedly transformed what was once a modest Eastside streetscape into a vista of shining urban modernity.

The main entrance of the Center opened onto an art-enhanced, easily negotiated lobby and reception area. Off to one side was a well-appointed gift shop and a chapel. Off to the other were two cafeterias—one for visitors and one for staff.

The second and third floors housed offices, conference rooms, and a major medical library open to the public.

The fourth floor housed all the laboratories—pioneering research remaining at the heart of the Manhattan East mission—plus the kitchens in which all patient meals were prepared.

The fifth and sixth floors held private rooms, small lounges, and operating and procedure rooms for the Center's adult patients. The seventh floor offered similarly thoughtfully-conceived amenities for its pediatric patients and the caregivers who accompanied them.

Half the roof was covered by a fleet of solar panels that contributed toward the Center's energy needs, and half by a Japanese rock garden, a meditation maze, the greenhouse that supplied much of the organic produce served to its patients, and a small patio suitable for outdoor events.

Serach exited the Q train at 63rd Street and found her way to the building's glittering front façade. She slipped between the wings of the automatic revolving door and was delivered into the lobby. She approached the massive front desk at which a small dark-haired man in his mid-forties presided over all arrivals and departures. He wore a well-fitted pearl-gray uniform, a snow-white shirt, a pearl-gray tie, and a pair of large-framed black, tinted, rectangular glasses. The tag on his chest stated that his name was Gary.

"Good morning," said Gary, as Serach approached. "How can I help you?"

"I'm here to see Paloma Rodriguez," she said. "She's the Nurse Manager for…"

"Oh, I know who Ms. Rodriguez is," said Gary, suddenly grinning. "I've only just started to work here and don't know everyone yet. But that Ms. Rodriguez—everyone knows who she is. She's a hard one to miss."

"That she is," Serach sighed.

"Whom shall I say is here?" Gary continued, lightly emphasizing the "m" of whom.

"Serach."

"Just Serach?"

Serach bit her lower lip.

"Yes—just Serach."

Gary stared with open curiosity at the small, tough, androgynous figure standing before him and pondered what relationship she could possibly have with the glamorous Ms. Rodriguez. He punched in the number, waited a moment, and then spoke.

"Yes, hello, Ms. Rodriguez. There's a certain Serach here to see you. Shall I send her up?"

He nodded several times and then said: "Okay" and put the phone down.

"She says she's just about to go into the third-floor conference room to lead a staff meeting. Twenty minutes? Maybe half an hour? There's a bench right outside the room she'll be in where you can wait for her. It's just down the hall as you get off the elevator."

"Thank you."

She turned away from him and headed for the hospital directory on the far side of the lobby.

"Hey! The elevators are in the other direction!" Gary called after her.

"I know," Serach said, waving back at him.

She briefly perused the directory, walked back to the elevators, punched in the number "7" on the panel at the center of the wall, and waited for the right elevator to take her to her first destination.

Twenty-six nurses exited the third-floor conference room at exactly 12:15—Paloma at the front, with her head thrown back in a mighty peal of laughter. One of the nurses, her hand resting gently on Paloma's shoulder, was laughing almost as hard as Paloma was and a second one was shaking his head and grinning hard as he trailed after them both.

Every nurse was dressed in identical, square-cut gray scrubs, gray caps, and white Croc shoes. Still, Paloma somehow managed to escape the dreariness of that muted uniformity. The scrubs' boxy lines only served to highlight her ample curves. The dullness of the cap made the color and vivacity of her features stand out even further. And that laugh! Any taint of grim conventionality evaporated in its radiant wake.

Once everyone had re-assembled in the corridor, however, Paloma suddenly stopped laughing, turned to face the group, and began speaking in a tone that brought them all quickly to attention.

"Okay team," she said. "Thanks for a great meeting. I think we're all clear on the changes we have to make today. Go to it!"

The other nurses nodded in unison, donned their masks, and filed forward toward the elevator bank. Paloma might invite—might even encourage—a degree of casual intimacy from those whom she supervised, but she also clearly knew how to control the troops.

Serach stood up from the bench as the group dispersed and waited for her partner to turn around. It took a few moments for Paloma to do so—and another few for her to fully register how perturbed (and how frightened) she suddenly felt at Serach's intrusion into her workspace—and her overstretched workday. It was so unlike Serach to be impulsive and inconsiderate.

"Serach, why on earth are you here? What is so terrible that you couldn't just call me?"

"It's something that needs to be said in person, Paloma."

"But I have Rounds coming up!"

"It won't take long."

Paloma drew a long breath. "Okay. I guess I can manage a minute. But let's go somewhere more private than this hallway, shall we?"

She motioned to the Conference Room from which she had just exited, and in they went.

Once inside, Serach stood very still for a moment, gazing all around her. It was a marvelous, airy, high-ceilinged space. There was a big, plain oak table at its center, encircled by a set of green-cushioned oak chairs. Three of its walls were covered in artwork that had clearly been selected by someone who had access to major collections. The fourth was less a wall than a single, glinting, floor-to-ceiling pane of glass, fronted by a well-curated collection of potted trees and opening out on a view of startlingly bright sunlight and lush green gardens.

Serach eventually stopped looking and pulled off her mask, her jacket, and her sunglasses. She shook out her curls. Her armor removed, she looked pale and small and slight.

"I need you to do something for me," she said.

"Sure, Baby," replied Paloma, smiling back at her partner. "Whatever you need."

She couldn't help herself. When Serach looked tough and edgy, it thrilled her—but when she assumed her fragile gamine look, she melted.

"Still," she added, "please do talk fast! Rounds wait for no one."

She gestured to two adjacent chairs and sat down in one. Serach nodded and took the other.

"Paloma, Shmuely Skyped me this morning."

"Oh my God!" Paloma gasped. "A total miracle! The prodigal brother returns!"

Serach looked so hurt that Paloma lowered her eyes.

"Sorry," she said. "But you have to admit that it's a...."

"It's not something to laugh about, Paloma. It's something really terrible. They think that his daughter—his little three-and-a-half-year-old daughter—has childhood leukemia. Like I had. Except that mine wasn't exactly 'childhood leukemia.' I mean, I was twenty. I had some coping mechanisms in place. But she's so young! What can she possibly understand of what she's going through—or what she's going to go through?"

She paused to collect herself.

"Shmuely was utterly devastated when I had it. It was ages ago, but I sometimes think he's never fully recovered. I can't even begin to imagine what he must be feeling now."

She paused again.

"Well, certainly devastated enough to reach out to me, despite all the factors that make it so difficult for him to do so. Devastated enough to carry out that particular act of rebellion."

Paloma clamped her lips shut to prevent herself from retorting in the way she was immediately inclined to do. An act of rebellion? Sobbing on your older sister's shoulder after all those years of total and cruel negligence—an act of rebellion? More like an act of *chutzpah*!

Still, there was no denying it: this was truly rough stuff. She steeled herself to offer a response that would be more appropriately sympathetic.

"That is terrible news," she said, carefully extending a hand to clasp Serach's shoulder.

But then—ever the nurse: "What else did he say? What kind of care is he arranging for her?"

"He's bringing her to New York on Monday to be treated at Maimonides Hospital."

This time Paloma couldn't help herself.

"New York? Maimonides? Why on earth?"

"Because that's where I was treated, Paloma. And cured." Serach sighed.

"I know. It sounds like magical thinking."

"So how did you respond to this nonsensical plan?"

"I told him that she would be much better off at Manhattan East than at Maimonides. And then," she drew a breath, "I promised him that I'd get her a bed, here."

"You did what?" asked Paloma, suddenly back to ground level on the sympathy scale. "You told him that you'd get her into Manhattan East? Just like that?"

She shook her head.

"And what exactly made you think that would be possible?"

"Well," Serach said slowly, "I was hoping that you'd help." Paloma colored.

"Serach. I'm just the Nurse Manager of Manhattan East's Adult Department. I have no powers of admission. I certainly don't have them in the Pediatric Department—I never even go up there. Not if I can help it. Not my thing—children's care. As you know."

"Yes, but... surely you must know some of the staff, there. Surely, there's some way you could..."

"Yes, of course I know some of them," said Paloma, briskly. "All of them, actually. This is a small, intimate facility, for all its outsized presence on the cancer research and treatment scene. But knowing the staff is one thing and being able to influence them is quite another."

"Paloma! Please! I know that you can! Who do you know there?"

Paloma looked at Serach's yearning face and sighed.

"Well. There's my counterpart Nurse Manager—Amalia Bonilla," she said, cautiously. "We're not close friends or anything, but we do go way back a while—worked together for a bit at Sloane Kettering before we were both tapped to come here."

"See? I knew it. Who else?"

Paloma looked away for a moment and then a dimple gleamed within one of her cheeks.

"Well," she said slowly. "I have what you might call a 'lunchtime' relationship with one of the Admitting Doctors— Sherman Silverstein. He plops himself down at my table whenever he sees me in the staff cafeteria and tries to trap me into conversation. I can generally steer him away from discussing his pending divorce or what I'm doing on Saturday night and onto things like how bad the staff cafeteria food is. But it's always a struggle."

Serach reached for Paloma's hand and squeezed it.

"You see? I knew you had 'ins' that you could draw on."

She breathed deeply.

"Paloma, you have to help me. Shoshi needs to be here. She deserves to be here. That seventh floor is clearly a place where miracles occur. It's the place that she should be."

"Serach, how would you know? You've never even been on the seventh floor."

"Oh, but I have," Serach said, eagerly. "Before coming here to find you, I went up there and took a look around."

"You what?" said Paloma, shaking off Serach's hand. "What made you think you could just go and do that? You could have gotten yourself into real trouble. And me, too, if anyone suspected who you were. Didn't anyone question you? Tell you to leave?"

"No," said Serach. She looked down for a moment and then looked up again to meet Paloma's horrified look with an innocent smile. "No one even said a word to me."

She paused.

"Why does that surprise you? Aren't you the one who always says I have the obscene advantage of being a small white female of no obvious ethnicity? That I can slip into almost any situation without anyone paying much attention to me or thinking that I'm up to no good? That I can get away with just about anything as long as it seems like I know what I'm doing?"

Paloma grinned. She couldn't help it. It was true. She had often made that observation.

"So that's what I counted on—and it worked. I got off the elevator, toured around a bit—looking purposeful but making no waves—and then left again, with no one the wiser."

"Still, Serach! There are some very sick children up there. They can't have unauthorized people just wandering around spewing germs at them."

"I wore my mask. I didn't go into any of the rooms. I didn't breathe on anyone. Paloma, I had to do it! I had to see where Shoshi might..."

Paloma looked so fierce that Serach looked away.

"Anyway," she eventually forged ahead, "while I was doing that, I noticed that there were four empty patient rooms. Four of the fifteen pediatric beds are empty right now, Paloma!"

She looked beseechingly at her partner.

"Paloma, Shoshi is arriving in New York in just three days. All four of those beds can't possibly fill up in so short a time, can they? There could be a place available for her!"

Paloma shook her head.

"Paloma, couldn't you somehow work with Dr. Silverstein or with your friend Amalia to..."

"Serach—it is one thing for me to say 'hello-how-are-you' to Amalia when I bump into her at an all-nurses staff meeting. Or to give Sherman the occasional lunch-time thrill by talking to him about the quality of the sandwiches we are eating. It is quite another thing for me to ask either of them to reserve a bed in New York City's most exclusive pediatric oncology ward for a foreign kid who will be arriving here in three days without so much as a credible referral, the necessary medical records, or—in all likelihood—the proper insurance coverage."

Serach smiled gently as she contemplated how well-prepared she was to counter Paloma's objections. She permitted herself a single short moment of self-satisfaction before standing up, wriggling her hand into her jeans pocket, fishing out the flash drive, and handing it over.

"All of Shoshi's medical records are scanned and stored and available for anyone who needs them, right here on this device," she said, smiling a bit deeper. "They come from a very credible referring pediatrician, trust me. Shmuely's wife would insist on the best. Shmuely e-mailed them to me this morning."

Paloma arched an eyebrow.

"Meanwhile, as to your other points," Serach continued, "yes, of course, Israel is a foreign country as far as you are concerned. But for a middle-aged New York Jewish doctor with a name like Sherman Silverstein, I'd warrant not so much. There are bound to be deep ties there. Maybe Sherman celebrated his Bar Mitzvah at the Wailing Wall. Or maybe his sons did. Or maybe he sent them all on Birthright trips. One thing is for sure: he joins with scores of other American Jews in concluding every Passover Seder with the words: 'Next year in Jerusalem.'"

"Serach, you surprise me. I thought you didn't believe in communal stereotypes."

"I don't, generally," Serach said, sighing. "And these days, that particular stereotype is especially full of holes. But for Jews of a certain vintage, I promise you, it still holds true. I'm banking on that being the case with Sherman."

She put her hand back on her partner's.

"Finally, Manhattan East needn't worry about the money," she continued. "You can reassure anyone who is worried that Shmuely's father-in-law will pay whatever it costs. In full. In cash."

Paloma's eyes widened.

"We're talking potentially tens of thousands of dollars, Serach."

"The father-in-law is in diamonds. Seriously in diamonds. Money is no obstacle."

"Money does talk in this place."

"Where doesn't it?"

Serach caught her breath.

"So Paloma—will you do it? Will you at least try?"

"It's a lot of chips for me to be squandering on a schmucky little brother who's never even had the decency to..."

"It's not for Shmuely that you'll be doing it, Paloma. It's for me."

"Indeed."

Paloma tightened her lips.

"Well," she said, "But there is one small but make-it-or-break-it detail that we have to clarify before I promise anything."

"Sure. What?"

"Did you at any point as much as hint that I, myself, would have any part in taking care of Shmuely's darling little daughter? Because that far ... I mean, forget it. Not to mention the fact that I wouldn't be allowed to do so. Wrong department. Wrong function. I don't take direct care of patients anymore. As you know."

"Paloma, I didn't even tell him that you worked here. I left my connections to this place very vague. Said I was a big donor. That I 'knew some higher ups.'"

Paloma guffawed.

"In fact, I'd be surprised if Shmuely even remembers that you're a nurse—let alone where you might be working. He's not exactly interested in the details of my life. Or of yours."

"Well thank God for small favors."

"Paloma. All I'm asking is for you to try to get Shoshi in here. For that alone I will be—"

"Oh, please!"

Paloma glanced down at her watch and gasped.

"Sweet Jesus! I have exactly ninety-two seconds to meet up with the group going out on Rounds. If I miss those Rounds, goodbye to any clout I might possibly have with anyone around here. I'll see you at home!"

She leaned over and gave Serach a brief kiss in passing.

"Paloma—"

"No worries, Serach. I'll do it. Even if it means bringing Dr. Silverstein homemade lunches for a year while listening to all the reasons why he needs to leave his wife. But, please! Now I've really got to run!"

Serach watched Paloma fly out of the room and then looked carefully around her one more time, taking in all the striking details of her partner's new sphere of influence. She then stood up herself, walked back into the corridor, pulled the Conference Room door shut behind her and headed for the elevators.

September 2023: Manhattan

- 3 -

If someone had asked Paloma just how it was that she arrived in the Manhattan East lobby at exactly the moment that she did, her answer would undoubtedly have been: "Coincidence." Or: "I always go down at that time to get my second cup of coffee."

A bit of persistence on the part of the questioner might have revealed that once Paloma had learned the ETA for the El Al red-eye that morning, it would not have been too difficult for her to gauge how long it might take for a passenger to get from Kennedy International Airport to Manhattan's East Sixties, just off York Avenue.

Nonetheless, beyond that, Paloma would have held her ground. There was no way, after all, that she could have precisely predicted the length of the queue at Customs or in the Baggage Claim area. Or known in advance the density of morning traffic on the FDR Drive that day.

The chances of miscalculation were endless, in short. Coincidence had to have played a role.

Whatever the real story, the fact remains that just at the point that Paloma was stepping out of the elevator, Shmuely was heading toward the reception desk with a big, blanketed bundle slung over his left shoulder and a little pink backpack swinging from his free hand.

Okay, Paloma thought, adjusting her mask and flattening herself against the wall. Now I know that they've arrived, safe and sound. I can report back to Serach that everything is in order. I can grab my coffee and head upstairs again. I can wash my hands of this whole crazy business.

When Shmuely pivoted toward the elevator bank, however—and the little girl on his shoulder suddenly lifted her head to capture Paloma's black-eyed gaze within her own deep gray one—everything shifted irrevocably.

The after-image of that shockingly familiar little face persisted long after the elevator doors closed tightly behind father and child. It remained vividly present as Paloma made her way into the staff cafeteria to stand in line at the coffee station. As she filled her mug with that murky liquid. As she stumbled over to an empty table on the far side of the room, sat herself down, and tried to take a sip.

Her hands were shaking so ferociously that it was a long while before she could manage it.

- 4 -

Amalia Bonilla, the sturdy no-nonsense Nurse Manager for Manhattan East's Pediatric Oncology Department, was aware of Serach's existence—but only just. The subject of Paloma's home life had come up once or twice when they had worked together at Memorial Sloane Kettering, but she'd never felt either curiosity or censure. She had more important things to do than keep track of her colleagues' romantic relationships.

While initially miffed at Amalia's indifference, Paloma was now grateful for it. It meant there was no need for explanation, bluffing, or the tediousness of catching up. She could just stride up to the Nurses' Station on the seventh floor and get right to the point.

"Amalia, I have a big favor to ask."

"Yes?" Amalia muttered, without looking up from the chart she was perusing.

"Last Friday, I lobbied Dr. Silverstein to find a bed for a little girl from Israel," Paloma continued. "The girl's name is Shoshana Gottesman and I understand that she was admitted here on Monday for suspected acute lymphoblastic leukemia."

"Yes?" Amalia repeated, eyes still down on the chart. "And?"

"Well, the little girl is my partner Serach's niece. That's why I did the lobbying."

Amalia slowly raised her head and pushed her glasses up to meet Paloma's eyes.

"The girl's father is a religious fanatic," Paloma continued. "As you would know if you've ever seen him. And as you can probably imagine, he doesn't approve of how Serach's living her life. He can't bear the thought of me. But he temporarily ditched his scruples to ask his sister to help him get the best oncological care that New York has to offer."

Amalia had no idea where Paloma was headed. She glanced back down at the desk.

"What does that have to do with me, Paloma?" she said.

Paloma took a breath.

"Serach would love to keep tabs on the kid's progress," she said. "Which I obviously can't help her do, since I'm not the girl's nurse. Also, since I can't let Shoshana's father think that I am in any way involved. Just the thought of that would cause him to immediately snatch her out of here and install her in Maimonides Hospital, safe from my malevolent presence."

Amalia kept her gaze firmly on her paperwork. She didn't like where this was going at all.

"So I was wondering," Paloma forged ahead, "whether you could perhaps help me out? Keep an eye on the kid and then keep me in the loop about it, so I can give Serach periodic updates?"

Amalia finally had to lift her head.

"Paloma, I—"

"I don't want to see her chart or anything, Amalia. I know the rules. But you do supervise her nurse, don't you? You do have access to what's happening with her in ... general terms. You might even have some idea of what has gone on so far. Please, Amalia? Please share what you can? Serach is so pre-occupied and it's so hard for me to say 'no' to her."

Amalia sighed again. She was beginning to see where Paloma's reputation came from. It was hard to say 'no' to her as well.

"Let's go somewhere less public," she sighed, motioning them away from the nurses' station to a more secluded spot.

"As you say, I can't share particulars," Amalia began, carefully. "Only things that I'm sure you already know. Like what happens when children first arrive with that potential diagnosis."

"Refresh my memory. I haven't thought about what happens to children for years."

"A child admitted to rule out A.L.L.," Amalia continued, in the tone she used when training her staff, "gets an immediate bone marrow aspirate and a biopsy. Then a spinal tap. Then a first dose of chemo. Then a port-o-cath inserted into her chest to make it easier to deliver fluids and drugs and to obtain blood samples, over time. Why are you shutting your eyes, Paloma?"

Paloma—who had dealt with many a port-o-cath in her day—found herself fiercely pushing away the image of a hole being dug into the soft pale chest of Serach's miniature double.

"You're a stronger soul than me, Amalia," she said, taking a breath. "I'm no fan of kids, as you know—it's why I don't work on this floor. And, like I said, I'm no fan of this particular kid's father. But she's only three and a half. Barely. The idea of someone so young..."

Amalia gave her colleague a small empathetic smile.

"The fact that she's so young is actually a good thing," she said. "We have a remarkable track record with children her age. Plus, we're a world leader on the frontiers of pediatric drug titration. As you must also know. Patients here have an excellent chance of avoiding the potentially damaging long-term effects of the treatment modalities we employ."

"Indeed." said Paloma. "Which is why our niece is here."

She gave Amalia her best smile and continued.

"So ... what more can you tell me?"

"Nothing, Paloma. That's truly as far as I can go."

But Paloma had heard the crack in her colleague's voice and pressed forward.

"Look, Amalia," she continued, slowly. "I know that you can't tell me the results of those initial procedures, and I'm not going to ask you for them. But surely, you've walked by the kid's room from time to time and gotten a glimpse of her. Or seen her in the halls. Surely, you've talked with her nurse. Gotten some basic impressions of how she is doing."

Amalia shook her head.

"Oh, please, Amalia. Just some impressions. No one can get on your case for that."

"Well, I guess I can tell you one thing, because it's pretty much general knowledge around here," Amalia sighed. "Her nurse is in total awe of her. Says she's the smartest, bravest little trouper she's ever met."

She glanced up at Paloma and saw an expression of such relief and—yes—such pride on her colleague's face that she couldn't help herself.

"Okay, Paloma. I tell you what. Why don't you and I just take a little stroll down to your niece's room so you can have a look for yourself? The door is usually open."

"Oh, no—not that, Amalia! That really is going too far. Too risky, altogether."

"Not if you're with me. We're just two colleagues taking a little tour of the seventh floor."

"I'm not talking about the risks from our supervisors. I'm talking about the risks of running into the father."

"Oh, no worries about that. He never arrives before 9:00 p.m.— long past the time that the girl generally goes to sleep. Then he takes off again by 6:00 a.m.— generally before she wakes up. It's his older sister who's here during the long stretch in-between. When everything tends to happen. When someone is really needed."

Paloma snorted.

"Naturally," she said. "Can't expect the greatest scholar of all time to bother with the heavy lifting."

"Well," said Amalia. "The way the aunt explains it, it's because he is obligated to go to synagogue to pray three times a day. He'd be out as much as he was in if he took the day shift. Women aren't mandated to do that, so the aunt is able to provide a steadier presence."

"How convenient when a religion keeps men free from the main burdens of child-rearing," said Paloma, before realizing what she'd just said—and coloring. Hadn't she constructed her own life in such a way as to ensure that same freedom, after all?

"Well, be that as it may," said Amalia, ignoring Paloma's blush. "The point is that you have nothing to worry about. The father won't be there right now. It will be the aunt. Unless it's possible that she'll recognize you, as well."

Paloma shook her head.

"She has no idea who I am. It's just a fluke that Shmuely— that the father—does. Serach is dead as far as all her other siblings are concerned. And I've never as much as existed."

"Okay, then. She's nice, by the way, the aunt. Seems to get along very well with the little girl and also with everyone on staff here. She comes to the nurse's station to ask questions from time to time, and they're always good questions. Concerned but not hysterical."

Paloma nodded.

"Come on," said Amalia. "Let's go see how they're both doing."

She led Paloma down the corridor, past the operating and procedure rooms, past the rooms for the child-life specialists and the teachers who help patients keep up with their schoolwork. Past the on-site pharmacy, the computer room, the toy room, the art room, and the parents' lounge.

Eventually they arrived at the corridor with all the individual patients' rooms and walked down to the far end.

As Amalia had predicted, the door was wide open and sunlight was streaming in from the flimsily-shaded windows, illuminating every detail of that interior space.

On a chair off to one side sat a tall, thin, kerchiefed woman dressed in a long dark skirt and big-sleeved white blouse. Her track-shoe-clad feet were planted firmly on the ground and her face bent closely over a little book.

On the other side—on a hospital bed cluttered with gadgets and levers and tubes—sat a tiny, curly-haired girl in a tiny pink hospital gown, playing with a set of enormous lavender and white pop-beads. She was pushing the beads together into long strings and then popping them apart again, an expression of fierce concentration on her face. A perfect pared-down version of her Aunt Serach wrestling with some challenging accounting issue.

Paloma stood mesmerized until the sheer magnetism of her regard drew Shoshi's face upward to meet it. Startled and embarrassed, Paloma ducked back behind the doorframe and Shoshi immediately burst into a peal of giggles.

Paloma turned away, but then—unable to help herself—peered in a second time. Shoshi once again raised her eyes from the pop beads, Paloma darted back, and Shoshi let out another peal.

"She's playing peekaboo with you," said Amalia, smiling.

Paloma gave her a puzzled look.

"Peekaboo. You know. Peekaboo?"

Paloma shrugged.

"Goodness, Paloma. Don't you know what peekaboo is? Didn't your mother ever play it with you?"

"No."

"Well, the rules are pretty simple. You appear, you disappear, the kid giggles. Go on! Do it again! Or just use your hands. You cover your face – then you uncover it...."

Paloma peered around the doorframe and then darted dramatically out of sight. The giggles surged and Beile stood up, walked to the door, and peered out at the two nurses.

"What's going on? Is Shoshi due for another procedure, *chas v'cholileh*?"

"No," said Amalia. "We're just playing peekaboo with her."

"I didn't know that was part of the standard hospital routine."

"It's not, we're just...."

"Well come on in already if this is just a friendly visit. We could use some distraction."

Amalia strode forward and Paloma trailed behind her. Paloma looked at Shoshi, covered her face briefly with her hands and then pulled them away and Shoshi clapped her hands together and giggled louder than ever.

"Are you going to be Shoshi's new nurse? I haven't seen you before," said Beile.

"No, I'm not. I'm just ... I was just...looking around."

"Well, now that you're here, get a good look. What's your name?"

"Paloma."

"That's a funny name," came a voice from Shoshi's bed. It was as sweet as her giggles.

"No, it is not," said Paloma.

"Yes, it is! What does it mean?" said the girl.

"What do you mean, 'what does it mean'?" asked Paloma.

"My name means 'lily,'" said the girl. "What does Paloma mean?"

"It means 'dove,'" said Paloma, slowly. "Do you know what a dove is?"

"Like Noah's dove?"

Paloma nodded, looking fixedly at the child.

"Yes. I guess. Like Noah's dove."

"Then where's your rainbow? Noah's dove brought a rainbow! Where's yours?"

"I don't have it with me today," Paloma said, taking in the girl's quick-wittedness with wonder. "But next time I come, I'll bring it."

"Watch out—she'll remember that you promised," said Beile. Her eyes emitted a quick, faint blast of mischief. "She'll hold you to it."

Brooklyn

- 5 -

"Can I help?" asked Serach as she moved toward the kitchen table.

Paloma, frazzled and sweaty, shoved a stack of plates out of the way, hauled a sheet pan of turkey parts out of the oven and onto a trivet on that table, and turned to her partner.

"Yes," she said. "Stand guard at the front door and—when the others arrive, which will happen any moment now—keep them out of my way. I need at least a half hour more to finish everything up and I can't function with people crowding all around me."

Serach nodded and—right on cue—the doorbell rang and she went to answer it.

"Hey, Tía," said Negrito, leaving a trail of some delicious aftershave behind him as he breezed in to plant a firm kiss on one of Serach's cheeks. Gloria followed suit—though she expanded the gesture to include a parallel kiss on Serach's other cheek. Gordito came in last and immediately wriggled his way in between them all to pull his aunt firmly toward him and squeeze her tight.

"Paloma is still in the kitchen," said Serach, gently prying herself free from his arms. "She's not ready for us. Why don't you all go off into the living room and wait?"

"Don't be silly," said Gloria. "I'll go in and help her."

"I'll come with you," said Negrito.

"Me too," said Gordito.

"No, it's—Paloma doesn't—" began Serach, but they were already three quarters of the way into the kitchen before she had finished.

"Oh, well."

Paloma shook her head at their entrance but she didn't kick them out. Gordito soon found himself transferring the rice from its pot to a serving dish while Gloria expertly skinned and sliced the turkey and placed the slices on a second clean, well-parchmented sheet pan.

"Okay, team," said Paloma once she had inspected Gordito's serving and Gloria's slicing and found it all adequate. "You've been a big help and I thank you, but now I need you to get out of here. I mean it. The last procedures for this meal are both crucial and precise and I'll need to concentrate."

She strode to the pot on the front burner, reached for the mixing spoon and gave the contents a few brisk stirs before beginning to ladle it over the turkey. No one moved.

"Out!" she said to Negrito again. "Out!" she snapped at Gordito.

"Huh-uh," said Gloria, standing stanchly by the stove. "We're not moving—at least, I'm not moving—till you spill all the secrets of this feast. It's a real *mole poblano de guajolote* that you're making, isn't it?"

"Gloria..." said Paloma.

"Please! I am so curious! It smells so divine! You are so wonderful to do all this for us!"

Paloma took her time wiping her hands on the dishtowel that was hanging on the oven door.

"All right," she finally said. "But only if you listen carefully because I won't say it twice. You need twenty-six different ingredients for this dish, including four kinds of chile, several types of seeds, nuts and spices, and the authentic chocolate of Mexico that you can only get in certain parts of the South Bronx. Or maybe in Sunset Park. You need to carry out just about every cooking process ever invented—soaking, chopping, toasting, grinding, boiling, sauté-ing, deep-frying, baking, and broiling. You need to do it in a very special order."

Gloria looked suitably enthralled.

"And of course," concluded Paloma, "you need all the fine instincts of a master chef to successfully carry it off."

She gave a small, mock-modest smile.

"Now please! Move yourselves into the living room and let me finish up!"

Negrito walked up close to his aunt, put his arm around her.

"I'm impressed as hell, Tía, and it smells like some truly heavenly shit. But really—there was no need to go all out on this ethnic stuff. Gloria's people are not fresh-off-the-boat Mexicans. They're Texans, through and through. They wear ten-gallon hats and cowboy boots, for God's sake. If you wanted authenticity, you could have just ordered in from Dallas Jones Bar-B-Q."

"Shut up, Oscar," said Gloria. "I think it's perfectly lovely that Paloma is honoring my roots like this."

She paused.

"What's more, *Querido*," she added, "Mole Poblano is not 'ethnic stuff.' It's haute cuisine."

Negrito gave a little shrug.

"Whatever," he said. "Just saying."

He leaned over to give Paloma a conciliatory kiss on the cheek. Paloma brushed it off with the back of her knuckles.

"You're right about one thing, however, Gloria," Negrito added, ignoring his aunt's rebuke. "Tía Paloma is most definitely a marvel. She never disappoints."

Paloma glowered at him, he smiled beguilingly back at her, and—looping one hand around Gloria's waist and the other over Gordito's shoulder—he escorted them both out of the room.

The next arrival in the kitchen was Frank, who ambled in just as Paloma was returning the turkey to the oven and turning the gas up to "broil" for the turkey's final browning.

"I thought this was supposed to be a major celebratory event," he said. "An event so important that you asked me to postpone the recital part of the evening for a good hour, so that you-all would have enough time to rejoice."

He cleared his throat.

"Yet, I just peeked into the living room and nobody is acting the least bit joyful. The nephews are plopped down on the couch, looking bored. Serach is sitting on one of the Louis Quinze chairs, staring into the distance. And Gloria—the person evidently responsible for all the fuss—is standing all by her lonesome, solemn as a nun, inspecting your wall of Virgin Mary portraits. I find myself bewildered."

"Frank, please stop complaining," Paloma sighed. "Gloria was desperate to get the family together for whatever it is that she's announcing, and this was the only evening that everyone was free. Anyway, there's no reason you can't begin playing a bit later than usual tonight, because—for once—we don't have to worry about getting Frayda home at a decent time. She called up a little while ago to say that she won't be able to attend—even if we start the music at nine instead of at eight. She has to stay late at work to help with some dental emergency."

"You mean my performance will just be just for you and Serach?" Frank said, making a face. "What kind of recital will it be without Frayda here? We will have to re-schedule."

"I was actually going to suggest that," Paloma grinned, as she took in just how much Frank had grown to value their friend's presence. "Frayda was totally devastated about having to miss it—kept saying how it was just because the patient is ninety-three and he has this heart condition and the procedure can take hours and it will require all sorts of post-operative monitoring and yada-yada-yada."

She shook her head.

"I'll call her after dinner to say we're postponing. She'll be thrilled."

"So ... what do you think Gloria's going to announce?" Frank asked, temporarily placated. "Do we hear the tinkle of wedding bells? Will dear old Aunt Paloma be serving as matron of honor, all dolled up in some hot pink, totally over-the-top dress?"

"I suppose that it's possible—minus the totally over-the-top-hot-pink part. Gloria has an impeccable sense of style. As you know."

Paloma opened the oven door again and peered in.

"I'm very happy for them if that's what it is," she said, squinting at the turkey. "And I hope to God that it finally spurs them to move out of my brother's house. I can't imagine how they've put up with living in Gordito's old bedroom all this time. Or with living under the same roof as Beatriz, for that matter. Of course, I also sometimes wonder how Gloria puts up with Negrito."

"Well, he's clearly someone who is going places," murmured Frank. "That can be very persuasive. Then, of course, there's the matter of his breathtakingly good looks and utterly intoxicating scent. I might have trouble resisting him myself, under the right circumstances."

Paloma reached into the oven, carefully extracted the sheet pan, placed it on the counter and began transferring its contents to a serving dish.

"Okay, *Viejo Verde*, TMI," she muttered. "Anyway, we'll know what they are up to soon enough. Meanwhile, why don't you make yourself useful by setting the table and then bringing out the food platters and rounding everyone up?"

Frank sighed audibly and reached for the silverware drawer.

"Always with the demands," he said. But he did what he was asked.

Judith's dining room had not been so splendidly decked out since the days when the leading opera stars of New York had routinely convened there for a post-performance supper.

The crystal goblets shone, the Limoges plates and serving dishes gleamed cobalt blue and gold, the linens were pristinely pressed, the silverware glinted. In an act of reckless generosity Frank had even bolted upstairs, retrieved the vase of white roses that he kept permanently fresh on his nightstand, and placed it dead center on the tablecloth.

"Come in, everyone!" he said, poking his head into the living room once everything was set up and he'd had time to sufficiently admire his handiwork. "Dinner is served!"

He then strode to the head of the table and took his seat.

Negrito took the chair immediately to his left, Gloria at his side. Gordito and Serach took the seats to his right. Paloma emerged a few moments later—the two last serving dishes in hand—and sat down beside Gloria. She began passing around the platters of food, while Serach sprang up to pour the water and wine.

Once everyone had everything they needed, they all clinked glasses and then no one said another word for a very long time.

"Well, Tía," Negrito finally sighed, as he rubbed a tortilla vigorously around his plate one last time, polished it off, and gave a small, gentlemanly belch, "I must say that you have totally outdone yourself. I have never eaten anything so delicious in all my life. On behalf of myself, my brother, and the lovely Gloria, let me thank you. I also take back everything mean that I have ever said about your menu planning or choice of cuisine."

"Okay, *Pendejo*, you're forgiven for your stupidity and your rudeness," said Paloma. "But only because I love you so dearly."

She then gazed around the room.

"Are we all done for now?" she asked.

Several people nodded, and Gordito—reaching once again for the turkey platter—said, "I'm not, but never mind me."

"Then enough with the suspense. Gloria? You've called us all together. Now tell us why. What monumental announcement do you have to make?"

Negrito made a grand gesture out of putting his arm around Gloria's shoulders while she gave a small, deep smile and looked down for a moment at the tablecloth.

"We're pregnant," she said.

Gordito gasped and clapped his hands. Paloma and Frank grinned at each other.

"Bingo!" said Frank. "We suspected something like that, didn't we, Paloma dear? So when is the wedding? Or am I sounding totally dated, talking about marriage to you modern folks?"

"Oh," said Gloria, looking hard at Negrito for a moment. "We are definitely getting married."

"So which church will it be held in? Which reception hall will you be renting? Should I be getting my tux dry-cleaned for the occasion?"

"No need for that, Frank," said Gloria, softly—still looking at Negrito. "We're just going to go to City Hall. The officiant, two witnesses, and us. Maybe a party, sometime later on. We—"

"We don't need all that bougie crap to prove we're committed to one another," interjected Negrito. "We're saving all our money to invest into our start-ups."

Frank turned his gaze slowly toward Gloria and conjured up an image of her swanning her way down the aisle of some lovely little church in some glorious minimalist frock—like a second Carolyn Bessette. He sighed loudly at the opportunity lost.

Was there an echo of similar regret within Gloria's sleekly chignoned head? Hard to tell.

"Please, Frank," said Serach. "Please, everyone. The proper response to Gloria's wonderful news is not a bunch of silly questions. It's simply: '*Mazel tov!*' And perhaps—if someone is feeling particularly forward: 'When is the baby due?'"

Gloria looked up at Serach with gratitude.

"Thank you, Serach," she said. "He's due in four months. And yes, it's a 'he'—at least for now. We wanted you and Paloma—and Roberto, of course—to be the first to know. Even before my parents. Or Beatriz."

Gordito gave a grunt.

"We also," said Negrito, beaming, "wanted to ask Tía Paloma about doing something for us before we move on to tell Gloria's parents."

Paloma gave Gloria a startled glance.

"I thought we were going to do that part after dinner, Oscar," Gloria murmured, her undertone fierce. "In private. In case…"

"In case what?" said Negrito, blithely. "This is my Tía Paloma we're talking about. You can ask her anything. In front of anyone. Besides, we're all family, here."

Gloria took a breath and relaxed her glare.

"Okay, Oscar," she said. "You know her best. But let me do it."

She looked straight at Paloma, black eyes to black eyes.

"We want—I want—you to be our son's *madrina*," she said, half challenge and half plea.

Frank raised an eyebrow to Negrito: "*Madrina?*" he mouthed.

"Godmother," said Negrito, and Frank promptly burst out laughing.

"I love it!" he giggled. "Gloria, you are a genius! Paloma—a godmother!"

But Paloma was shaking her head.

"I don't ... I mean ... I don't even know what a godmother does!"

"Really? Didn't you have one?" asked Gloria.

"I barely had a real mother."

"The godmother is the person who oversees a child's Catholic upbringing," said Frank, folding his hands and looking beatific as a choirboy. "Makes sure that he stays on the Right Path."

Paloma looked up at him sharply and then turned her gaze to Gloria.

"I'm not the person to do that, Gloria. I'm hardly a functioning Catholic, myself."

"Of course you are, dear," said Frank. "Your faith has been jostled a bit, of late, but your core love for the Blessed Virgin Mother—and hers for you—is ... inviolable."

Paloma shivered and looked away.

"I will confess that religion is not really my thing, either," Gloria said, looking curiously at Paloma. "Nor is it Oscar's. But we—at least, I—wanted to..."

"Hedge your bets?" said Frank.

"I guess you could put it that way. Mostly, however, it's an act of appeasement."

She paused.

"My parents and I ... we don't see eye-to-eye on many things. They hate New York. They think fashion is frivolous. They were appalled that I applied to FIT—and that I got in.

They have no respect for my dreams for *Alta Costura—Alta Ambición*. Their big dream for me was that I should stay in Corpus Christi, get a business degree from Del Mar College, marry a local boy in our local Catholic church, and go work for Sam Kane Beef Processors, like everyone else in that town. They might have expected me to end up someplace in management there, with my college degree and all. But that's about as far as their ambitions for me might reach."

She paused again.

"After much time and many battles, they finally accepted that I wanted to go away for school and that I didn't marry that local boy," she sighed. "It's going to be tough reconciling them to the fact that Oscar and I don't want a traditional church wedding. The least I can offer them is the reassurance that our son will have a godmother. That—"

"That you haven't turned your back completely on Our-Lord-Jesus-Christ," said Frank, slipping into the drawl that was never too far away from his speech. "Wise move when dealing with folk in that part of the world."

Negrito gave him a grin of appreciation, and Gloria looked down.

"Tía," she eventually resumed, turning to face Paloma directly. "I've felt that we were on the same page in so many ways from the first time that I met you, under that terrible downpour, at your poor brother's funeral. And tonight, when I stood in your living room and saw all those Virgin Mary's smiling down at me, my feelings were confirmed. You clearly love the BVM as deeply—as naturally—as I do, even as we both reject certain other aspects of our religion."

She smiled.

"And the fact that those Mary's were interspersed with all those saucy nudes only made me more certain of our shared views about who is who and what is worthy of attention and what can be safely cast aside. I'm sure that whatever tenets of Catholicism you choose to pass on to our son, I will be comfortable with them. Which is what Oscar thinks too. Don't you, Oscar?"

"Yeah," said Negrito. "Tía Paloma and I don't agree about everything, but she's definitely the coolest person I know."

"So please—won't you at least consider it? Please?"

Paloma nodded briefly—almost imperceptibly—and then looked quickly away.

How could Gloria claim to understand Paloma's feelings about Catholicism right then? About how her once rock-solid faith in the BVM had been ground to dust within the Church of St. Nicholas of Tolentine after seeking out Mary's tender comfort and finding only a plaster statue with cold, empty eyes? How—ever since then—Paloma had taken to avoiding any and all representations of the Madonna (including, even, those familiar, beloved portraits on her own living-room wall) for fear of registering the same chilling indifference within their gaze?

No, Paloma sighed. Gloria couldn't possibly know anything about all that. Nor was she eager to enlighten her. Certainly not that evening, when the girl's radiant hopes were suffusing the room.

"Are we finally all finished?" she asked, instead, looking at Gordito.

He nodded.

"Would anyone like coffee? Should I bring in the dessert?"

She then stacked all the dinner dishes and carried them swiftly out of the room—along with orders for three coffees and five flans.

Gloria shot a startled glance at Serach.

"Did she just agree to do it or not?" she asked.

"She did," said Serach. "But you have to give her some time to digest it all."

Gloria nodded.

"Well," said Frank brightly, after a brief silence. "Anyone else have anything to add?"

There was a long silence but finally Gordito spoke up.

"I do," he said, louder than necessary.

He cleared his throat.

"I miss my little brother," he continued. "I miss Anteojitos. I want to know how he is. I want to see him. He finally came back into our family, and now he's gone again. He should have been here today to hear that he's going to be an uncle."

No one said a word for a moment, but Serach leaned toward Gordito, put her arm around him and rested her head against his shoulder.

Before anyone could say anything further however, the doorbell rang, Paloma appeared with the tray of dessert dishes and coffees, and Serach let Gordito go, stood up, and went to see who could possibly be arriving at that hour.

A moment later she re-appeared in the doorway with Frayda perched on her arm, panting slightly and sweating a great deal.

"Am I too late for the music?" she asked, looking shyly around her at the crowd.

"Absolutely not!" said Frank, standing at her entrance. "We were just about to eat dessert. After which everyone not directly involved in the recital will depart—leaving you, me, Serach, and Paloma to revel in Bach and Ravel."

Negrito took a long, curious look at the scrawny, drab woman hesitating in the doorway. He tilted his head toward Frank and raised one eyebrow.

Frank—pleased at Negrito's acknowledgement of his insiders' expertise—beamed back at him.

"You are quite right to ask what is going on, Oscar. Let me make some introductions."

He waved his hand in an arc that took in the two brothers and Gloria.

"Oscar? Roberto? Gloria? The lovely lady who just arrived here is Frayda Goldblatt. She's a dear family friend. She is also the guardian angel who has taken Ramon under her wing as he finds his way within his new world. Take note of her, Roberto. She holds the keys to your brother's happiness."

He nodded at Frayda and continued: "Meanwhile, Frayda, these two young men are Paloma and Serach's nephews. Oscar and Roberto. Older brothers to Ramon. And the lovely young woman to Oscar's left is Oscar's fiancée, Gloria."

He paused and looked benevolently around, before catching himself.

"But—silly me—what am I doing leaving you just standing there like a flagless flagpole in the wind, dear Frayda?" he said. "Come in and join us."

He rushed to the foot of the table, pulled out the last available chair, and swept his hand toward it. Frayda regarded him for a moment, inched toward the chair, and lowered herself down as everyone else returned to the gratifying task of savoring Paloma's dessert.

When all had finished, Frank stood up once more.

"Well," he said, "I think we are finally ready to move on. Frayda, Serach, Paloma—into the living room! Everyone else—say your fond farewells!"

"I guess that's our cue," said Gloria, watching him sweep off toward his piano. She stood as well, took Negrito's hand to coax him to his feet, and walked over to Serach.

"Thank you for giving me such a warm welcome, Tía," she said, giving her a kiss. "I'm so glad to be joining a family that has you in it."

"Goodness!" replied Serach, returning the kiss. "Well, the feeling is mutual—and I can't wait to be a great aunt!"

She then headed for the living room, while Gloria floated toward Paloma.

"Tia, I need to thank you for everything that you did for us tonight," she said, hugging her aunt gently. "It was all so lovely—so right. I only hope that you'll…"

Paloma cut Gloria off with a raised hand and a small smile, kissed her vaguely on the cheek, disengaged herself and turned to follow Serach.

Frayda meanwhile sat frozen in place for a moment, narrowing her eyes at Gordito—who was still rocking from foot to foot, looking perturbed. She rose from her chair and marched up to him.

"You mustn't worry about your little brother, young man" she said, giving him her fiercest stare. "Not for one single moment. Ramon is doing just fine. Better than he ever has."

Gordito gave her a sideways glance, rocked some more, then looked away again.

"He has everything that he needs," Frayda continued. "And if he ever should want for something, I will be there to make sure that he gets it. I will also be there," she added, "to get help him find his way again, whenever he loses it. He tends to do that, you know."

She gave Gordito one of her rare full smiles.

"He listens to me," she said definitively, and then turned and headed for the living room.

Gordito stood silently in place till he felt another firm hand on his shoulder.

"Party's over, Hermano," said Negrito, as he gently but firmly began steering Gordito and Gloria toward the front door. "We need to get out of here. And listen—stop worrying about our little brother. If Frank says that that Frayda person is Anteojitos' guardian angel, then she's his guardian angel. He'll be okay."

Gordito gave his brother a disbelieving look and Negrito grinned.

"Yeah, I know," Negrito continued, as he opened the door and ushered his brother and fiancée out. "She looks like something the cat dragged in and Frank's a total *pajaro*. But the man knows a thing or two. Trust me."

Frank, meanwhile, had installed himself on his piano bench—spine straight and feet poised just above the pedals—while Serach and Paloma took their places on the sofa just across from him and Frayda took the armchair to his left.

He spread the score open with one practiced hand, positioned his fingers over the keys, and lowered his feet. He drew a deep breath. He began to play.

Brooklyn and Manhattan

- 6 -

"Paloma, this is Serach speaking. Don't tell me that there's nothing wrong. You've been pacing back and forth like a caged leopard ever since taking that call. Please. Sit down and drink your coffee before it grows stone cold. Then tell me what's bothering you."

Paloma stopped moving, but she didn't sit down and she didn't immediately respond.

"Serach, please," she finally said, turning to her partner. "You'd pace, too, if people kept bugging you to do things you didn't want to do. What's wrong with them, anyway?"

"Paloma, are you still fuming about Gloria asking you to be her son's godmother? Was that who was on the phone again?"

"No. I mean yes. I mean, yes, I'm still fuming. But no, that wasn't Gloria."

"Well, then, who was it and what did they ask you to do?"

Paloma bit her lip.

"It was Amalia," she said, after a long pause during which she searched in vain for a way to avoid going any further without actually bending the truth.

"Amalia—the Nurse Manager on Shoshi's ward?" asked Serach, suddenly blanching. "Why did she call? Is there bad news about Shoshi?"

"Serach, calm down. Your niece is fine," said Paloma—but carefully. Amalia's daily progress reports, while far from dire, had never been one hundred percent encouraging. Shoshi had yet to turn a real corner. "Or as fine as she can be, under the circumstances," she added.

"Then what? What did Amalia want? What did she ask you to do?"

Paloma sighed.

The problem right now wasn't telling Serach about Shoshi's reports. That could wait—should wait—till everything was a bit further along and clearer. No. The challenge was presenting the sticky new issue raised by Amalia's call. The issue that Serach had so clearly picked up on and couldn't be distracted away from. Serach could be a real bulldog when she spotted something in need of clarification. It was one of the reasons she was so good at parsing a tax return.

Paloma lifted her cup took a sip, made a face, and placed it back in its saucer.

"Okay, so I haven't been entirely honest with you about Amalia and Shoshi," she began. "Jesus, Serach! Don't give me the evil eye."

She tried a second sip and gave up for good. Definitely stone cold. Serach continued glaring.

"Serach, please! It's not as if I've actually lied to you about anything. I've just omitted a few details—details that wouldn't have made much of a difference and that could have made things really complicated and ... Serach! Let me explain myself."

Serach stood, walked to the kitchen window, and stayed there with her back to Paloma. How could Paloma have held back anything related to Shoshi—no matter how small— knowing the agony she'd been in?

"Please, Serach," said Paloma. "Don't be so quick to condemn me. Just listen, okay?"

"I am listening. I just don't want to look at you."

Paloma grinned.

"Okay, fair enough. So, one day—right at the beginning of this whole ordeal—Amalia asks if I want to see your niece for myself. I didn't want to do it. I really didn't. But she kept asking and eventually she wore me down so I went with her to take a peek."

Serach drew a breath.

"It was just going to be a peek—I swear it—but then your sister catches me at it and orders me to come in and introduce myself."

"You must have been peeking particularly hard," said Serach, finally turning partway round.

"Or maybe she's just a real *yenta*, your sister," Paloma countered. "Has to know everybody's business at all times."

Serach didn't intend to loosen the tight line of her mouth, but she couldn't help herself. She had no idea that Paloma even knew that word—let alone when and how to use it.

Paloma smiled back knowingly. She decided there was nothing to lose by giving a blow-by-blow description of what had happened up there in Shoshi's room—and she knew she was right when she reached the part about the rainbow and Serach spun fully around and clapped.

"But that's just what I would have asked when I was her age!" she exclaimed. "Shmuely, too! What did you answer her?"

"I told her that I didn't have my rainbow with me right then but that I'd bring it the next time I came."

She paused.

"Then I left. Before anyone could ask anything else."

"And then?"

"Then nothing."

"You didn't go back there after you said you would?"

"No, I did not. I only saw her that once."

"But why not? Why didn't you go back?"

Paloma remained silent.

"Paloma—she must have been expecting you all this time! How long has it been since you made that promise?"

It had been two and a half weeks. Paloma took her time answering.

"Serach, I just couldn't do it," she finally said, quietly. "I couldn't go back there. That little girl—that niece of yours—looks just like you did when you were so ill. Those same great gray eyes. That same pale face. That same frail little frame. Those same golden curls. Except that she's not twenty, she's only three. Just like you said when you first told me about her. Three years old and having to deal with everything she's going through!"

She swallowed.

"When I first saw her, they had basically just started all the tests and procedures. By now, they'll be in full swing. She'll be even weaker than she was when I first saw her. All her hair will have fallen out. Shit, Serach. Those curls! Those beautiful curls!"

She closed her eyes.

"I haven't wanted to—haven't been able to..."

Serach came back to the table and sat down, right next to her partner.

"Which is also the reason I didn't tell you anything about meeting her," Paloma added, after a moment. "I knew that if I did, you'd start doing exactly what you're doing now. Telling me to go back. Asking how she looks—asking me how she seems. I couldn't. Just couldn't."

Serach put her hand on Paloma's.

"So what happened just now? What does all that have to do with Amalia's call?"

"Amalia called to say that I was evidently a real hit with your niece," Paloma sighed. "That she keeps asking for me."

Serach smiled back at her.

"But why would she do that?" asked Paloma. "I only met her that one time! And barely."

"I'm afraid I understand," answered Serach, drily. "You tend to have that effect."

Paloma shrugged.

"Anyway," she continued, "it seems that being that the kid liked me so much, Beile wants me to come and babysit her this evening, so that she—Beile—can attend this prayer service that they're offering in the first-floor chapel of the hospital to anyone who's interested. What did she say it was called? Kol something? It sounded familiar. Maybe I heard about it when I was working at Maimonides? Maybe you've told me about it?"

"*Kol Nidre*," said Serach, nodding. "It's the opening service for the holiday of Yom Kippur—the Day of Atonement—which is the holiest day in the whole Jewish calendar. So sure, I've probably mentioned it to you at some point."

She sighed before going on.

"It's a really moving service, besides being so important. It's where we begin making our last serious plea for forgiveness—begin begging God to inscribe us in the Book of Life for another year."

She swallowed, while she thought about Shoshi's chances.

"The tune used in the service's central prayer is really haunting," she finally went on. "And the whole thing opens with this provocative proclamation that 'it is permissible to pray in the company of sinners.'"

She swallowed again.

"When I was young, I didn't understand what all that meant or why it was necessary to proclaim it, but over time I realized that it's there because if we were allowed to skip out so as not to be caught sitting with sinners, no one would show up. And then where would our community be? So it is better for everyone to stop obsessing about whether they are sitting next to some transgressor, to just focus on their own failings, and to leave the task of sin-counting to God."

She drew a breath while Paloma refrained from pointing out that Shmuely would do well to live by that code.

"There's a little synagogue just across Ocean Parkway," Serach continued, "that's run by this Hasidic sect that tries to bring all Jews back into the Orthodox fold by offering super-easy-to-attend services. You don't need be a member or reserve seats or anything. You just walk in and sit down."

She hesitated again before forging onward.

"When I first moved in here with you and was still a bit … homesick for certain things," she finally added in a musing—almost dreamy—tone, "there were times when I felt tempted to take advantage of those open doors. The longing got pretty intense around *Kol Nidre* time."

"For heavens' sake, Serach!" said Paloma, coloring. "You should have gone! I wouldn't have stopped you. In fact—you should go tonight, if you like."

Serach looked up abruptly. It was so unlike Paloma to suggest such a thing.

"Goodness," she replied, after a moment. "Well, thanks, but I couldn't just do that. I'd have to prepare myself."

She gave the beginnings of a grin.

"And even were I fully prepared," she continued, grinning further, "I don't know that I could do it alone. I might have to ask you to come, too. You know—for moral support?"

Paloma looked back at her, startled, and Serach allowed her to squirm a bit before continuing.

"No worries, love," she finally relented. "I won't do it. Certainly not tonight. Not when you have something so much more important to do."

Paloma remained silent.

"Well? Don't you? Aren't you going to go off to the hospital to take care of Shoshi? Didn't you tell Amalia 'yes'?"

Paloma drew a breath.

"No, I did not," she answered.

Serach raised an eyebrow.

"Well, heck, Serach—why should I? Aren't there—like— eighteen other sisters in your family who could do it far better than I could?"

"Just three," said Serach, calmly. "All of whom will want to go to tonight's services, themselves. None of whom would be permitted to commute into Manhattan on a religious holiday. And—most importantly—none of whom would be anywhere near as appealing to Shoshi as a beautiful nurse who's promised to give her a rainbow."

Serach reached across the table and took both of Paloma's hands in hers.

"Paloma." she said. "Call Amalia back and say that you'll be there. Put on your scrubs, so you'll look the same as you did the first time that Shoshi saw you—and go.

Paloma shook her head.

"If you won't do it for Beile or for Shoshi," said Serach, "then do it for me. If even that isn't enough, then do it because it's the right thing to do."

Paloma turned her face away from those pleading, accusatory eyes for a long moment before forcing herself to look back.

"Okay," she said. "Okay."

The late afternoon sunlight was just beginning to dim through the various floor-to-ceiling windows of the Pediatric Department when Paloma got off the elevator—scrubs, cap, and mask in place—to find her way down the hall with all the patients' rooms.

Before she took that last turn, however, she stopped in at the Art Room.

It was empty, save for a very thin, very white-skinned girl—perhaps ten years old—seated at one of the tables next to a woman who must have been her mother. The girl was wearing a bubble-gum-pink sweat suit and a Mets cap over what was clearly a hairless head. She was determinedly pounding a piece of clay into a flat, nearly perfect circle, crushing it back up into a ball, and then pounding it out again.

"Hi," said Paloma, sitting down on the girl's other side.

The girl didn't respond, though the mother gave Paloma a brief piercing stare.

"I was wondering if you could do me a favor."

The girl looked up at her for a moment and then, quickly, down again.

"I was wondering if you could draw me a rainbow," continued Paloma. "I am ashamed to say I don't know the right order of the colors. But I bet you do."

The girl nodded, almost unwillingly. The mother relaxed her gaze.

"Of course I do," the girl muttered. "Any moron knows the order."

Paloma blinked but maintained her calmly seductive tone.

"If I brought you a piece of paper and some magic markers, would you be willing to do it for me? Make me a nice big rainbow in the right color order?"

The mother gently nudged her daughter.

"Of course she would," she said. "Emma! This nice nurse is asking you for a favor. You needn't be rude to her. You know you love rainbows."

The girl shrugged.

"Sure," she said, smashing the clay down even more forcefully than before.

Paloma brought over the paper and markers and Emma pulled them in front of her and slowly and deliberately began uncapping the markers.

"Purple. Indigo. Blue. Green. Yellow. Orange. Red," she said as she uncapped each one and lined them up in a row. She then pinched her lips together and drew and filled in each colored arc with precision.

"There," she said, handing Paloma the paper and recapping the markers as painstakingly as she had uncapped them. "Now you know the order of the colors."

"Now I'm not a moron anymore," said Paloma, smiling. "Thank you."

"I'm sorry for her rudeness," murmured the mother.

"Please! I'm sorry that she ... is having to go through all this," said Paloma. "She can't be feeling great."

Then she brought her head down toward the girl's ear.

"You've saved my life," she said. "Or, at least, my reputation. Thanks again."

The girl shrugged, Paloma clutched the picture she'd drawn, returned the markers to their box on the shelf, and began making her way down the hall toward Shoshi's room.

"*Baruch Ha-Shem*, you finally arrived!" said Beile, as Paloma leaned into the doorway. "I was beginning to lose hope. Shoshi, look who is here!"

Shoshi looked up and gave a mammoth sigh.

"My dove," she said, not yet ready to smile. "You never came back. Why didn't you come back?"

"But I did!" said Paloma. "I'm here!"

Shoshi was, in fact, now completely bald and she looked half the size that she had been only two and a half weeks previously. Paloma took a deep breath and walked up close.

"What's more—" she said, extending her hand to the child, "I've brought you your rainbow."

Shoshi took the drawing in her own small hand and regarded it.

"It's pretty," she said and Paloma took in another breath and let it out again very slowly.

"I'll be going now or I'll miss the opening, *chas v'cholileh*," said Beile, standing up, walking over to her niece, and drawing her hand gently across that small bald head. "The opening is the best part."

She turned to Paloma.

"I can't thank you enough. I'll be back as soon as it's over."

She turned back to Shoshi. "Be good, Shoshi. Be good with Nurse Paloma."

Shoshi nodded and her aunt bent down to kiss her before tightening the white turban around her own head, re-checking the buttons on her white sweater, and striding swiftly out the door.

"So," said Paloma, suddenly very self-conscious as she considered the next step. What the hell do you do with a three-and-a-half-year-old cancer patient, once you've given her a rainbow? What do you say to her? 'How are you?' 'How's the chemo going?' Sweet Jesus!

"Put my rainbow on the wall!" said Shoshi.

"Put it up where?" said Paloma, marveling at the strength with which the child had issued that command. "And with what? Do you have any thumb tacks? Any scotch tape?"

Shoshi shrugged.

Paloma looked around dazedly and then remembered where she was. *Silly me!* She marched over to the little supply cabinet in the corner of the room and pulled out a roll of surgical tape. She expertly tore off four pieces, doubled them into rings—sticky side out—and applied them to the four back corners of the drawing.

"Should we put it up here—on the wall behind your bed?" she said.

"No," said Shoshi. "Put it up over there! Put it over Tatteh's bed!"—and she pointed to a place on the wall over the cot directly across from her. "So I can see it!"

Paloma did as she was told and then turned to Shoshi again.

"Well..." she began. "Here we are. What's next? What would you like to do?"

"Tell me a story!" said Shoshi. "Tell me a story like Tatteh does!"

"What kind of stories does he tell?"

"Torah stories!"

Paloma bit her lip.

"Torah stories aren't really my thing," she said.

Shoshi looked at her with surprise. Then she got serious again

"So tell me a different story!"

Paloma shivered. What story could she possibly tell this child? Storytelling—particularly storytelling appropriate for children—had not been part of her life experience.

Then, suddenly, she recalled the time—years before—when her sister-in-law Beatriz had told her a story. A children's story. A little girl's story. Beatriz had done it with the intent of humiliating Paloma, but perhaps it didn't have to be done in that way.

"Actually, I do know one story," she said. "A Latina story."

"What's 'Latina'?"

Paloma gazed at the child, curiously. Well, why would she know such a thing, after all?

"Latina means something that's from ... Latin America. From the countries to the south of this one. It's where my people come from."

"I come from Israel."

"Yes, I know," Paloma said. "But my people come from a place called Latin America."

Shoshi said nothing.

"It's a story called *La Cucarachita Mandinga*."

"That's a funny name."

"No it's not. Well, maybe it is. I'll tell you what it means. A '*cucarachita*' is a little cockroach. Do you know what a cockroach is?"

Shoshi shook her head solemnly as Paloma sat down on the bed beside her.

"No, I bet you wouldn't. Not given the eat-off-the-floor cleanliness of your parents' house."

Shoshi was not surprised that Paloma knew all about the cleanliness of her home. Why shouldn't she? Grown-ups knew all sorts of things. There was no need, therefore, for Paloma to explain how she had bulldozed her way past Ruchel's poor housekeeper, Dalisay, so many years before, as she attempted to orchestrate a reconciliation between Shmuely and his broken-hearted oldest sister.

"A cockroach is a little brown bug," she continued.

"*Ichs*! Bugs! They're dirty."

"Not this one. This one was a very, very clean bug. And very, very pretty."

"Like you."

Paloma shook her head in amazement at the child—at those porcelain cheeks and those big gray lash-less eyes.

"No," she said after a moment. "Like you."

"And *Mandinga*?" asked Shoshi. "What does *Mandinga* mean?"

"*Mandinga* is an African name."

"What's 'African'?"

"Africa is another place—a continent of countries—far, far away from here. The *Mandigos* were a group of African people who were captured and brought to Latin America to be ... enslaved. Do you know what a slave is?"

"Yes!" said Shoshi, nodding hard. "We were slaves in Egypt!"

"So you were. Well, the *Mandingos* were enslaved in the Americas. But *La Cucarachita Mandinga* wasn't a slave. In fact, she was very proper little lady, living in a very nice house that she kept very, very clean. Like Dalisay keeps your house."

Shoshi nodded, again. Why shouldn't Paloma know Dalisay? Didn't everyone?

"So one day, *La Cucarachita Mandinga* was sweeping her living room when suddenly she saw a shiny coin on the floor, and she said: 'Oh my goodness! A coin that I didn't know I had! What should I buy with this coin? Should I buy some candy?' But then she thought: 'Oh, no! Not candy! I don't want to get fat!'"

Shoshi giggled.

"Then she thought: 'Well, then, should I buy some nice jewelry?' but then she remembered that a single coin wouldn't be enough money to buy nice jewelry. Jewelry is very expensive."

Shoshi nodded sagely. Her mother, her grandmother, and her grandfather all worked in the jewelry business. She had often heard how expensive that jewelry was. She looked up at Paloma and waited for her to tell her some more of the story.

"So," Paloma continued, "*La Cucarachita Mandinga* thought and thought and finally said. 'I know! I can buy myself a little tin of rouge and some lipstick and make myself even prettier than I am. Then, I can go sit on my front porch and see what happens.' So that is just what she did. She bought the rouge and the lipstick and she put them on and she went to sit down on her porch. And no sooner than she had done that, but who should come around but *Señor Perro*—Mr. Dog?"

She looked at Shoshi and arched her eyebrow and Shoshi responded just the way she wanted.

"Mr. Dog," she repeated, nodding.

"That's right. And Mr. Dog went right up to *La Cucarachita Mandinga* and said: 'Oh, *Cucarachita Mandinga*, how pretty you are! Would you like to be my wife?' And *La Cucarachita Mandinga* said: 'Well, that's all very nice, but how will you speak to me once we are married?' And Mr. Dog said: 'I'll speak to you like this'—and what do dogs say, Shoshi?"

"They say: 'Hav-hav-hav-hav!'" said Shoshi, very loudly.

"That's right. And *La Cucarachita Mandinga* said: 'Oh, no! That's much too loud—it hurts my ears! I can't possibly marry you if you're going to talk to me like that!' And Mr. Dog went away and was very sad."

"Very sad," said Shoshi.

"The next animal to come was *Señor Gallo*—Mr. Rooster. Do you know what a rooster is?"

Shoshi shook her head.

"It's a—it's a man chicken. You know what a chicken is, don't you?"

Shoshi nodded.

"Well, Mr. Rooster said exactly the same thing that Mr. Dog had said. That *La Cucarachita* was so pretty. That he wanted to marry her. And—just like with Mr. Dog—*La Cucarachita Mandinga* asked him how he would talk to her after they were married. And he said...."

Shoshi shrugged.

"No roosters in your part of town, huh? Okay, I'll show you. He said: 'COCOROCORO!' Now you do it!"

Shoshi giggled.

"COCOROCORO!"

"That's right. And *La Cucarachita Mandinga* said: 'Oh, no! That's a terrible way to speak to a lady! I could never live with a husband who spoke like that.' And once again, her suitor went away, very sadly."

Shoshi nodded again. She wasn't sure what 'suitor' meant, but by now she was much too caught up in the story to ask.

"One by one, all the animals came by," Paloma continued. "Some spoke too much. Some spoke too sadly. Some spoke too softly—they mumbled! One of them— *Señor Tortuga*— Mr. Turtle—didn't speak at all, but only pulled his head back into his shell after *La Cucarachita Mandinga* asked her question. That wouldn't do, at all."

Paloma looked down at Shoshi and was temporarily incapable of going on. The intensity of that little girl's gaze! The fierceness of her concentration! Pure Serach. Pure, unadulterated, miniature Serach.

"*La Cucarachita Mandinga* was about to give up hope," she resumed, after a small moment's pause. "But then— finally—*El Ratoncito Pérez* arrived. *Ratoncito* means 'little mouse' and 'Pérez' means ... well, it doesn't mean anything. It was just his name. *El Ratoncito Pérez*—unlike the other animals—had put on his best clothes to go visit *La Cucarachita Mandinga*. A beautiful long coat and a wonderful big hat with a big red plume. He looked very handsome. He said: 'Cucarachita Mandinga, you are so pretty and so hard-working and I admire you so much. Won't you be my wife?' And *La Cucarachita Mandinga* said..."

"'How will you talk to me after we are married?'" yelled Shoshi.

"That's right. And *El Ratoncito Pérez* answered: 'I will talk to you like this: 'Eee, eee, eee.' And *La Cucarachita Mandinga* said: 'Oh, yes, *Ratoncito*! If you talk like that to me, I will be glad to marry you!' So they had a big wedding with lots of food and lots of music and lots of dancing and all the animals came—even the animals whom *La Cucarachita Mandinga* had turned down. Everyone had a wonderful time."

Paloma looked down at Shoshi for a moment and saw those big gray eyes looking at her with such anticipation and trust that she couldn't resist. She reached over and stroked her head, just once, just as Beile had done—and as she herself had done for Serach, so very long ago when Serach had been just as hairless as Shoshi now was from all the chemo she had received.

She took a breath, drew back her hand, and continued.

"*La Cucarachita Mandinga* and *El Ratoncito Pérez* were very happy in their marriage until one day when *La Cucarachita Mandinga* was making an enormous pot of rice pudding on the stove—do you know what rice pudding is? It's like—like a *kugel*. Made of rice."

Shoshi nodded.

"And *El Ratoncito Pérez* climbed up onto the rim of the pot to take a whiff of the pudding and he fell in and was cooked to death."

Until that moment, Paloma had never realized the full, fierce cruelty of the folk tale that Beatriz had recounted to her. But one look at the crumpled face of the little girl whom she had been trying to entertain suddenly made the brutal nature of that tale perfectly clear.

Shoshi didn't just cry. She wailed. She howled. She pounded her fists on the blanket.

"No he didn't! No he didn't! He didn't die! He didn't!"

Paloma gulped. How the hell could she have been so stupid as to mention death in this particular hospital room with this particular little girl? She quickly took Shoshi's hand.

"No, no, of course not. He didn't die. It just looked that way for a very short moment. A moment just long enough to make *La Cucarachita Mandinga* spring into action. She dashed to the other side of the kitchen to find something with which she could pull her poor beloved husband out of that pot. And she grabbed—what did she grab? A spoon?"

Shoshi gave one last sob.

"No!" she said. "A fork!"

"A fork! Yes, of course! A fork! She grabbed that fork and dangled it into the pot and *El Ratoncito Pérez* saw it out of the corner of one eye and grabbed the other end. *La Cucarachita Mandinga* pulled and pulled and pulled *El Ratoncito Pérez* out and he landed right on the kitchen counter."

Shoshi eyed Paloma suspiciously. What was coming next?

"He didn't look very good at that point—it's true," said Paloma. "He was very red and very wet and ... he'd lost all his hair."

Shoshi gasped and put her hand up to her own head.

"Like me," she said.

"Yes, like you. But *La Cucarachita Mandinga* knew that he was going to be fine and that his hair was all going to grow back and that he would be as handsome as he ever was. She KNEW it. But just to make sure, she had to give him a very special kiss and say a very special prayer."

Shoshi nodded.

"So she leaned over—like this—and gave him a very special kiss on his forehead—like this—and she said that very special prayer to herself, very softly."

Paloma—almost inaudibly—mouthed the most fervent prayer for healing that she had ever offered to the Virgin Mary. Then she sat up again and looked at Shoshi's face.

"And he got all better," said Shoshi.

"Yes," said Paloma, taking Shoshi's hand again and turning her own face away for a moment, so that Shoshi wouldn't see her cry. "He got all better."

Shoshi nodded and closed her eyes.

"I'm sleepy," she said.

Which is why, when Beile came back from the *Kol Nidre* service, that is just how she found them. Paloma sitting on the bed with her hand around Shoshi's hand—and Shoshi sound asleep.

October 1, 2023: Brooklyn

- 7 -

As soon as the glint of the first three night-time stars brought the second day of *Sukkoth* observance to a close, the men of Boro Park began pouring out of their synagogues and onto the sidewalks to enjoy a last bit of *shmoozing* before heading home.

Shmuely knew he had barely enough time to grab a bite at Beile's before going off to take his usual shift at the hospital. Still, he felt he deserved a few more moments with the group with whom he now felt so re-connected—having *davened* with them three times a day, ever since coming back to Brooklyn. It was thus with a flash of sharp annoyance that he glanced up to see Beile's oldest daughter, Bluma, hurtling toward him at top speed—her long dull-brown braids flying out behind her and her pleated, plaid school-girl skirt whirling about her shins.

What could she possibly want from him?

He had become begrudgingly accustomed to her antics over the past few weeks. She was a girl who seemingly felt no compunction about interrupting him—and for the most trivial of reasons—while he was conversing with her father or even studying his texts. This latest incursion, however, was more brazen than anything she had attempted to date.

He watched her grimly out of the corner of one eye as she slammed to a halt some six feet away from him.

"*Onkel* Shmuely!" she hissed between ragged breaths.

Shmuely snuck a look around. No one else had looked up—no one seemed to have heard her. Good. I'll pretend I didn't hear her either. Perhaps she'll give up and go away.

But no. She just needed to get her wind back.

"*Onkel* Shmuely!" she repeated, this time at full volume. Several men turned to stare—first at her, then at him. Shmuely detached himself from his peers and reluctantly approached her.

"What is it, Bluma?" he growled. "What can't wait till I get home?"

"*Onkel* Shmuely," she said, looking straight at him. "Mama texted me as soon as the holiday ended to say that you need to call her immediately."

She extended one long-sleeved arm toward him—an i-phone carefully cradled in her hand.

"Here. I've brought you your device."

Shmuely's skin went from porcelain-toned to deathly white. This had to be bad news. It took him several seconds to reach out for the phone and—when he finally did so—he clutched it to his chest and turned brusquely away from his niece.

"Don't you need to go home to finish making dinner?" he barked back at her over one shoulder.

"Yes, *Onkel* Shmuely," she responded.

Yes, Onkel Shmuely. I know just what I need to do. Haven't I been the one who has been shopping for everyone, and cooking for everyone (you included), and minding all my younger brothers and sisters, and doing all the laundry, and keeping the house clean—ever since Mama started staying in the city with Shoshi every day?

She spun on her heel and sped down the three blocks to her house.

Meanwhile Shmuely spun himself around as well—this time to distance himself a bit from the group. He took a long breath and punched in Beile's number. He spoke with her briefly, disconnected, and then—suddenly, phone dangling precipitously in his hand—lost all self-control.

For several moments, his shoulders shook spasmodically and tears ran freely into his beard. It was a disconcerting sight and no one seemed prepared to say a word. Eventually, however, Reb Ephraim—a man who had known Shmuely since he was a child—stepped forward to put a hand on that thin, quaking back.

"Rav Gottesman," he said in his kind, hoarse voice, "is everything all right?"

At that sound and that touch, Shmuely emerged from his daze, realized where he was and what he had been doing, and straightened up.

"Thank you, Reb Ephraim," he sighed, wiping his cheeks with the handkerchief that he always kept at the ready in his coat pocket. "But these are tears of joy, not of sorrow. I have just learned from my sister that today's lab tests show that my daughter is totally free of the cancer." He choked one last time and then gathered himself together again. "There is not one single trace of it left. She can leave the hospital tomorrow. We can fly back home."

"A *Sukkos* miracle!" breathed Reb Ephraim.

"*Baruch Ha-Shem*!" a number of the others immediately added.

"And now," said Reb Ephraim, making a few brisk shooing motions with his hands, "I think it only right that we give Rav Gottesman the chance to deal with what he has learned. I am sure there are many people whom he needs to inform and many tasks that he needs to attend to."

The others nodded in agreement.

"Thank you again, Reb Ephraim," Shmuely said as they dispersed. "What you say is true."

The task most immediately before him was to text Ruchel as she lay in her own hospital bed, back in Jerusalem, desperately awaiting word from him. He swiftly typed in a message asking after her health, after their son Asher's health, and after the health of their newborn daughter—and then repeating what Beile had told him.

The second task—just as urgent (for if he thought about it too much, he would never do it)—was to call Beile back and make certain arrangements that only now were feasible. To implement a strategy that only now was fully crystalizing in his mind.

"Listen," he said, when she answered. "I need to begin booking a flight back to Jerusalem for me and Shoshi. You know how hard it is to secure tickets at this time of year with everyone needing to complete their travels before *Shemini Atzereth* begins. Who knows when I will be able to get to the hospital tonight? Better you should just stay over and I'll set out in the morning after services to bring you both back home."

Beile grunted what appeared to be assent. Shmuely grunted back. Then he got off the phone before she could begin posing questions. Beile's knack for interrogation could quickly uncover the weak spot in his assertions and cause his whole fragile plan to fall apart.

It was not as if he was claiming anything blatantly false. He truly did need to obtain those tickets as quickly as he could. It was, in fact, truly next-to-impossible for most people to do that on such short notice at that time of year. It could take hours of trying to pin El Al Airlines down.

What wasn't quite accurate was the implication that he was "most people." That he didn't have the tools with which to cut through all that red tape. That he couldn't just make a single simple call to his father-in-law, Yehuda, and ask him to please take care of everything. That—in turn—Yehuda (a man of both extraordinary means and total devotion to his favorite son-in-law) couldn't see to it with the greatest efficiency and speed.

Well, never mind all that. Beile's nosiness had been temporarily diverted. The plane tickets would soon be in hand. He had finally created the space and the means with which to carry out the act that had been insistently, temptingly—disturbingly—on his mind from the very first moment his plane had touched down at JFK.

The act of traversing the twenty-six blocks that separate the universe of Boro Park from the universe of Prospect Park South. Of once again finding himself in Serach's vibrant, flesh-and-blood presence—of receiving the irrefutable proof that total healing can and does take place. Of hearing the sister who had raised him tell him (and he knew that she would do so, for she had always known how to comfort him) that—yes—Shoshi would really be all right. That she would survive and flourish and live to grow up. Just as Serach had done, herself.

Shmuely closed his eyes so tightly that he saw floating specks of light when he finally opened them again. He shivered in his long black coat as he allowed the waves of deeply suppressed desire to sweep over him.

Then he turned and began walking forward—bargaining steadily with himself as he went.

If I don't actually enter that house of sin—if I insist that Serach come out on the porch and speak with me in the open air—it will all be fine.

If I do not allow her to touch me, it will all be fine.

If I only knock—if I do not ring the bell—and if I turn around and leave immediately if no one answers, it will all be fine.

If our meeting lasts for only a very few minutes—and I can quickly return to Beile's house to eat and to ask my father-in-law to arrange for those plane reservations—it will all be fine.

By the time he had finished conducting all those persuasive interior arguments, Shmuely had covered a good part of the distance that he needed to go. Even more importantly, he had covered it without anyone of any note spotting him and asking why he was speeding off in altogether the wrong direction from Beile's house.

It was all going to be fine.

"Well, Paloma—I wasn't even sure it was a knock, at first. I was immersed in my thoughts. I thought it might have been the wind. Or a raccoon. Or ... my own heartbeat. When I finally realized what was happening, it had already stopped, and by the time I opened the door..."

Paloma paused in reaching for the corkscrew and looked at Serach's fallen face.

"Yes, of course, by the time you got to the door he had bolted. I can just picture it. What I can't picture, however, is you just standing there and staring as your brother scurried madly down Marlborough Road with his hand on his hat and his coat flapping all around him. Why didn't you just yell at him to stop? Or dash after him and grab him?"

"He was running very fast, Paloma. He was already far away by the time I spotted him—I doubt I could have caught up. And I ... you don't yell at Shmuely. Or grab him. It isn't..."

"Respectful?"

Serach nodded.

"Jesus, Serach."

"Why do you think he came, Paloma?"

"He came to share the good news that Shoshi had made it through, of course. He must have learned about it this evening, same as we did—but had no way of knowing that Amalia had already told us and that we were breaking out the chilled Prosecco."

She waved the bottle around. Serach ignored it.

"But then why did he have to leave like that?" she said, her voice breaking. "To not even give me a chance to get to him? Why did he have to run away so fast?"

"How should I know, Baby? But if I had to guess, I'd say that he took it as a sign of Divine disapproval that you weren't already standing in the doorway waiting to welcome him in—despite giving you no advance warning that he was coming."

"It didn't take me all that long to get there."

"Well, it was clearly too long for someone so wimpy that he couldn't even ring the doorbell like a normal person but only tap-tap-tap on the wood, like a tiny moth fluttering against a lightbulb."

"Shmuely is not a wimp, Paloma," Serach said, looking away. "It took great courage for him to come here at all. Whatever way he did it."

Paloma caught the misery on Serach's face and stopped herself from contradicting her.

"Well," she said, instead, "I suppose that—in the world he moves in—what he managed to do might well pass for courage."

She looked at Serach for half a moment, waiting for a protest, and—hearing none—picked up the corkscrew and began twisting it firmly into the cork of the Prosecco bottle.

"Meanwhile," she continued, pulling the cork out with a satisfying pop, "can we please go back to celebrating this wonderful event without Shmuely totally wrecking it for us? An hour ago, we were both completely teary-eyed with happiness about Shoshi's lab results, so please let's simply focus on that."

Serach nodded.

"And listen, Babe. Even if Shmuely was too lily-livered to actually connect with you—he clearly wanted to, on some level. So take comfort from the fact that he made it as far as our front porch. As you say, that in itself was big-time for him."

Serach nodded again.

Paloma poured out the Prosecco and began serving up Serach's favorite *bacalao a la vizcaína* with white rice and peas. They sat peacefully together without having to say a word, eating and drinking and occasionally looking at one another.

"Shoshi's recovery was never a complete slam-dunk, you know," Paloma finally ventured, as they finished up the last of their almond cookies along with a cup of tea (for Serach) and a cup of espresso (for herself). "If I've learned anything in the past couple of years of rampant illness and heart-breaking death, it's that a hundred million things can go wrong, even under the best of circumstances and in the best of facilities. Sherman basically worked a miracle."

"It's only God who works miracles, Paloma," said Serach, softly.

"Well then, God worked the miracle," Paloma smiled. "Or—if you're going to get technical about it—God's mother."

It took Serach a few beats to grasp what Paloma was saying, but when she finally did, she let out a peal of delighted laughter.

"You prayed to the Virgin for Shoshi's recovery, didn't you?"

Paloma shut her eyes and nodded slowly.

"I did."

"You trusted her to help with Shoshi!"

"Desperate times require desperate means."

Serach reached out and took Paloma's hand.

"I know how hard that prayer must have been. I've watched how abandoned you have felt. How betrayed. Faith can be challenging like that. Relationships, too."

She smiled.

"But you and the Virgin are clearly back in synch. Back to being the unbeatable team that once you were."

Paloma sat very still for a moment, feeling Serach's words washing over her, like balm.

"Well, be that as it may," she finally said, briskly. "But in the meantime, I'd like to return to the topic of Shmuely for a moment. There's one last thing I'd like to note."

"I don't know that I want to hear anything more about him," said Serach, suddenly becoming very quiet.

"Oh, I think you'll want to hear this," said Paloma.

Serach bowed her head.

"You will, Serach. Trust me."

Paloma gave her a kind glance.

"Look," she said. "I'm sure you're still hurting like crazy over how he's treated you, ever since he arrived here. How he's never as much as thanked you for getting his daughter into Manhattan East. Or called to update you on her progress, knowing how worried you must have been. How he didn't even have the guts to stick around tonight to give you the good news."

Serach continued to look down.

"Worst of all, you may be fearing that you've lost the last chance of ever seeing him again—that this was it and now it's gone."

Did Serach nod? Paloma couldn't be sure, but it sure looked that way.

"But no fears, Baby. Not the last chance. Guaranteed."

This time, Serach unmistakably shook her head.

"Shmuely has his whole way of life pulling him away from me. His whole reputation. His—"

"Serach! Shmuely will never give you the satisfaction of confessing it, but he needs you. You're the only one in the entire world who truly understands him—the only one whom he can turn to when life throws him off course. One day he'll be wrestling with some new life-changing crisis or event and he'll be right back on your doorstep. On our doorstep, God help me."

Serach said nothing while Paloma poured herself the last few drops of Prosecco and drank them down.

"Babe—don't you get it? Everyone always comes back to us. When they need comfort. Or advice. Or approval. Or a place to stay. Or a really good meal. When they need someone to be the godmother to their kid. Or the babysitter for their niece."

Paloma guffawed.

"We've become the home base. For everyone. Haven't you noticed?"

"Not for everyone," Serach finally answered, in a very small voice. "Not for Ramon. Not anymore. He'll never come back."

She breathed deeply.

"I don't begrudge it to him," she said, quietly. "Even as it breaks my heart."

Paloma arched an eyebrow. It was the first time Serach had brought up that loss, all on her own. Certainly, the first time she'd been so candid about how deeply it had wounded her.

"Never say 'never,'" she countered. "But yes, Anteojitos may well be the exception to everything I just proclaimed. After a long struggle against tough odds, the boy who never fit in where God originally placed him has finally found his way. Doing just what he should be doing. In exactly the right company."

She paused for a moment before taking Serach's hands in hers.

"As have we, my darling."

Serach looked back at her and offered the small, beatific smile that Paloma could never resist.

"As have we," she whispered.

EPILOGUE: Swapping Places

*"I have set My rainbow in the clouds, and it will be the sign
of the covenant between Me and the earth."*

Genesis 9:13-16

October 4-5, 2023: Somewhere Over the Atlantic Ocean

The crew members of El Al's Kennedy-to-Ben-Gurion-Airport flights know better than to interfere with all the reshuffling. When passengers first board, they wave them perfunctorily into the seats that are officially posted on their tickets. Then they duck swiftly out of the way, leaving the Haredi men who dominate those passenger lists to make their own arrangements.

Two of those men take their places, one at the head of each aisle. They place their enormous hatboxes temporarily down on the nearest seats and begin swaying back and forth in their big black coats as they survey the lay of the land.

"You two—over there—" one man will shout to a pair of kerchiefed women sitting next to a very uncomfortable-looking man holding his own hat box tensely on his lap— "move into the aisle!"

"Now you—yes, you!" the other man will shout, motioning to two men on the far side of the cabin— "go over there and take their places!"

"And you!" the first one will add—pointing to a woman with a squiggling toddler seated beside her— "you go wait over there. Yes, there!" He will then shoo two skinny *yeshiva bochers* into the vacated seats next to the old man who had been strenuously leaning away from both mother and child— while the mother and child are scuttled into place next to another woman.

Row by row, swiftly and cleanly—men clasping their hat boxes, women clasping their children, and the few hapless secular passengers cluelessly following orders—the entire passenger list will be re-assembled into neat, single-gender rows.

The men will then all stand up and reverently place their hatboxes into the appropriate compartments over their re-assigned seats, the women will jam their hand luggage and their children's paraphernalia into whatever spaces remain, and the flight attendants will emerge from the rear of the plane.

The cabin doors will then be slammed shut, as will the overhead compartments. All seats will be placed in an upright position, all seatbelts securely fastened, and all extra bags tucked neatly under the seats in front of their owners. The giant blue and white El Al aircraft will begin taxi-ing down the runway and—when all is cleared—it will take off for Israel.

On the fateful night of Wednesday October 4th, at 11:45 p.m., Shmuely boarded the flight home—hatbox in hand and half-asleep child slung over his shoulder. He strode to the premium seats on the far-right side of the cabin for which his father-in-law had paid some outrageously large last-minute price, put his hatbox and his *tallis* and *tefillin* bags into the overhead compartment, along with Shoshi's little pink backpack, settled Shoshi into the window seat, tucked the two navy-blue, cardboard-stiff airline blankets around her tiny frame, and settled into the middle seat beside her.

He knew all about the seating drill ahead but he also knew that he could confidently ignore it. Who was going to interfere with a father and his little girl? More to the point—where could they possibly be moved that wouldn't make somebody uncomfortable?

The man directing the seating plan on the right-hand side of the plane watched Shmuely's progress with wariness ("where is that child's mother?") and made the same calculation that Shmuely had. He then resignedly gestured an oversized fellow with a massive black beard out of his untenable position in a female-dominated row across the aisle and three rows down and waved him into the aisle seat to Shmuely's left.

The man gave Shoshi a single brief disapproving glance, stuffed his hatbox into the overhead compartment—as far away as possible from the little pink backpack—settled himself into his seat, pulled out a prayer book from one of his coat pockets, and buried himself within the text without a single word.

Just as Shmuely himself would have done, had he found himself in the same unfortunate bind of being seated in the same row as a small, strange female child.

The first half of the flight passed without incident. The safety instructions were delivered in crisp Hebrew and English—along with many clever visuals—on the screens in front of every passenger's seat. Drinks and then dinner arrived without a hitch and Shmuely managed to eat a swallow of the chicken dish before pocketing the cookie for later, re-wrapping everything and handing it back to the flight attendant when she passed back down the aisle.

The man to Shmuely's left fell sound asleep as soon as he had polished off every last bite of the meal on his tray— his heavy head listing perilously toward Shmuely's shoulder several times before Shmuely managed to shove it off with sufficient emphasis to force the man to reposition himself.

The lights dimmed, everyone fell silent, and the aircraft proceeded on its way.

For several hours all was quiet, all was dark, until— suddenly—the screens on every seatback began to flash the message that the plane had reached the latitude, longitude and altitude that put it in direct line with the impending dawn.

It may still have been the middle of the night back in New York—it may already have been late morning in Jerusalem—but on a plane full of Haredi men heading across the Atlantic at 35,000 feet and going nearly 600 miles an hour, the sun was just about to come into view and it was time for morning prayers.

Within seconds of that announcement, all the plane's lights came back on. Every *Haredi* man popped up from his seat, opened the appropriate overhead compartment, fished out his hatbox and his *tallis* and *tefillin*, removed the hat from its box, put it on and pushed it to the back of his head, said the appropriate blessings, strapped his *tefillin* onto his forehead, unfurled—and then re-furled himself into—his *tallis*, and joined the crowd congregating around the restrooms.

The women whom they left behind in their segregated rows also did their bit. The ones whose children were old enough to stay still pulled out their own prayer books. The others murmured comfort and endearments—and produced the cookies, the boxes of juices, and the books that would keep their crankily-awakened toddlers quietly occupied.

There was, however, no woman seated beside Shoshi to comfort her when the sudden blaze of light and commotion sprang her out of her slumbers. The two seats immediately adjacent to hers were empty, of course, now that her father and his burly neighbor had joined the crowd of mumbling, bowing men. The rows directly in back, in front and across the aisle from her were empty as well. No woman seated elsewhere would have dared to shove herself through the wall of male *daveners* solidly blocking the aisles to reach an inexplicably alone and fretful child.

Softly at first—then louder and louder—Shoshana's voice made itself heard above the droning of the men. Distaste and annoyance began showing across every bearded face. What was that child's mother doing while her child was causing such a ruckus in the middle of the morning's devotions?

Shmuely himself remained obliged to keep *davening* the prayers in the prescribed order at the prescribed time and, in any event—just like the women—he would never have disturbed the men who surrounded him. Though the wailing thoroughly de-railed him, though—for the first time that he could remember—he struggled to focus on what he was doing, he kept his eyes fixed on the *siddur* and his lips moving when they needed to move.

When the last word of the last prayer was spoken, however, he knew what he had to do.

He elbowed his way through the crowd, zipped back to his seat, and—torn between concern, annoyance, and fear—drew the now-hysterical child into his arms.

"Sha-sha-sha, Mameleh!" he murmured. "Why are you making such a fuss? Don't you know that Tatteh was davening? That the whole plane was davening? What were you thinking, Mameleh, interrupting us like that?"

"Where is she?" Shoshi was wailing. "She was right here with me! But now she's gone!"

"Mameleh—please!" he said, smoothing her head with difficulty. "What are you talking about? Where is who? Who is gone? No one was here with you. You were just having a dream, Mameleh. Just a dream!"

"NO!" wailed Shoshi. "It wasn't a dream! She was right here! She was holding my hand and telling me a story!"

"Do you mean Mama? Were you dreaming about Mama? We'll be seeing her soon, you know, Shoshele. We'll be home again and seeing her before you know it!"

"Not Mama!" Shoshi's wailed even louder. "Not Mama!"

"Shoshi, please! Not so loud!"

Shoshi drew in a ragged breath.

"Not Mama," she repeated, rubbing her eyes. "It was my dove with her pretty hair and her pretty eyes! She was here with me. But then the lights came on and—"

She began to sob quietly.

Shmuely drew his hand across his own brow. What was his daughter going on about? What nonsense was this? Could this be the effect of all the medications she'd been taking?

"Shoshi, Mameleh, what dove could you possibly mean?" he said, trying to keep his own voice down. "What dove was right here with you?"

"My dove!" she repeated, shaking her head. "She was here—right here! Where is she? I want her to come back!"

By this time, the burly man to Shmuely's left had re-seated himself and was glaring fiercely at his two seatmates. What man in his right mind takes a child on a plane if he can't keep her quiet? Where was that child's mother?

"Mameleh!" said Shmuely, his own face growing as red as Shoshi's. "Please stop crying! You had a dream, that is all. And then you woke up. You shouldn't be causing a *ganze balagan* over someone in a dream—someone who isn't even real!"

With great effort, Shoshi stopped wailing and looked up at her father with her great, gray, tear-filled eyes.

"No, Tatteh!" she said. "My dove is real! She brought me a rainbow and she told me a story—and now she came back again! She was here! Where did she go?"

Shmuely—thankful that his daughter had at least finally brought her voice down—put his arm around her shoulders and began murmuring in her ear.

"Mameleh, you aren't making any sense," he said.

He smiled at her.

"Who do you think you are, anyway, with your doves and your rainbows? Do you think that you are Noah—the ancestor of all humanity? Do you think that we are on an ark instead of on a great big El Al airplane? Are you now going to start asking where the elephants have gone?"

Shoshi shook her head briskly back and forth again.

"No!" she said. "I don't want an elephant—I want my dove!"

Shmuely looked down at his stubborn, impossible, miraculously-alive daughter—at the daughter he had prayed so fervently to be taking home like this—and shook his own head. He leaned toward her and pulled her even closer.

"Mameleh, Mameleh...."

"Bring her back to me, Tatteh!" Shoshi said, looking up at him. "Bring back my dove!"

"Sha-sha-sha, Mameleh," he said again, as the lights began dimming, and the talking around them stopped. "Look! The lights are going off. It's time to be quiet!"

He breathed in deeply and stroked her cheek, thinking how much easier it had been to tend Shoshi while she slept at Manhattan East—to leave it up to Beile to handle any baffling flights of girlish imagination.

"I have no idea what you are talking about," he sighed. "But when we get back to Israel and we are both more rested, we will do our best to figure it all out and make it all right."

He stroked her cheek again.

"We will? You'll help me bring my dove back again, Tatteh? Do you promise?"

Shmuely hesitated. Vows, oaths—even promises to an extent—are sacrosanct. There are terrible penalties for breaking them. But here was his beloved daughter—so totally precious, so totally fragile, so totally distraught. He couldn't just leave her like that. He had to do something to reassure her.

"I do," he said.

GLOSSARY

Abuela - grandmother

aglio-olio - with garlic and olive oil

alta - high, tall

alte-kaker - old man (implied: grouchy old man)

ambición - ambition

Amidah - a central Jewish weekday, Shabbos, and holiday prayer—always said standing

bacalao a la vizcaína - a classic salt cod recipe from the Basque country

bachata - a dance from the Dominican Republic, now popular in all Latin countries and beyond

balagan - mess

Bar Mitzvah - the ritual marking a Jewish boy's transition to religious adulthood

Baruch Ha-Shem - thank God

bazorgt - worried, anxious

bentch, bentching - bless, say the blessings that conclude a meal

Borchu - the call to worship, said standing up

bris - Jewish ritual circumcision

B'sevah Tovah - good old age

BVM - Blessed Virgin Mother

chas v'cholileh - God forbid

chutzpah - nerve, thick skin

conjunto - a musical ensemble; iterally: "joint, combined"

costura - sewing, fashion, couture

cucarachita - little cockroach

cumbia - a form of music popular in Colombia

daven, davening, daveners - pray, praying, people praying

dummkopf - blockhead

farmisht - befuddled

fonfedik-ing - snuffling

frum - religiously observant

the whole megillah, the ganze megillah - the whole thing

gonif - thief

goyishe - non-Jewish

¡Hablame! or ¡Hablame duro! - Speak up!

Haftarah - portions from the Prophets paired with Shabbos and holiday Torah readings

Hasidic Judaism - a religious spiritual revival movement arising in the 18th century

Hermano, Hermana - brother, sister

kashrut - the Jewish ritual laws of cooking and eating

kichel - a little egg-based cookie in the shape of a bow-tie

kiddush - the blessing said over wine; also, refreshment served after a Shabbos service

Kosher - conforming to the Jewish ritual laws of cooking and eating

Kol Nidre - the evening service for Yom Kippur—the Day of Atonement

kugel - a kind of pudding based around something starchy—generally potatoes or noodles

kvelling - taking pride in, bragging about

kvetching - complaining

lashon hara - evil gossip

macher - influential person, "doer"

macho - tough, manly

madrina - godmother

Mameleh - term of endearment; literally "little Mama"

mamzer - an untrustworthy person, literally: a person born of certain forbidden unions

Mandinga - an ethnic group in West Africa

marimba - a Latin-American percussion instrument

mazel tov - congratulations; literally: good luck

mea culpa - part of the prayer of confession in the Catholic faith, literally: 'my fault'

mensch - a person of integrity, a good person

meshugge, meshugas - nutty, nutty stuff

merengue - a style of dancing, rooted in Africa and based on a repeating five-beat rhythmic pattern. It is the national dance of the Dominican Republic

mi shebeirach - Jewish prayer used to request a blessing from God

mierda - excrement

mitzvah - a commandment; a good deed

mole poblano de guajolote - turkey in mole sauce; said by some to be Mexico's national dish

muchacho - boy

Onkel - uncle

pajaro - pejorative Latino slang for gay man; literally: bird'

Papito - term of endearment; literally: "little father."

parve - containing neither dairy nor meat and therefore able to be eaten with either one

Passover seder - Passover ceremonial dinner

pendejo - idiot; literally: "pubic hair"

pura Rodriguez - pure Rodriguez

Querido, Querida - dear, darling

ratoncito - little mouse

Rav - an honorific title for a teacher or scholar

Reb - a Jewish title of respect, equivalent to 'Mister'

saumon Wellington en croute - salmon fillets and

mushrooms wrapped in a puff pastry

schmaltz - rendered poultry fat

schmoozing - making small talk

schmuck - terrible person; literally; "penis"

Señor Perro - Mr. Dog

Señor Gallo - Mr. Rooster

Señor Tortuga - Mr. Turtle

Shabbos - the Jewish Sabbath, lasting from sundown Friday till nightfall Saturday, and observed through twenty-five hours of strictly regulated rest, activities, and prayer

shanda - shame

Shefele - term of endearment; literally: "little lamb"

Sh'ma - one of the central prayers of the Jewish service Shemini Atzereth the second to last day of the eight-day holiday of Sukkoth

shlemiel - fool, incompetent person

shmooze, shmoozing - chat, chatting

shokolad - chocolate

shul - synagogue

shtetl - a Jewish town or village in eastern Europe

siddur - prayer book

¡Suave—suave! - keep cool!; literally: "gentle, gentle!"

¡Suerte! - luck! (good luck!)

Sukkah - shelter

Sukkoth, Sukkos - an eight-day-long Jewish festival that commemorates the journey of the Israelites through   the desert after leaving enslavement in Egypt. It begins four days after Yom Kippur and—during its first two and last two days—those who are observing it are forbidden to use electronic devices, to travel, or to carry out any type of work.

tallis, tallitot - prayer shawl(s) used by observant Jews during morning services

Talmud - a central text of Rabbinic Judaism

Tatteh - Daddy

Tatteleh - a term of endearment used for a grown man—literally: "little father"

tefillin - little leather boxes that contain selected scriptural passages.

toi, toi, toi - an expression used to ward off the evil eye.

Torah - the first five books of the Jewish Bible

Torah service - a prayer service at which a   portion of the Torah is read

tostones - double-fried green plantain rounds

trayf - something not kosher

tsoris - trouble, grief

vallenato - a form of music popular in Colombia

viejo verde - dirty old man, literally 'green old man'

yarmulke - Jewish skullcap

yenta - gossip or busybody

yeshiva bocher - yeshiva boy, young (male) student at a Jewish school

About the Author

S.W. Leicher grew up in the Bronx in a bi-cultural (Latina and Jewish) home. She moved to Manhattan after graduate school and raised her family on the Upper West Side, where she still lives with her husband and black cat. When not dreaming up fiction, she writes about social justice issues for nonprofit organizations.

www.swleicher.com
@susanleicher

Acknowledgments

Four astute readers contributed crucial recommendations—alerting me to where logic faltered and offering suggestions regarding plot, character, pacing, and word choice. Renée Caffiero, Susan Eagan, Sandra Matthews, Lori Ubell—your perceptive, detailed advice made all the difference.

Elena Belli—concert and choral pianist extraordinaire—your recital programming suggestions were flawless.

Dr. Jeffrey Moskow—Senior Oncology Drug Development Consultant and Former Chief, Investigational Drug Branch at the National Cancer Institute—clarified the course and treatment of pediatric leukemia and helped me dream up an ideal facility.

Dr. Cynthia Nutall—Chief Nurse Academic Affairs, Professional Practice and Research at the New Mexico VA Healthcare System—illuminated the functions and qualifications of a Nurse Manager working in a major medical center.

Rabbi Lewis Warshauer vetted the Hebrew, the Yiddish, and the depictions and definitions of observance, while offering a host of wise and witty tips regarding plot and overall tone.

Elba Montalvo graciously vetted my Spanish and my portrayals of Latino culture.

Whatever is true and authentic in this book is due to the support of those wonderful experts. The inaccuracies remain mine alone.

Once again, I felt a surge of confidence when Joan Leggitt—a publisher of impeccable skill and insight—agreed to take this project on.

Tony: your unshakeable support, brilliant editing, and unfailing patience as I prattled on endlessly about imaginary people and events, mean more than I can say.

Thank you and bless you all!

www.ingramcontent.com/pod-product-compliance
Lightning Source LLC
Chambersburg PA
CBHW030559170726
48283CB00002B/398